RIPLEY KNEW WHAT
WAS GOING ON.
KNEW WHAT
WAS COMING.

She could sense it even if they couldn't see it, like a wave rushing a black sand beach at night.

She found her voice and the mike simultaneously.

"Pull your team out, Gorman. Get them out of there *now*."

The lieutenant spared her an irritated glare. "Don't give me orders, lady. I know what I'm doing."

"Maybe, but you don't know what's being *done*."

Down on C-level the walls and ceiling of the alien chamber were coming to life. Biomechanical fingers extended talons that could tear metal. Slime lubricated jaws began to flex, pistoning silently as their owners awoke. Uncertain movements dimly glimpsed through smoke and steam by the nervous human intruders.

Master Sergeant Apone found himself starting to back up. "Go to infrared. Look sharp, people!"

"Multiple signals," Comtech Corporal Hudson declared, "all around. Closing from all directions."

The medtech's nerves snapped and she whirled to retreat. As she turned something tall and immensely powerful loomed above the smoke to wrap long arms around her . . .

Also by Alan Dean Foster

ALIENS

a novelization by
ALAN DEAN FOSTER
based on the screenplay by
JAMES CAMERON

WARNER BOOKS

ISBN 0 7088 3182 6

Printed in England by Clays Ltd, St Ives plc

Warner
A Division of
Little, Brown and Company (UK) Limited
165 Great Dover Street,
London SE1 4YA

For H. R. Giger
Master of the sinister airbrush.
Who reveals more about us than we wish to know.
From ADF and points west.

Two dreamers.

Not so very much difference between them despite the more obvious distinctions. One was of modest size, the other larger. One was female, the other male. The mouth of the first contained a mixture of sharp and flat teeth, a clear indication that it was omnivorous, while the maxillary cutlery of the other was intended solely for slicing and penetrating. Both were the scions of a race of killers. This was a genetic tendency the first dreamer's kind had learned to moderate. The other dreamer remained wholly feral.

More differences were apparent in their dreams than in their appearance. The first dreamer slept uneasily, memories of unmentionable terrors recently experienced oozing up from the depths of her subconscious to disrupt the normally placid stasis of hypersleep. She would have tossed and turned dangerously if not for the capsule that contained and restrained her movements—that and the fact that in deep sleep, muscular activity is reduced to a minimum. So she tossed and turned mentally. She was not aware of this. During hypersleep one is aware of nothing.

Every so often, though, a dark and vile memory would rise to the fore, like sewage seeping up beneath a city street. Temporarily it would overwhelm her rest. Then she would moan within the capsule. Her heartbeat would increase. The computer that watched over her like an electronic angel would note the accelerated activity and respond by lowering her body temperature another degree while increasing the flow of stabilizing drugs to her system. The moaning would stop. The dreamer would quiet and sink back into her cushions. It would take time for the nightmare to return.

Next to her the small killer would react to these isolated episodes by twitching as if in response to the larger sleeper's distress. Then it, too, would relax again, dreaming of small, warm bodies and the flow of hot blood, of the comfort to be found in the company of its own kind, and the assurance that this would come again. Somehow it knew that both dreamers would awaken together or not at all.

The last possibility did not unsettle its rest. It was possessed of more patience than its companion in hypersleep, and a more realistic perception of its position in the cosmos. It was content to sleep and wait, knowing that if and when consciousness returned, it would be ready to stalk and kill again. Meanwhile it rested.

Time passes. Horror does not.

In the infinity that is space, suns are but grains of sand. A white dwarf is barely worthy of notice. A small spacecraft like the lifeboat of the vanished vessel *Nostromo* is almost too tiny to exist in such emptiness. It drifted through the great nothing like a freed electron broken loose from its atomic orbit.

Yet even a freed electron can attract attention, if others equipped with appropriate detection instruments happen to chance across it. So it was that the lifeboat's course took it close by a familiar star. Even so, it was a stroke of luck that it was not permanently overlooked. It passed very near another ship; in space, "very near" being anything less than a light-year. It appeared on the fringe of a range spanner's screen.

Some who saw the blip argued for ignoring it. It was too small to be a ship, they insisted. It didn't belong where it was. And ships talked back. This one was as quiet as the dead. More likely it was only an errant asteroid, a renegade chunk of nickel-iron off to see the universe. If it was a ship, at the very least it would have been blaring to anything within hearing range with an emergency beacon.

But the captain of the ranging vessel was a curious fellow. A minor deviation in their course would give them a chance to check out the silent wanderer, and a little clever bookkeeping would be sufficient to justify the detour's cost to the owners. Orders were given, and computers worked to adjust trajectory. The captain's judgment was confirmed when they drew alongside the stranger: it was a ship's lifeboat.

Still no sign of life, no response to polite inquiries. Even the running lights were out. But the ship was not completely dead. Like a body in frigid weather, the craft had withdrawn power from its extremities to protect something vital deep within.

The captain selected three men to board the drifter. Gently as an eagle mating with a lost feather, the larger craft sidled close to the *Narcissus*. Metal kissed metal. Grapples were applied. The sounds of the locking procedure echoed through both vessels.

Wearing full pressure suits, the three boarders entered their airlock. They carried portable lights and other equipment. Air being too precious to abandon to vacuum, they waited patiently while the oxygen was inhaled by their ship. Then the outer-lock door slid aside.

Their first sight of the lifeboat was disappointing: no internal lights visible through the port in the door, no sign of life within. The door refused to respond when the external controls were pressed. It had been jammed shut from inside. After the men made sure there was no air in the lifeboat's cabin, a robot welder was put to work on the door. Twin torches flared brightly in the darkness, slicing into the door from two sides. The flames met at the bottom of the barrier.

Two men braced the third, who kicked the metal aside. The way was open.

The lifeboat's interior was as dark and still as a tomb. A section of portable grappling cable snaked along the floor. Its torn and frayed tip ended near the exterior door. Up close to the cockpit a faint light was visible. The men moved toward it.

The familiar dome of a hypersleep capsule glowed from within. The intruders exchanged a glance before approaching. Two of them leaned over the thick glass cover of the transparent sarcophagus. Behind them, their companion was studying his instrumentation and muttered aloud.

"Internal pressure positive. Assuming nominal hull and systems integrity. Nothing appears busted; just shut down to conserve energy. Capsule pressure steady. There's power feeding through, though I bet the batteries have about had it. Look how dim the internal readouts are. Ever see a hypersleep capsule like this one?"

"Late twenties." The speaker leaned over the glass and murmured into his suit pickup. "Good-lookin' dame."

"Good-lookin', my eye." His companion sounded disappointed. "Life function diodes are all green. That means she's alive. There goes our salvage profit, guys."

The other inspector gestured in surprise. "Hey, there's something in there with her. Nonhuman. Looks like it's alive too. Can't see too clearly. Part of it's under her hair. It's orangish."

"Orange?" The leader of the trio pushed past both of them and rested the faceplate of his helmet against the transparent barrier. "Got claws, whatever it is."

"Hey." One of the men nudged his companion. "Maybe it's an alien life-form, huh? That'd be worth some bucks."

Ripley chose that moment to move ever so slightly. A few strands of hair drifted down the pillow beneath her head, more fully revealing the creature that slept tight against her.

The leader of the boarders straightened and shook his head disgustedly.

"No such luck. It's just a cat."

Listening was a struggle. Sight was out of the question. Her throat was a seam of anthracite inside the lighter pumice of her skull; black, dry, and with a faintly resinous taste. Her tongue moved loosely over territory long forgotten. She tried to remember what speech was like. Her lips parted. Air came rushing up from her lungs, and those long-dormant bellows ached with the exertion. The result of this strenuous interplay between lips, tongue, palate, and lungs was a small triumph of one word. It drifted through the room.

"Thirsty."

Something smooth and cool slid between her lips. The shock of dampness almost overwhelmed her. Memory nearly caused her to reject the water tube. In another time and place that kind of insertion was a prelude to a particularly unique and loathsome demise. Only water flowed from this tube, however. It was accompanied by a calm voice intoning advice.

"Don't swallow. Sip slowly."

She obeyed, though a part of her mind screamed at her to suck the restoring liquid as fast as possible. Oddly enough, she did not feel dehydrated, only terribly thirsty.

"Good," she whispered huskily. "Got anything more substantial?"

"It's too soon," said the voice.

"The heck it is. How about some fruit juice?"

"Citric acid will tear you up." The voice hesitated, considering, then said, "Try this."

Once again the gleaming metal tube slipped smoothly into her mouth. She sucked at it pleasurably. Sugared iced tea cascaded down her throat, soothing both thirst and her first cravings for food. When she'd had enough, she said so,

and the tube was withdrawn. A new sound assailed her ears:
the trill of some exotic bird.

She could hear and taste; now it was time to see. Her
eyes opened to a view of pristine rain forest. Trees lifted
bushy green crowns heavenward. Bright iridescent winged
creatures buzzed as they flitted from branch to branch. Birds
trailed long tail feathers like jet contrails behind them as they
dipped and soared in pursuit of the insects. A quetzal peered
out at her from its home in the trunk of a climbing fig.

Orchids bloomed mightily, and beetles scurried among
leaves and fallen branches like ambulatory jewels. An agouti
appeared, saw her, and bolted back into the undergrowth.
From the stately hardwood off to the left, a howler monkey
dangled, crooning softly to its infant.

The sensory overload was too much. She closed her eyes
against the chattering profusion of life.

Later (another hour? another day?) a crack appeared in
the middle of the big tree's buttressing roots. The split widened to obliterate the torso of a gamboling marmoset. A
woman emerged from the gap and closed it behind her, sealing
the temporary bloodless wound in tree and animal. She touched
a hidden wall switch, and the rain forest went away.

It was very good for a solido, but now that it had been
shut off, Ripley could see the complex medical equipment
the rain forest imagery had camouflaged. To her immediate
left was the medved that had responded so considerately to
her request for first water and then cold tea. The machine
hung motionless and ready from the wall, aware of everything
that was happening inside her body, ready to adjust medication, provide food and drink, or summon human help should
the need arise.

The newcomer smiled at the patient and used a remote
control attached to her breast pocket to raise the backrest of
Ripley's bed. The patch on her shirt, which identified her as
a senior medical technician, was bright with color against the
background of white uniform. Ripley eyed her warily, unable

to tell if the woman's smile was genuine or routine. Her voice was pleasant and maternal without being cloying.

"Sedation's wearing off. I don't think you need any more. Can you understand me?" Ripley nodded. The medtech considered her patient's appearance and reached a decision. "Let's try something new. Why don't I open the window?"

"I give up. Why don't you?"

The smile weakened at the corners, was promptly re-charged. Professional and practiced, then; not heartfelt. And why should it be? The medtech didn't know Ripley, and Ripley didn't know her. So what. The woman pointed her remote toward the wall across from the foot of the bed.

"Watch your eyes."

Now there's a choice non sequitur for you, Ripley thought. Nevertheless, she squinted against the implied glare.

A motor hummed softly, and the motorized wall plate slid into the ceiling. Harsh light filled the room. Though filtered and softened, it was still a shock to Ripley's tired system.

Outside the port lay a vast sweep of nothingness. Beyond the nothingness was everything. A few of Gateway Station's modular habitats formed a loop off to the left, the plastic cells strung together like children's blocks. A couple of communications antennae peeped into the view from below. Dominating the scene was the bright curve of the Earth. Africa was a brown, white-streaked smear swimming in an ocean blue, the Mediterranean a sapphire tiara crowning the Sahara.

Ripley had seen it all before, in school and then in person. She was not particularly thrilled by the view so much as she was just glad it was still there. Events of recent memory suggested it might not be, that nightmare was reality and this soft, inviting globe only mocking illusion. It was comforting, familiar, reassuring, like a worn-down teddy bear. The scene was completed by the bleak orb of the moon drifting in the background like a vagrant exclamation point: planetary system as security blanket.

"And how are we today?" She grew aware that the med-tech was talking to her instead of at her.

"Terrible." Someone or two had told her once upon a time that she had a lovely and unique voice. Eventually she should get it back. For the moment no part of her body was functioning at optimum efficiency. She wondered if it ever would again, because she was very different from the person she'd been before. That Ripley had set out on a routine cargo run in a now vanished spacecraft. A different Ripley had returned, and lay in the hospital bed regarding her nurse.

"Just terrible?" You had to admire the medtech, she mused. A woman not easily discouraged. "That's better than yesterday, at least. I'd call 'terrible' a quantum jump up from atrocious."

Ripley squeezed her eyelids shut, opened them slowly. The Earth was still there. Time, which heretofore she hadn't given a hoot about, suddenly acquired new importance.

"How long have I been on Gateway Station?"

"Just a couple of days." Still smiling.

"Feels longer."

The medtech turned her face away, and Ripley wondered whether she found the terse observation boring or disturbing. "Do you feel up to a visitor?"

"Do I have a choice?"

"Of course you have a choice. You're the patient. After the doctors you know best. You want to be left alone, you get left alone."

Ripley shrugged, mildly surprised to discover that her shoulder muscles were up to the gesture. "I've been alone long enough. Whattheheck. Who is it?"

The medtech walked to the door. "There are two of them, actually." Ripley could see that she was smiling again.

A man entered, carrying something. Ripley didn't know him, but she knew his fat, orange, bored-looking burden.

"Jones!" She sat up straight, not needing the bed support now. The man gratefully relinquished possession of the big tomcat. Ripley cuddled it to her. "Come here, Jonesey, you ugly old moose, you sweet ball of fluff, you!"

The cat patiently endured this embarrassing display, so typical of humans, with all the dignity his kind was heir too. In so doing, Jones displayed the usual tolerance felines have for human beings. Any extraterrestrial observer privy to the byplay would not have doubted for an instant which of the two creatures on the bed was the superior intelligence.

The man who'd brought the good orange news with him pulled a chair close to the bed and patiently waited for Ripley to take notice of him. He was in his thirties, good-looking without being flashy, and dressed in a nondescript business suit. His smile was no more or less real than the medtech's, even though it had been practiced longer. Ripley eventually acknowledged his presence with a nod but continued to reserve her conversation for the cat. It occurred to her visitor that if he was going to be taken for anything more than a delivery man, it was up to him to make the first move.

"Nice room," he said without really meaning it. He looked like a country boy, but he didn't talk like one, Ripley thought as he edged the chair a little closer to her. "I'm Burke. Carter Burke. I work for the Company, but other than that, I'm an okay guy. Glad to see you're feeling better." The last at least sounded as though he meant it.

"Who says I'm feeling better?" She stroked Jones, who purred contentedly and continued to shed cat hair all over the sterile bed.

"Your doctors and machines. I'm told the weakness and disorientation should pass soon, though you don't look particularly disoriented to me. Side effects of the unusually long hypersleep, or something like that. Biology wsn't my favorite subject. I was better at figures. For example, yours seems to have come through in pretty good shape." He nodded toward the bed covers.

"I hope I look better than I feel, because I feel like the inside of an Egyptian mummy. You said 'unusually long hy-

persleep.' How long was I out there?" She gestured toward
the watching medtech. "They won't tell me anything."

Burke's tone was soothing, paternal. "Well, maybe you
shouldn't worry about that just yet."

Ripley's hand shot from beneath the covers to grab his
arm. The speed of her reaction and the strength of her grip
clearly surprised him. "No. I'm conscious, and I don't need
any more coddling. How *long*?"

He glanced over at the medtech. She shrugged and turned
away to attend to the needs of some incomprehensible tangle
of lights and tubes. When he looked back at the woman lying
in the bed, he found he was unable to shift his eyes away
from hers.

"All right. It's not my job to tell you, but my instincts
say you're strong enough to handle it. Fifty-seven years."

The number hit her like a hammer. Fifty-seven too many
hammers. Hit her harder than waking up, harder than her
first sight of the home world. She seemed to deflate, to lose
strength and color simultaneously as she sank back into the
mattress. Suddenly the artificial gravity of the station seemed
thrice Earth-normal, pressing her down and back. The air-
filled pad on which she rested was ballooning around her,
threatening to stifle and smother. The medtech glanced at her
warning lights, but all of them stayed silent.

Fifty-seven years. In the more than half century she'd
been dreaming in deepsleep, friends left behind had grown
old and died, family had matured and faded, the world she'd
left behind had metamorphosed into who knew what. Gov-
ernments had risen and fallen; inventions had hit the market
and been outmoded and discarded. No one had ever survived
more than sixty-five years in hypersleep. Longer than that
and the body begins to fail beyond the ability of the capsules
to sustain life. She'd barely survived; she'd pushed the limits
of the physiologically possible, only to find that she'd outlived life.

"Fifty-seven!"

"You drifted right through the core systems," Burke was telling her. "Your beacon failed. It was blind luck that that deep salvage team caught you when they . . ." he hesitated. She'd suddenly turned pale, her eyes widening. "Are you all right?"

She coughed once, a second time harder. There was a pressure—her expression changed from one of concern to dawning horror. Burke tried to hand her a glass of water from the nightstand, only to have her slap it away. It struck the floor and shattered. Jones's fur was standing on end as the cat leapt to the floor, yowling and spitting. His claws made rapid scratching sounds on the smooth plastic as he scrambled away from the bed. Ripley grabbed at her chest, her back arching as the convulsions began. She looked as if she were strangling.

The medtech was shouting at the omnidirectional pickup. "Code Blue to Four Fifteen! Code Blue, Four One Five!"

She and Burke clutched Ripley's shoulders as the patient began bouncing against the mattress. They held on as a doctor and two more techs came pounding into the room.

It couldn't be happening. It couldn't!

"No—noooooo!"

The techs were trying to slap restraints on her arms and legs as she thrashed wildly. Covers went flying. One foot sent a medtech sprawling while the other smashed a hole in the soulless glass eye on a monitoring unit. From beneath a cabinet Jones glared out at his mistress and hissed.

"Hold her," the doctor was yelling. "Get me an airway, stat! And fifteen cc's of—!"

An explosion of blood suddenly stained the top sheet crimson, and the linens began to pyramid as something unseen rose beneath them. Stunned, the doctor and the techs backed off. The sheet continued to rise.

Ripley saw clearly as the sheet slid away. The medtech fainted. The doctor made gagging sounds as the eyeless, toothed worm emerged from the patient's shattered rib cage.

It turned slowly until its fanged mouth was only a foot from its host's face, and screeched. The sound drowned out every-thing human in the room, filling Ripley's ears, overloading her numbed cortex, echoing, reverberating through her entire being as she...

...sat up screaming, her body snapping into an upright position in the bed. She was alone in the darkened hospital room. Colored light shone from the insectlike dots of glowing LEDs. Clutching pathetically at her chest she fought to regain the breath the nightmare had stolen.

Her body was intact: sternum, muscles, tendons, and ligaments all in place and functional. There was no demented horror ripping itself out of her torso, no obscene birth in progress. Her eyes moved jerkily in their sockets as she scanned the room. Nothing lying in ambush on the floor, nothing hiding behind the cabinets waiting for her to let down her guard. Only silent machines monitoring her life and the com-fortable bed maintaining it. The sweat was pouring off her even though the room was pleasantly cool. She held one fist protectively against her sternum, as if to reassure herself constantly of its continued inviolability.

She jumped slightly as the video monitor suspended over the bed came to life. An older woman gazed anxiously down at her. Night-duty medtech. Her face was full of honest, not merely professional, concern.

"Bad dreams again? Do you want something to help you sleep?" A robot arm whirred to life left of Ripley's arm. She regarded it with distaste.

"No. I've slept enough."

"Okay. You know best. If you change your mind, just use your bed buzzer." She switched off. The screen darkened.

Ripley slowly leaned back against the raised upper sec-tion of mattress and touched one of the numerous buttons set in the side of her nightstand. Once more the window screen that covered the far wall slid into the ceiling. She could see out again. There was the portion of Gateway, now brilliantly lit by nighttime lights and, beyond it, the night-shrouded globe of the Earth. Wisps of cloud masked distant pinpoints of light. Cities—alive with happy people blissfully ignorant of the stark reality that was an indifferent cosmos.

Something landed on the bed next to her, but this time she didn't jump. It was a familiar, demanding shape, and she hugged it tightly to her, ignoring the casual *meowrr* of protest.

"It's okay, Jones. We made it, we're safe. I'm sorry I scared you. It'll be all right now. It's going to be all right."

All right, yes, save that she was going to have to learn how to sleep all over again.

Sunlight streamed through the stand of poplars. A meadow was visible beyond the trees, green stalks splattered with the brightness of bluebells, daisies, and phlox. A robin pranced near the base of one tree, searching for insects. It did not see the sinewy predator stalking it, eyes intent, muscles taut. The bird turned its back, and the stalker sprang.

Jones slammed into the solido of the robin, neither acquiring prey nor disturbing the image, which continued its blithe quest for imaged insects. Shaking his head violently, the tomcat staggered away from the wall.

Ripley sat on a nearby bench regarding this cat-play. "Dumb cat. Don't you know a solido by now when you see one?" Although maybe she shouldn't be too hard on the cat. Solido design had improved during the last fifty-seven years. Everything had been improved during the last fifty-seven years. Except for her and Jones.

Glass doors sealed the atrium off from the rest of Gateway Station. The expensive solido of a North American temperate forest was set off by potted plants and sickly grass underfoot. The solido looked more real than the real plants, but at least the latter had an honest smell. She leaned slightly toward one pot. Dirt and moisture and growing things. Of cabbages and kings, she mused dourly. Horsepucky. She wanted off Gateway. Earth was temptingly near, and she longed to put blue sky between herself and the malign emptiness of space.

Two of the glass doors that sealed off the atrium parted to admit Carter Burke. For a moment she found herself regarding him as a man and not just a company cipher. Maybe that was a sign that she was returning to normal. Her appraisal of him was mitigated by the knowledge that when the *Nostromo* had departed on its ill-fated voyage, he was two decades short of being born. It shouldn't have made any difference. They were approximately the same physical age.

"Sorry." Always the cheery smile. "I've been running behind all morning. Finally managed to get away."

Ripley never had been one for small talk. Now more than ever, life seemed too precious to waste on inconsequential banter. Why couldn't people just say what they had to say instead of dancing for five minutes around the subject?

"Have they located my daughter yet?"

Burke looked uncomfortable. "Well, I was going to wait until after the inquest."

"I've waited fifty-seven years. I'm impatient. So humor me."

He nodded, set down his carrying case, and popped the lid. He fumbled a minute with the contents before producing several sheets of thin plastic.

"Is she . . . ?"

Burke spoke as he read from one of the sheets. "Amanda Ripley-McClaren. Married name, I guess. Age sixty-six at . . . time of death. That was two years ago. There's a whole history here. Nothing spectacular or notable. Details of a pleasant, ordinary life. Like the kind most of us lead, I expect. I'm sorry." He passed over the sheets, studied Ripley's face as she scanned the printouts. "Guess this is my morning for being sorry."

Ripley studied the holographic image imprinted on one of the sheets. It showed a rotund, slightly pale woman in her mid-sixties. Could have been anyone's aunt. There was noth-

ing distinctive about the face, nothing that leapt out and
shouted with familiarity. It was impossible to reconcile the
picture of this older woman with the memory of the little girl
she'd left behind.

"Amy," she whispered.

Burke still held a couple of sheets, read quietly as she
continued to stare at the hologram. "Cancer. Hmmm. They
still haven't licked all varieties of that one. Body was cremated. Interred Westlake Repository, Little Chute, Wiscon-
sin. No children."

Ripley looked past him, toward the forest solido but not
at it. She was staring at the invisible landscape of the past.

"I promised her I'd be home for her birthday. Her elev-
enth birthday. I sure missed that one." She glanced again at
the picture. "Well, she'd already learned to take my promises
with a grain of salt. When it came to flight schedules, anyway."

Burke nodded, trying to be sympathetic. That was difficult for him under ordinary circumstances, much more so
this morning. At least he had the sense to keep his mouth
shut instead of muttering the usual polite inanities.

"You always think you can make it up to somebody—
later, you know." She took a deep breath. "But now I never
can. I never can." The tears came then, long overdue. Fifty-
seven years overdue. She sat there on the bench and sobbed
softly to herself, alone now in a different kind of space.

Finally Burke patted her reassuringly on her shoulder,
uncomfortable at the display and trying hard not to show it.
"The hearing convenes at oh-nine-thirty. You don't want to
be late. It wouldn't make a good first impression."

She nodded, rose. "Jones. Jonesey, c'mere." Meowing,
the cat sauntered over and allowed her to pick him up. She
wiped self-consciously at her eyes. "I've got to change. Won't
take long." She rubbed her nose against the cat's back, a
small outrage it suffered in silence.

"Want me to walk you back to your room?"

"Sure, why not?"

He turned and started for the proper corridor. The doors parted to permit them egress from the atrium. "You know, that cat's something of a special privilege. They don't allow pets on Gateway."

"Jones isn't a pet." She scratched the tom behind the ears. "He's a survivor."

As Ripley promised, she was ready in plenty of time. Burke elected to wait outside her private room, studying his own reports, until she emerged. The transformation was impressive. Gone was the pale, waxy skin; gone the bitterness of expression and the uncertain stride. Determination? he wondered as they headed for the central corridor. Or just clever makeup?

Neither of them said anything until they neared the sublevel where the hearing room was located. "What are you going to tell them?" he finally asked her.

"What's to tell that hasn't already been told? You read my deposition. It's complete and accurate. No embellishments. It didn't need any embellishments."

"Look, *I* believe you, but there are going to be some heavyweights in there, and every one of them is going to try to pick holes in your story. You got feds, you got Interstellar Commerce Commission, you got Colonial Administration, insurance company guys—"

"I get the picture."

"Just tell them what happened. The important thing is to stay cool and unemotional."

Sure, she thought. All of her friends and shipmates and relatives were dead, and she'd lost fifty-seven years of reality to an unrestoring sleep. Cool and unemotional. Sure.

Despite her determination, by midday she was anything but cool and collected. Repetition of the same questions, the same idiotic disputations of the facts as she'd reported them, the same exhaustive examination of minor points that left the major ones untouched—all combined to render her frustrated and angry.

As she spoke to the somber inquisitors the large videoscreen behind her was printing out mug shots and dossiers. She was glad it was behind her, because the faces were those of the *Nostromo*'s crew. There was Parker, grinning like a goon. And Brett, placid and bored as the camera did its duty. Kane was there, too, and Lambert. Ash the traitor, his soulless face enriched with programmed false piety. Dallas . . .

Dallas. Better the picture behind her, like the memories.

"Do you have earwax or what?" she finally snapped. "We've been here three hours. How many different ways do you want me to tell the same story? You think it'll sound better in Swahili, get me a translator and we'll do it in Swahili. I'd try Japanese, but I'm out of practice. Also out of patience. How long does it take you to make up your collective mind?"

Van Leuwen steepled his fingers and frowned. His expression was as gray as his suit. It was approximated by the looks on the faces of his fellow board members. There were eight of them on the official board of inquiry, and not a friendly one in the lot. Executives. Administrators. Adjusters. How could she convince them? They weren't human beings. They were expressions of bureaucratic disapproval. Phantoms. She was used to dealing with reality. The intricacies of politicorporate maneuvering were beyond her.

"This isn't as simple as you seem to believe," he told her quietly. "Look at it from our perspective. You freely admit to detonating the engines of, and thereby destroying, an M-Class interstellar freighter. A rather expensive piece of hardware."

The insurance investigator was possibly the unhappiest member of the board. "Forty-two million in adjusted dollars. That's minus payload, of course. Engine detonation wouldn't leave anything salvageable, even if we could locate the remains after fifty-seven years."

Van Leuwen nodded absently before continuing. "It's

not as if we think you're lying. The lifeboat shuttle's flight
recorder corroborates some elements of your account. The
least controversial ones. That the *Nostromo* set down on LV-
426, an unsurveyed and previously unvisited planet, at the
time and date specified. That repairs were made. That it
resumed its course after a brief layover and was subsequently
set for self-destruct and that this, in fact, occurred. That the
order for engine overload was provided by you. For reasons
unknown."

"Look, I told you—"

Van Leuwen interrupted, having heard it before. "It did
not, however, contain any entries concerning the hostile alien
life-form you *allegedly* picked up during your short stay on
the planet's surface."

"We didn't 'pick it up,'" she shot back. "Like I told
you, it—"

She broke off, staring at the hollow faces gazing stonily
back at her. She was wasting her breath. This wasn't a real
board of inquiry. This was a formal wake, a post-interment
party. The object here wasn't to ascertain the truth in hopes
of vindication, it was to smooth out the rough spots and make
the landscape all nice and neat again. And there wasn't a
thing she could do about it, she saw now. Her fate had been
decided before she'd set foot in the room. The inquiry was
a show, the questions a sham. To satisfy the record.

"Then somebody's gotten to it and doctored the recorder.
A competent tech could do that in an hour. Who had access
to it?"

The representative of the Extrasolar Colonization Administration was a woman on the ungenerous side of fifty.
Previously she'd looked bored. Now she just sat in her chair
and shook her head slowly.

"Would you just listen to yourself for one minute? Do
you really expect us to believe some of the things you've
been telling us? Too much hypersleep can do all kinds of
funny things to the mind."

Ripley glared at her, furious at being so helpless. "You want to hear some funny things?"

Van Leuwen stepped in verbally. "The analytical team that went over your shuttle centimeter by centimeter found no physical evidence of the creature you describe or anything like it. No damage to the interior of the craft. No etching of metal surfaces that might have been caused by an unknown corrosive substance."

Ripley had kept control all morning, answering the most inane queries with patience and understanding. The time for being reasonable was at an end, and so was her store of patience.

"That's because I blew it out the airlock!" She subsided a little as this declaration was greeted by the silence of the tomb. "Like I said."

The insurance man leaned forward and peered along the desk at the ECA representative. "Are there any species like this 'hostile organism' native to LV-426?"

"No." The woman exuded confidence. "It's a rock. No indigenous life bigger than a simple virus. Certainly nothing complex. Not even a flatworm. Never was, never will be."

Ripley ground her teeth as she struggled to stay calm. "I told you, it wasn't indigenous." She tried to meet their eyes, but they were having none of it, so she concentrated on Van Leuwen and the ECA rep. "There was a signal coming from the surface. The *Nostromo*'s scanner picked it up and woke us from hypersleep, as per standard regulations. When we traced it, we found an alien spacecraft like nothing you or anyone else has ever seen. *That* was on the recorder too.

"The ship was a derelict. Crashed, abandoned . . . we never did find out. We homed in on its beacon. We found the ship's pilot, also like nothing previously encountered. He was dead in his chair with a hole in his chest the size of a welder's tank."

Maybe the story bothered the ECA rep. Or maybe she

was just tired of hearing it for the umpteenth time. Whatever, she felt it was her place to respond.

"To be perfectly frank, we've surveyed over three hundred worlds, and no one's ever reported the existence of a creature, which, using your words"—and she bent to read from her copy of Ripley's formal statement—"'gestates in a living human host' and has 'concentrated molecular acid for blood.'"

Ripley glanced toward Burke, who sat silent and tight-lipped at the far end of the table. He was not a member of the board of inquiry, so he had kept silent throughout the questioning. Not that he could do anything to help her. Everything depended on how her official version of the *Nostromo*'s demise was received. Without the corroborating evidence from the shuttle's flight recorder the board had nothing to go on but her word, and it had been made clear from the start how little weight they'd decided to allot to that. She wondered anew who had doctored the recorder and why. Or maybe it simply had malfunctioned on its own. At this point it didn't much matter. She was tired of playing the game.

"Look, I can see where this is going." She half smiled, an expression devoid of amusement. This was hardball time, and she was going to finish it out even though she had no chance of winning. "The whole business with the android— why we followed the beacon in the first place—it all adds up, though I can't prove it." She looked down the length of the table, and now she did grin. "Somebody's covering their Ash, and it's been decided that I'm going to take the muck for it. Okay, fine. But there's one thing you can't change, one fact you can't doctor away.

"Those things *exist*. You can wipe me out, but you can't wipe that out. Back on that planet is an alien ship, and on that ship are thousands of eggs. *Thousands*. Do you understand? Do you have any idea what that implies? I suggest you go back there with an expedition and find it, using the flight recorder's data, and find it fast. Find it and deal with it, preferably with an orbital nuke. before one of your survey teams comes back with a little surprise."

"Thank you, Officer Ripley," Van Leuwen began, "that will be—"

"Because just one of those things," she went on, stepping on him, "managed to kill my entire crew within twelve hours of hatching."

The administrator rose. Ripley wasn't the only one in the room who was out of patience. "*Thank* you. That will be all."

"That's not all!" She stood and glared at him. "If those things get back here, that *will* be all. Then you can just kiss it goodbye, Jack. Just *kiss it goodbye!*"

The ECA representative turned calmly to the administrator. "I believe we have enough information on which to base a determination. I think it's time to close this inquest and retire for deliberation."

Van Leuwen glanced at his fellow board members. He might as well have been looking at mirror images of himself, for all the superficial differences of face and build. They were of one mind.

That was something that could not be openly expressed, however. It would not look good in the record. Above all, everything had to look good in the record.

"Gentlemen, ladies?" Acquiescent nods. He looked back down at the subject under discussion. Dissection was more like it, she thought sourly. "Officer Ripley, if you'd excuse us, please?"

"Not likely." Trembling with frustration, she turned to leave the room. As she did so, her eyes fastened on the picture of Dallas that was staring blankly back down from the videoscreen. Captain Dallas. Friend Dallas. Companion Dallas.

Dead Dallas. She strode out angrily.

There was nothing more to do or say. She'd been found guilty, and now they were going to go through the motions of giving her an honest trial. Formalities. The Company and its friends loved their formalities. Nothing wrong with death and tragedy, as long as you could safely suck all the emotion out of it. Then it would be safe to put in the annual report. So the inquest had to be held, emotion translated into sanitized figures in neat columns. A verdict had to be rendered. But not too loudly, lest the neighbors overhear.

None of which really bothered Ripley. The imminent demise of her career didn't bother her. What she couldn't forgive was the blind stupidity being flaunted by the all-powerful in the room she'd left. So they didn't believe her. Given their type of mind-set and the absence of solid evidence, she could understand that. But to ignore her story totally, to refuse to check it out, that she could never forgive. Because there was a lot more at stake than one lousy life, one unspectacular career as a flight transport officer. And they didn't care. It didn't show as a profit or a loss, so they didn't care.

She booted the wall next to Burke as he bought coffee and doughnuts from the vending machine in the hall. The machine thanked him politely as it accepted his credcard. Like practically everything else on Gateway Station, the machine had no odor. Neither did the black liquid it poured. As for the alleged doughnuts, they might once have flown over a wheat field.

"You had them eating out of your hand, kiddo." Burke was trying to cheer her up. She was grateful for the attempt, even as it failed. But there was no reason to take her anger out on him. Multiple sugars and artificial creamer gave the ersatz coffee some taste.

"They had their minds made up before I even went in there. I've wasted an entire morning. They should've had scripts printed up for everyone to read from, including me. Would've been easier just to recite what they wanted to hear instead of trying to remember the truth." She glanced at him. "You know what they think?"

"I can imagine." He bit into a doughnut.

"They think I'm a headcase."

"You are a headcase," he told her cheerfully. "Have a doughnut. Chocolate or buttermilk?"

She eyed the precooked torus he proffered distastefully. "You can taste the difference?"

"Not really, but the colors are nice."

She didn't grin, but she didn't sneer at him, either.

The "deliberations" didn't take long. No reason why they should, she thought as she reentered the room and resumed her seat. Burke took his place on the far side of the chamber. He started to wink at her, thought better of it, and aborted the gesture. She recognized the eye twitch for what it almost became and was glad he hadn't followed through.

Van Leuwen cleared his throat. He didn't find it necessary to look to his fellow board members for support.

"It is the finding of this board of inquiry that Warrant Officer Ellen Ripley, NOC-14672, has acted with questionable judgment and is therefore declared unfit to hold an ICC license as a commercial flight officer."

If any of them expected some sort of reaction from the condemned, they were disappointed. She sat there and stared silently back at them, tight-lipped and defiant. More likely they were relieved. Emotional outbursts would have to be recorded. Van Leuwen continued, unaware that Ripley had reattired him in black cape and hood.

"Said license is hereby suspended indefinitely, pending review at a future date to be specified later." He cleared his throat, then his conscience. "In view of the unusual length of time spent by the defendant in hypersleep and the concomitant indeterminable effects on the human nervous system, no criminal charges will be filed at this time."

At this time, Ripley thought humorlessly. That was corporatese for "Keep your mouth shut and stay away from the media and you'll still get to collect your pension."

"You are released on your own recognizance for a six-

month period of psychometric probation, to include monthly
review by an approved ICC psychiatric tech and treatment
and or medication as may be prescribed."

It was short, neat, and not at all sweet, and she took it
all without a word, until Van Leuwen had finished and departed. Burke saw the look in her eye and tried to restrain
her.

"Lay off," he whispered to her. She threw off his hand
and continued up the corridor. "It's over."

"Right," she called back to him as she lengthened her
stride. "So what else can they do to me?"

She caught up with Van Leuwen as he stood waiting for
the elevator. "Why won't you check out LV-426?"

He glanced back at her. "Ms. Ripley, it wouldn't matter.
The decision of the board is final."

"The heck with the board's decision. We're not talking
about me now. We're talking about the next poor souls to
find that ship. Just tell me why you won't check it out."

"Because I don't have to," he told her brusquely. "The
people who live there checked it out years ago, and they've
never reported any 'hostile organism' or alien ship. Do you
think I'm a complete fool? Did you think the board wouldn't
seek some sort of verification, if only to protect ourselves
from future inquiries? And by the way, they call it Acheron
now."

Fifty-seven years. Long time. People could accomplish
a lot in fifty-seven years. Build, move around, establish new
colonies. Ripley struggled with the import of the administrator's words.

"What are you talking about? What people?"

Van Leuwen joined the other passengers in the elevator
car. Ripley put an arm between the doors to keep them from
closing. The doors' sensors obediently waited for her to remove it.

"Terraformers," Van Leuwen explained. "Planetary engineers. Much has happened in that field while you slept,

Ripley. We've made significant advances, great strides. The cosmos is not a hospitable place, but we're changing that. It's what we call a shake-'n'-bake colony. They set up atmosphere processors to make the air breathable. We can do that now, efficiently and economically, as long as we have some kind of resident atmosphere to work with. Hydrogen, argon— methane is best. Acheron is swimming in methane, with a portion of oxygen and sufficient nitrogen for beginning bonding. It's nothing now. The air's barely breathable. But given time, patience, and hard work, there'll be another habitable world out there ready to comfort and succor humanity. At a price, of course. Ours is not a philanthropic institution, though we like to think of what we do as furthering mankind's progress.

"It's a big job. Decades worth. They've already been there more than twenty years. *Peacefully.*"

"Why didn't you tell me?"

"Because it was felt that the information might have biased your testimony. Personally I don't think it would have made a bit of difference. You obviously believe what you believe. But some of my colleagues were of a differing opinion. I doubt it would have changed our decision."

The doors tried to close, and she slammed them apart. The other passengers began to exhibit signs of annoyance.

"How many colonists?"

Van Leuwen's brow furrowed. "At last count I'd guess sixty, maybe seventy, families. We've found that people work better when they're not separated from their loved ones. It's more expensive, but it pays for itself in the long run, and it gives the community the feeling of a real colony instead of merely an engineering outpost. It's tough on some of the women and the kids, but when their tour of duty ends, they can retire comfortably. Everyone benefits from the arrangement."

"Sweet Jesus," Ripley whispered.

One of the passengers leaned forward, spoke irritably. "Do you mind?"

Absently she dropped her arm to her side. Freed of their responsibility, the doors closed quietly. Van Leuwen had already forgotten her, and she him. She was looking instead into her imagination.

Not liking what she saw there.

It was not the best of times, and it certainly was the worst of places. Driven by unearthly meteorological forces, the winds of Acheron hammered unceasingly at the planet's barren surface. They were as old as the rocky globe itself. Without any oceans to compete with they would have scoured the landscape flat eons ago, had not the uneasy forces deep within the basaltic shell continually thrust up new mountains and plateaus. The winds of Acheron were at war with the planet that gave them life.

Heretofore there'd been nothing to interfere with their relentless flow. Nothing to interrupt their sand-filled storms, nothing to push against the gales instead of simply conceding mastery of the air to them—until humans had come to Acheron and claimed it for their own. Not as it was now, a landscape of tortured rock and dust dimly glimpsed through yellowish air, but as it would be once the atmosphere processors had done their work. First the atmosphere itself would be transformed, methane relinquishing its dominance to oxygen and nitrogen. Then the winds would be tamed, and the surface. The final result would be a benign climate whose offspring would take the form of snow and rain and growing things.

That would be the present's legacy to future generations. For now the inhabitants of Acheron ran the processors and struggled to make a dream come true, surviving on a ration of determination, humor, and oversize paychecks. They would not live long enough to see Acheron become a land of milk and honey. Only the Company would live long enough for that. The Company was immortal as none of them could ever be.

The sense of humor common to all pioneers living under difficult conditions was evident throughout the colony, most notably in a steel sign set in concrete pylons outside the last integrated structure:

HADLEY'S HOPE - Pop. 159
Welcome to Acheron

Beneath which some local wag had, without official authorization, added in indelible spray paint "Have a Nice Day." The winds ignored the request. Airborne particles of sand and grit had corroded much of the steel plate. A new visitor to Acheron, courtesy of the atmosphere processors, had added its own comment with a brown flourish: the first rains had produced the first rust.

Beyond the sign lay the colony itself, a cluster of bunkerlike metal and plasticrete structures joined together by conduits seemingly too fragile to withstand Acheron's winds. They were not as impressive to look upon as was the surrounding terrain with its wind-blasted rock formations and crumbling mountains, but they were almost as solid and a lot more homey. They kept the gales at bay, and the still-thin atmosphere, and protected those who worked within.

High-wheeled tractors and other vehicles crawled down the open roadways between the buildings, emerging from or disappearing into underground garages like so many communal pillbugs. Neon lights flickered fitfully on commercial buildings, advertising the few pitiful, but earnest, entertainments to be had at outrageous prices that were paid without comment. Where large paychecks are found, there are always small businesses operated by men and women with outsize dreams. The company had no interest in running such penny-ante operations itself, but it gladly sold concessions to those who desired to do so.

Beyond the colony complex rose the first of the atmosphere processors. Fusion-powered, it belched a steady storm of cleansed air back into the gaseous envelope that surrounded the planet. Particulate matter and dangerous gases were removed either by burning or by chemical breakdown; oxygen and nitrogen were thrown back into the dim sky. In with the bad air, out with the good. It was not a complicated process, but it was time-consuming and very expensive.

But how much is a world worth? And Acheron was not as bad as some that the Company had invested in. At least it possessed an existing atmosphere capable of modification. Much easier to fine-tune the composition of a world's air than to provide it from scratch. Acheron had weather and near normal gravity. A veritable paradise.

The fiery glow that emanated from the crown of the volcanolike atmosphere processor suggested another realm entirely. None of the symbolism was lost on the colonists. It inspired only additional humor. They hadn't agreed to come to Acheron because of the weather.

There were no soft bodies or pallid, weak faces visible within the colony corridors. Even the children looked tough. Not tough as in mean or bullying, but strong within as well as without. There was no room here for bullies. Cooperation was a lesson learned early. Children grew up faster than their Earthbound counterparts and those who lived on fatter, gentler worlds. They and their parents were a breed unto themselves, self-reliant yet interdependent. They were not unique. Their predecessors had ridden in wagons instead of starships.

It helped to think of oneself as a pioneer. It sounded much better than a numerical job description.

At the center of this ganglion of men and machines was the tall building known as the control block. It towered above every other artificial structure on Acheron with the exception of the atmosphere processing stations themselves. From the outside it looked spacious. Within, there wasn't a spare square meter to be found. Instrumentation was crowded into corners and sequestered in the crawl spaces beneath the floors and the serviceways above the suspended ceilings. And still there was never enough room. People squeezed a little closer to one another so that the computers and their attendant machines could have more room. Paper piled up in corners despite unceasing efforts to reduce every scrap of necessary information to electronic bytes. Equipment shipped out new from the factory quickly acquired a plethora of homey scratches, dents, and coffee-cup rings.

Two men ran the control block and therefore the colony. One was the operations manager, the other his assistant. They called one another by their first names. Formality was not in vogue on frontier worlds. Insistence on titles and last names and too much supercilious pulling of rank could find a man lost outside without a survival suit or communicator.

Their names were Simpson and Lydecker, and it was a toss-up as to which looked more harried than the other. Both wore the expression of men for whom sleep is a teasing mistress rarely visited. Lydecker looked like an accountant haunted by a major tax deduction misplaced ten years earlier. Simpson was a big, burly type who would have been more comfortable running a truck than a colony. Unfortunately he'd been stuck with brains as well as brawn and hadn't managed to hide it from his employers. The front of his shirt was perpetually sweat-stained. Lydecker confronted him before he could retreat.

"See the weather report for next week?" Simpson was chewing on something fragrant, which stained the inside of his mouth. Probably illegal, Lydecker knew. He said nothing about it. It was Simpson's business, and Simpson was his boss. Besides, he'd been considering borrowing a chew. Small vices were not encouraged on Acheron, but as long as they didn't interfere with a person's work, neither were they held up to ridicule. It was tough enough to keep one's sanity, hard enough to get by.

"What about it?" the operations manager said.

"We're going to have a real Indian summer. Winds should be all the way down to forty knots."

"Oh, good. I'll break out the inner tubes and the suntan lotion. Heck, I'd settle for just one honest glimpse of the local sun."

Lydecker shook his head, affecting an air of mock disapproval. "Never satisfied, are you? Isn't it enough to know it's still up there?"

"I can't help it; I'm greedy. I should shut up and count my blessings, right? You got something else on your mind, Lydecker, or are you just on one of your hour-long coffee breaks?"

"That's me. Goof off every chance I get. I figure my next chance will be in about two years." He checked a printed readout. "You remember you sent some wildcatters out to that high plateau out past the Ilium Range a couple days ago?"

"Yeah. Some of our dreamers back home thought there might be some radioactives out that way. So I asked for volunteers, and some guy named Jorden stuck up his mitt. I told 'em to go look if they wanted to. Some others might've taken off in that direction also. What about it?"

"There's a guy on the horn right now. Mom-and-pop

survey team. Says he's homing something and wants to know if his claim will be honored."

"Everybody's a lawyer these days. Sometimes I think I should've gone in for it myself."

"What, and ruin your sophisticated image? Besides, there's not much call for lawyers out-here. And you make better money."

"Keep telling me that. It helps." Simpson shook his head and turned to gaze at a green screen. "Some honch in a cushy office on Earth says go look at a grid reference in the middle of nowhere, we look. They don't say why, and I don't ask. I don't ask because it takes two weeks to get an answer from back there, and the answer's always 'Don't ask.' Sometimes I wonder why we bother."

"I just told you why. For the money." The assistant operations officer leaned back against a console. "So what do I tell this guy?"

Simpson turned to stare at a videoscreen that covered most of one wall. It displayed a computer-generated topographical map of the explored portion of Acheron. The map was not very extensive, and the features it illustrated made the worst section of the Kalahari Desert look like Polynesia. Simpson rarely got to see any of Acheron's surface in person. His duties required him to remain close to Operations at all times, and he liked that just fine.

"Tell him," he informed Lydecker, "that as far as I'm concerned, if he finds something, it's his. Anybody with the guts to go crawling around out there deserves to keep what he finds."

The tractor had six wheels, armored sides, oversize tires, and a corrosion-proof underbody. It was not completely Acheron-proof, but then, very little of the colony's equipment was. Repeated patching and welding had transformed the once-sleek exterior of the tractor into a collage composed of off-color metal blotches held together with solder and epoxy sealant. But it kept the wind and sand at bay and climbed steadily forward. That was enough for the people it sheltered.

At the moment it was chugging its way up a gentle slope, the fat tires kicking up sprays of volcanic dust that the wind was quick to carry away. Eroded sandstone and shale crumbled beneath its weight. A steady westerly gale howled outside its armored flanks, blasting the pitted windows and light ports in its emotionless, unceasing attempt to blind the vehicle and those within. The determination of those who drove combined with the reliable engine to keep it moving uphill. The engine hummed reassuringly, while the air filters cycled ceaselessly as they fought to keep dust and grit out of the sacrosanct interior. The machine needed clean air to breathe just as much as did its occupants.

He was not quite as weather-beaten as his vehicle, but Russ Jorden still wore the unmistakable look of someone who'd spent more than his share of time on Acheron. Weathered and wind-blasted. To a lesser degree the same description applied to his wife, Anne, though not to the two children who bounced about in the rear of the big central cabin. Somehow they managed to dart in and around portable sampling equipment and packing cases without getting themselves smashed against the walls. Their ancestors had learned at an early age how to ride something called a horse. The action of the tractor was not very different from the motion one has to cope with atop the spine of that empathetic quadruped, and the children had mastered it almost as soon as they learned how to walk.

Their clothing and faces were smeared with dust despite the nominally inviolable interior of the vehicle. That was a fact of life on Acheron. No matter how tight you tried to seal yourself in, the dust always managed to penetrate vehicles, offices, homes. One of the first colonists had coined a name for this phenomenon that was more descriptive than scientific. "Particulate osmosis," he'd called it. Acheronian science. The more imaginative colonists insisted that the dust was sentient, that it hid and waited for doors and windows to open a crack before deliberately rushing inside. Homemakers argued facetiously whether it was faster to wash clothes or scrape them clean.

Russ Jorden wrestled the massive tractor around boulders too big to climb and negotiated a path through narrow crevices in the plateau they were ascending. He was sustained in his efforts by the music of the Locater's steady pinging. It grew louder the nearer they came to the source of the electromagnetic disturbance, but he refused to turn down the volume. Each ping was a melody unto itself, like the chatter of old-time cash registers. His wife monitored the tractor's condition and the life-support systems while her husband drove.

"Look at this fat, juicy, magnetic profile." Jorden tapped the small readout on his right. "And it's mine, mine, mine. Lydecker says that Simpson said so, and we've got it recorded. They can't take that away from us now. Not even the Company can take it away from us. Mine, all mine."

"Half mine, dear." His wife glanced over at him and smiled.

"And half mine!" This cheerful desecration of basic mathematics came from Newt, the Jorden's daughter. She was six years old going on ten, and she had more energy than both her parents and the tractor combined. Her father grinned affectionately without taking his eyes from the driver's console.

"I got too many partners."

The girl had been playing with her older brother until she'd finally worn him out. "Tim's bored, Daddy, and so am I. When are we going back to town?"

"When we get rich, Newt."

"You always say that." She scrambled onto her feet, as agile as an otter. "I wanna go back. I wanna play Monster Maze."

Her brother stuck his face into hers. "You can play by yourself this time. You cheat too much."

"Do not!" She put small fists on unformed hips. "I'm just the best, and you're jealous."

"Am not! You go in places we can't fit."

"So? That's why I'm the best."

Their mother spared a moment to glance over from her bank of monitors and readouts. "Knock it off. I catch either of you two playing in the air ducts again, I'll tan your hides. Not only is it against colony regulations, it's dangerous. What if one of you missed a step and fell down a vertical shaft?"

"Aw, Mom. Nobody's dumb enough to do that. Besides, all the kids play it, and nobody's been hurt yet. We're careful." Her smile returned. "An' I'm the best 'cause I can fit places nobody else can."

"Like a little worm." Her brother stuck his tongue out at her.

She duplicated the gesture. "Nyah, nyah! Jealous, jealous." He made a grab for her protruding tongue. She let out a childish shriek and ducked behind a mobile ore analyzer.

"Look, you two." There was more affection than anger in Anne Jorden's tone. "Let's try to calm down for two minutes, okay? We're almost finished up here. We'll head back toward town soon and—"

Russ Jorden had half risen from his seat to stare through the windshield. Childish confrontations temporarily put aside, his wife joined him.

"What is it, Russ?" She put a hand on his shoulder to steady herself as the tractor lurched leftward.

"There's something out there. Clouds parted for just a second, and I *saw* it. I don't know what it is, but it's big. And it's ours. Yours and mine—and the kids'.."

The alien spacecraft dwarfed the tractor as the big six-wheeler trundled to a halt nearby. Twin arches of metallic glass swept skyward in graceful, but somehow disturbing, curves from the stern of the derelict. From a distance they resembled the reaching arms of a prone dead man, locked in advanced rigor mortis. One was shorter than the other, and yet this failed to ruin the symmetry of the ship.

The design was as alien as the composition. It might have been grown instead of built. The slick bulge of the hull still exhibited a peculiar vitreous luster that the wind-borne grit of Acheron had not completely obliterated.

Jorden locked the tractor's brakes. "Folks, we have scored big this time. Anne, break out the suits. I wonder if the Hadley Café can synthesize champagne?"

His wife stood where she was, staring out through the tough glass. "Let's check it out and get back safely before we start celebrating, Russ. Maybe we're not the first to find it."

"Are you kidding? There's no beacon on this whole plateau. There's no marker outside. Nobody's been here before us. Nobody! She's all ours." He was heading toward the rear of the cabin as he talked.

Anne still sounded doubtful. "Hard to believe that anything that big, putting out that kind of resonance, could have sat here for this long without being noticed."

"Bulll." Jorden was already climbing into his environment suit, flipping catches without hunting for them, closing seal-tights with the ease of long practice. "You worry too much. I can think of plenty of reasons why it's escaped notice until now."

"For instance?" Reluctantly she turned from the window and moved to join him in donning her own suit.

"For instance, it's blocked off from the colony's detectors by these mountains, and you know that surveillance satellites are useless in this kind of atmosphere."

"What about infrared?" She zipped up the front of her suit.

"What infrared? Look at it: dead as a doornail. Probably been sitting here just like that for thousands of years. Even if it got here yesterday, you couldn't pick up any infrared on this part of the planet; new air coming out of the atmosphere processor is too hot."

"So then how did Operations hit on it?" She was slipping on her equipment, filling up the instrument belt.

He shrugged. "How the heck should I know? If it's bugging you, you can winkle it out of Lydecker when we get back. The important thing is that we're the ones they picked to check it out. We lucked out." He turned toward the airlock door. "C'mon, babe. Let's crack the treasure chest. I'll bet that baby's insides are just crammed with valuable stuff."

Equally enthusiastic but considerably more self-possessed, Anne Jorden tightened the seals on her own suit. Husband and wife checked each other out: oxygen, tools, lights, energy cells, all in place. When they were ready to leave the tractor, she popped her wind visor and favored her offspring with a stern gaze.

"You kids stay inside. I mean it."

"Aw, Mom." Tim's expression was full of childish disappointment. "Can't I come too?"

"No, you cannot come too. We'll tell you all about it when we get back." She closed the airlock door behind her.

Tim immediately ran to the nearest port and pressed his nose against the glass. Outside the tractor, the twilight landscape was illuminated by the helmet beams of his parents.

"I dunno why I can't go too."

"Because Mommy said so." Newt was considering what to play next as she pressed her own face against another window. The lights from her parents' helmets grew dim as they advanced toward the strange ship.

Something grabbed her from behind. She squealed and turned to confront her brother.

"Cheater!" he jeered. Then he turned and ran for a place to hide. She followed, yelling back at him.

The bulk of the alien vessel loomed over the two bipeds as they climbed the broken rubble that surrounded it. Wind howled around them. Dust obscured the sun.

"Shouldn't we call in?" Anne stared at the smooth-sided mass.

"Let's wait till we know what to call it in as." Her husband kicked a chunk of volcanic rock out of his path.

"How about 'big weird thing'?"

Russ Jorden turned to face her, surprise showing on his face behind the visor. "Hey, what's the matter, honey? Nervous?"

"We're preparing to enter a derelict alien vessel of unknown type. You bet I'm nervous."

He clapped her on the back. "Just think of all that beautiful money. The ship alone's worth a fortune, even if it's empty. It's a priceless relic. Wonder who built it, where they came from, and why it ended up crashed on this godforsaken lump of gravel?" His voice and expression were full of enthusiasm as he pointed to a dark gash in the ship's side. "There's a place that's been torn open. Let's check her out."

They turned toward the opening. As they drew near, Anne Jorden regarded it uneasily. "I don't think this is the result of damage, Russ. It looks integral with the hull to me. Whoever designed this thing didn't like right angles."

"I don't care what they liked. We're going _in_."

A single tear wound its way down Newt Jorden's cheek. She'd been staring out the fore windshield for a long time now. Finally she stepped down and moved to the driver's chair to shake her sleeping brother. She sniffed and wiped away the tear, not wanting Tim to see her cry.

"Timmy—wake up, Timmy. They've been gone a long time."

Her brother blinked, removed his feet from the console, and sat up. He glanced unconcernedly at the chronometer set in the control dash, then peered out at the dim, blasted landscape. Despite the tractor's heavy-duty insulation, one could still hear the wind blowing outside when the engine was shut down. Tim sucked on his lower lip.

"It'll be okay, Newt. Dad knows what he's doing."

At that instant the outside door slammed open, admitting wind, dust, and a tall dark shape. Newt screamed, and Tim scrambled out of the seat as their mother ripped off her visor and threw it aside, heedless of the damage it might do to the delicate instrumentation. Her eyes were wild, and the tendons stood out in her neck as she shoved past her children. She snatched up the dash mike and yelled into the condenser.

"Mayday! Mayday! This is Alpha Kilo Two Four Niner calling Hadley Control. Repeat. This is Alpha Kil . . ."

Newt barely heard her mother. She had both hands pressed over her mouth as she sucked on stale atmosphere. Behind her, the tractor's filters whined as they fought to strain the particulate-laden air. She was staring out the open door at the ground. Her father lay there, sprawled on his back on the rocks. Somehow her mother had dragged him all the way back from the alien ship.

There was something on his face.

It was flat, heavily ribbed, and had lots of spiderlike chitinous legs. The long, muscular tail was tightly wrapped around the neck of her father's environment suit. More than anything else, the creature resembled a mutated horseshoe crab with a soft exterior. It was pulsing in and out, in and out, like a pump. Like a machine. Except that it was not a machine. It was clearly, obviously, obscenely alive.

Newt began screaming again, and this time she didn't stop.

It was quiet in the apartment except for the blare of the wallscreen. Ripley ignored the simpcom and concentrated instead on the smoke rising from her denicotined cigarette. It formed lazy, hazy patterns in the stagnant air.

Even though it was late in the day, she'd managed to avoid confronting a mirror. Just as well, since her haggard, unkempt appearance could only depress her further. The apartment was in better shape than she was. There were just enough decorative touches to keep it from appearing spartan. None of the touches were what another might call personal. That was understandable. She'd outlived everything that once might have been considered personal. The sink was full of dirty dishes even though the dishwasher sat empty beneath it.

She wore a bathrobe that was aging as rapidly as its owner. In the adjoining bedroom, sheets and blankets lay in a heap at the base of the mattress. Jones prowled the kitchen, hunting overlooked morsels. He would find none. The kitchen kept itself reasonably antiseptic despite a deliberate lack of cooperation from its owner.

"Hey, Bob!" the wallscreen bleated vapidly, "I heard that you and the family are heading off for the colonies!"

"Best decision I ever made, Phil," replied a fatuously grinning nonentity from the opposite side of the wall. "We'll be starting a new life from scratch in a clean world. No crime, no unemployment . . ."

And the two chiseled performers who were acting out this administration-approved spiel probably lived in an expensive Green Ring on the East Coast, Ripley thought sardonically as she listened to it with half an ear. In Cape Cod condos overlooking Martha's Vineyard or Hilton Head or some other unpolluted, high-priced snob refuge for the fortunate few who knew how to bill and coo and dance, yassuh, dance when imperious corporate chieftains snapped their fingers. None of that for her. No smell of salt, no cool mountain breezes. Inner-city Company dole, and lucky she was to have that much.

She'd find something soon. They just wanted to keep her quiet for a while, until she calmed down. They'd be glad to help her relocate and retrain. After which they'd conveniently forget about her. Which was just dandy keeno fine as far as she was concerned. She wanted no more to do with the Company than the Company wanted to do with her.

If only they hadn't suspended her license, she'd long since have been out of here and away.

The door buzzed sharply for attention and she jumped. Jones merely glanced up and meowed before trundling off toward the bathroom. He didn't like strangers. Always had been a smart cat.

She put the cigarette (guaranteed to contain no carcinogens, no nicotine, and no tobacco—harmless to your health, or so the warning label on the side of the packet insisted) aside and moved to open the door. She didn't bother to check through the peephole. Hers was a full-security building. Not that after her recent experiences there was anything in an Earthside city that could frighten her.

Carter Burke stood there, wearing his usual apologetic smile. Standing next to him and looking formal was a younger man clad in the severe dress-black uniform of an officer in the Colonial Marines.

"Hi, Ripley." Burke indicated his companion. "This is Lieutenant Gorman of the Co—"

The closing door cut his sentence in half. Ripley turned her back on it, but she'd neglected to cut power to the hall speaker. Burke's voice reached her via the concealed membrane.

"Ripley, we have to talk."

"No, we don't. Get lost, Carter. And take your friend with you."

"No can do. This is important."

"Not to me it isn't. Nothing's important to me."

Burke went silent, but she sensed he hadn't left. She knew him well enough to know that he wouldn't give up easily. The Company rep wasn't demanding, but he was an accomplished wheedler.

As it developed, he didn't have to argue with her. All he had to do was say one sentence.

"We've lost contact with the colony of Acheron."

A sinking feeling inside as she mulled over the ramifications of that unexpected statement. Well, perhaps not entirely unexpected. She hesitated a moment longer before opening the door. It wasn't a ploy. That much was evident in Burke's expression. Gorman's gaze shifted from one to the other. He was clearly uncomfortable at being ignored, even as he tried not to show it.

She stepped aside. "Come in."

Burke surveyed the apartment and gratefully said nothing, shying away from inanities like "Nice place you have here" when it obviously wasn't. He also forbore from saying, "You're looking well," since that also would have constituted an obvious untruth. She could respect him for his restraint. She gestured toward the table.

"Want something? Coffee, tea, spritz?"

"Coffee would be fine," he replied. Gorman added a nod.

She went into the compact kitchen and dialed up a few

cups. Bubbling sounds began to emanate from the processor as she turned back to the den.

"You didn't need to bring the Marines." She smiled thinly at him. "I'm past the violent stage. The psych techs said so, and it's right there on my chart." She waved toward a desk piled high with discs and papers. "So what's with the escort?"

"I'm here as an official representative of the corps." Gorman was clearly uneasy and more than willing to let Burke handle the bulk of the conversation. How much did he know, and what had they told him about her? she wondered. Was he disappointed in not encountering some stoned harridan? Not that his opinion of her mattered.

"So you've lost contact." She feigned indifference. "So?"

Burke looked down at his slim-line, secured briefcase. "It has to be checked out. Fast. All communications are down. They've been down too long for the interruption to be due to equipment failure. Acheron's been in business for years. They're experienced people, and they have appropriate backup systems. Maybe they're working on fixing the problem right now. But it's been no-go dead silence for too long. People are getting nervous. Somebody has to go and check it out in person. It's the only way to quiet the nervous Nellies.

"Probably they'll correct the trouble while the ship's on its way out and the whole trip will be a waste of time and money, but it's time to set out."

He didn't have to elaborate. Ripley had already gotten where he was going and returned. She went into the kitchen and brought out the coffees. While Gorman sipped his cup of brew she began pacing. The den was too small for proper pacing, but she tried, anyway. Burke just waited.

"No," she said finally. "There's no way."

"Hear me out. It's not what you think."

She stopped in the middle of the floor and stared at him in disbelief. "Not what I think? Not what I *think*? I don't have to think, Burke. I was reamed, steamed, and dry-cleaned by you guys, and now you want me to go back out *there*? Forget it!"

She was trembling as she spoke. Gorman misinterpreted the reaction as anger, but it was pure fear. She was scared. Gut-scared and trying to mask it with indignation. Burke knew what she was feeling but pressed on, anyway. He had no choice.

"Look," he began in what he hoped was his best conciliatory manner, "we don't know what's going on out there. If their relay satellite's gone out instead of the ground transmitter, the only way to fix it is with a relief team. There are no spacecraft in the colony. If that's the case, then they're all sitting around out there cursing the Company for not getting off its collective butt and sending out a repair crew pronto. If it is the satellite relay, then the relief team won't even have to set foot on the planet itself. But we don't know what the trouble is, and if it's *not* the orbital relay, then I'd like to have you there. As an adviser. That's all."

Gorman lowered his coffee. "You wouldn't be going in with the troops. Assuming we even have to go in. I can guarantee your safety."

She rolled her eyes and glanced at the ceiling.

"These aren't your average city cops or army accompanying us, Ripley," Burke said forcefully. "These Colonial Marines are some tough hombres, and they'll be packing state-of-the-art firepower. Man plus machine. There's nothing they can't handle. Right, Lieutenant?"

Gorman allowed himself a slight smile. "We're trained to deal with the unexpected. We've handled problems on worse worlds than Acheron. Our casualty rate for this kind of operation hovers right around zero. I expect the percentage to improve a little more after this visit."

If this declaration was intended to impress Ripley, it failed miserably. She looked back to Burke.

"What about you? What's your interest in this?"

"Well, the Company cofinanced the colony in tandem

with the Colonial Administration. Sort of an advance against
mineral rights and a portion of the long-term developmental
profits. We're diversifying, getting into a lot of terraforming.
Real estate on a galactic scale. Building better worlds and
all that."

"Yeah, yeah," she muttered. "I've seen the commer-
cials."

"The corporation won't see any substantial profits out
of Acheron until terraforming's complete, but a big outfit like
that has to consider the long term." Seeing that this was having
no effect on his host, Burke switched to another tack. "I hear
you're working in the cargo docks over Portside?"

Her reply was defensive, as was to be expected. "That's
right. What about it?"

He ignored the challenge. "Running loaders, forklifts,
suspension grates; that sort of thing?"

"It's all I could get. I'm crazy if I'm going to live on
charity all my life. Anyway, it keeps my mind off . . . everything. Days off are worse. Too much time to think. I'd rather
keep busy."

"You like that kind of work?"

"Are you trying to be funny?"

He fiddled with the catch on his case. "Maybe it's not
all you can get. What if I said I could get you reinstated as
a flight officer? Get you your license back? And that the
Company has agreed to pick up your contract? No more
hassles with the commission, no more arguments. The official
reprimand comes out of your record. Without a trace. As far
as anyone will be concerned, you've been on a leave of
absence. Perfectly normal following a long tour of duty. It'll
be like nothing happened. Won't even affect your pension
rating."

"What about the ECA and the insurance people?"

"Insurance is settled, over, done with. They're out of it.
Since nothing will appear on your record, you won't be considered any more of a risk than you were before your last

trip. As far as the ECA is concerned, they'd like to see you go out with the relief team too. It's all taken care of."

"*If* I go."

"*If* you go." He nodded, leaning slightly toward her. He wasn't exactly pleading. It was more like a practiced sales pitch. "It's a second chance, kiddo. Most people who get taken down by a board of inquiry never have the opportunity to come back. If the problem's nothing more than a busted relay satellite, all you have to do is sit in your cubbyhole and read while the techs take care of it. That, and collect your trip pay while you're in hypersleep. By going, you can wipe out all the unpleasantness and put yourself right back up there where you used to be. Full rating, full pension accumulation, the works. I've seen your record. One more long out-trip and you qualify for a captain's certificate.

"And it'll be the best thing in the world for you to face this fear and beat it. You gotta get back on the horse."

"Spare me, Burke," she said frostily. "I've had my psych evaluation for the month."

His smile slipped a little, but his tone grew more determined. "Fine. Let's cut the crap, then. I've read your evaluations. You wake up every night, sheets soaking, the same nightmare over and over—"

"No! The answer is no." She retrieved both coffee cups even though neither was empty. It was another form of dismissal. "Now please go. I'm sorry. Just go, would you?"

The two men exchanged a look. Gorman's expression was unreadable, but she had the feeling that his attitude had shifted from curious to contemptuous. The heck with him: what did he know? Burke mined a pocket, removed a translucent card, and placed it on the table before heading for the door. He paused in the portal to smile back at her.

"Think about it."

Then they were gone, leaving her alone with her thoughts. Unpleasant company. Wind. Wind and sand and a moaning sky. The pale disc of an alien sun fluttering like a paper cutout

beyond the riven atmosphere. A howling, rising in pitch and
intensity, coming closer, closer, until it was right on top of
you, smothering you, cutting off your breath.

With a guttural moan Ripley sat straight up in her bed,
clutching her chest. She was breathing hard, painfully. Suck-
ing in a particularly deep breath, she glanced around the tiny
bedroom. The dim light set in the nightstand illuminated bare
walls, a dresser, and a highboy, sheets kicked to the foot of
the bed. Jones lay sprawled atop the highboy, the highest
point in the room, staring impassively back at her. It was a
habit the cat had acquired soon after their return. When they
went to bed, he would curl up next to her, only to abandon
her soon after she fell asleep in favor of the safety and security
of the highboy. He knew the nightmare was on its way and
gave it plenty of space.

She used a corner of the sheet to mop the sweat from
her forehead and cheeks. Fingers fumbled in the nightstand
drawer until they found a cigarette. She flicked the tip and
waited for the cylinder to ignite. Something—her head
snapped around. Nothing there. Only the soft hum of the
clock. There was nothing else in the room. Just Jones and
her. Certainly no wind.

Leaning to her left, she pawed through the other nightstand drawer until she'd located the card Burke had left behind. She turned it over in her fingers, then inserted it into
a slot in the bedside console. The videoscreen that dominated
the far wall immediately flashed the words STAND BY at her.
She waited impatiently until Burke's face appeared. He was
bleary-eyed and unshaven, having been roused from a sound
sleep, but he managed a grin when he saw who was calling.

"Yello? Oh, Ripley. Hi."

"Burke, just tell me one thing." She hoped there was
enough light in the room for the monitor to pick up her
expression as well as her voice. "That you're going out there
to kill them. Not to study. Not to bring back. Just burn them
out, clean, forever."

He woke up rapidly, she noted. "That's the plan. If there's anything dangerous walking around out there, we get rid of it. Got a colony to protect. No monkeying around with potentially dangerous organisms. That's Company policy. We find anything lethal, anything at all, we fry it. The scientists can go suck eggs. My word on it." A long pause and he leaned toward his own pickup, his face looming large on the screen. "Ripley. Ripley? You still there?"

No more time to think. Maybe it was time to stop thinking and to *do*. "All right. I'm in." There, she'd gone and said it. Somehow she'd said it.

He looked like he wanted to reply, to congratulate or thank her. Something. She broke the connection before he could say a word. A thump sounded on the sheets next to her, and she turned to gaze fondly down at Jones. She trailed short nails down his spine, and he primped delightedly, rubbing against her hip and purring.

"And *you*, my dear, are staying right here."

The cat blinked up at her as he continued to caress her fingers with his back. It was doubtful that he understood either her words or the gist of the previous phone call, but he did not volunteer to accompany her.

At least one of us still has some sense left, she thought as she slid back beneath the covers.

IV

It was an ugly ship. Battered, overused, parts repaired that should have been replaced, too tough and valuable to scrap. Easier for its masters to upgrade it and modify it than build a new one. Its lines were awkward and its engines oversize. A mountain of metal and composites and ceramic, a floating scrap heap, weightless monument to war, it shouldered its way brutally through the mysterious region called hyperspace. Like its human cargo, it was purely functional. Its name was *Sulaco*.

Fourteen dreamers this trip. Eleven engaged in related morphean fantasies, simple and straightforward as the vessel that carried them through the void. Two others more individualistic. A last sleeping under sedation necessary to mute the effects of recurring nightmares. Fourteen dreamers—and one for whom sleep was a superfluous abstraction.

Executive Officer Bishop checked readouts and adjusted controls. The long wait was ended. An alarm sounded throughout the length of the massive military transport. Long dormant machinery, powered down to conserve energy, came back to life. So did long dormant humans as their hypersleep capsules were charged and popped open. Satisfied that his charges had survived their long hibernation, Bishop set about the business of placing *Sulaco* in a low geo-stationary orbit around the colony world of Acheron.

Ripley was the first of the sleepers to awake. Not because

she was any more adaptive than her fellow travelers or more used to the effects of hypersleep, but simply because her capsule was first in line for recharge. Sitting up in the enclosed bed, she rubbed briskly at her arms, then started to work on her legs. Burke sat up in the capsule across from her, and the lieutenant—what was his name?—oh, yeah, Gorman, beyond him.

The other capsules contained the *Sulaco*'s military complement: eight men and three women. They were a select group in that they chose to put their lives at risk for the majority of the time they were awake: individuals used to long periods of hypersleep followed by brief, but intense, periods of wakefulness. The kind of people others made room for on a sidewalk or in a bar.

PFC Spunkmeyer was the dropship crew chief, the man responsible along with Pilot-Corporal Ferro for safely conveying his colleagues to the surface of whichever world they happened to be visiting, and then taking them off again in one piece. In a hurry if necessary. He rubbed at his eyes and groaned as he blinked at the hypersleep chamber.

"I'm getting too old for this." No one paid any attention to this comment, since it was well known (or at least widely rumored) that Spunkmeyer had enlisted when underage. However, nobody joked about his maturity or lack of it when they were plummeting toward the surface of a new world in the PFC-directed dropship.

Private Drake was rolling out of the capsule next to Spunkmeyer's. He was a little older than Spunkmeyer and a lot uglier. In addition to sharing similarities in appearance with the *Sulaco*, likewise he was built a lot like the old transport. Drake was heavy-duty bad company, with arms like a legendary one-eyed sailor, a nose busted beyond repair by the cosmetic surgeons, and a nasty scar that curled one side of his mouth into a permanent sneer. The scar surgery could have fixed, but Drake hung on to it. It was one medal he was allowed to wear all the time. He wore a tight-fitting floppy cap, which no living soul dared refer to as "cute."

Drake was a smartgun operator. He was also skilled in the use of rifles, handguns, grenades, assorted blades, and his teeth.

"They ain't payin' us enough for this," he mumbled.

"Not enough to have to wake up to your face, Drake." This from Corporal Dietrich, who was arguably the prettiest of the group except when she opened her mouth.

"Suck vacuum," Drake told her. He eyed the occupant of another recently opened capsule. "Hey, Hicks, you look like I feel."

Hicks was the squad's senior corporal and second in command among the troops after Master Sergeant Apone. He didn't talk much and always seemed to be in the right place at the potentially lethal time, a fact much appreciated by his fellow Marines. He kept his counsel to himself while the others spouted off. When he did speak, what he had to say was usually worth hearing.

Ripley was back on her feet, rubbing the circulation back into her legs and doing standing knee-bends to loosen up stiffened joints. She examined the troopers as they shuffled past her on their way to a bank of lockers. There were no supermen among them, no overly muscled archetypes, but every one of them was lean and hardened. She suspected that the least among them could run all day over the surface of a two-gee world carrying a full equipment pack, fight a running battle while doing so, and then spend the night breaking down and repairing complex computer instrumentation. Brawn and brains aplenty, even if they preferred to talk like common street toughs. The best the contemporary military had to offer. She felt a little safer—but only a little.

Master Sergeant Apone was making his way up the center aisle, chatting briefly with each of his newly revived soldiers in turn. The sergeant looked as though he could take apart a medium-size truck with his bare hands. As he passed

Comtech Corporal Hudson's pallet, the latter voiced a complaint.

"This floor's _freezing_."

"So were you, ten minutes ago. I never saw such a bunch of old women. Want me to fetch your slippers, Hudson?"

The corporal batted his eyelashes at the sergeant. "Would you, sir? I'd be ever so grateful?" A few rough chuckles acknowledged Hudson's riposte. Apone smiled to himself as he resumed his walk, chiding his people and urging them to speed it up.

Ripley stayed out of their way as they trudged past. They were a tightly knit bunch, a single fighting organism with eleven heads, and she wasn't a part of their group. She stood outside, isolated. A couple of them nodded to her as they strode past, and there were one or two cursory hellos. That was all she had any right to expect, but it didn't make her feel any more relaxed in their company.

PFC Vasquez just stared as she walked past. Ripley had received warmer inspections from robots. The other smartgun operator didn't blink, didn't smile. Black hair, blacker eyes, thin lips. Attractive if she'd make half an effort.

It required a special talent; a unique combination of strength, mental ability, and reflexes, to operate a smartgun. Ripley waited for the woman to say something. She didn't open her mouth as she passed by. Every one of the troopers looked tough. Drake and Vasquez looked tough _and_ mean.

Her counterpart called out to her as she came abreast of his locker. "Hey, Vasquez, you ever been mistaken for a man?"

"No. Have you?"

Drake proffered an open palm. She slapped it, and his fingers immediately clenched right around her smaller fingers. The pressure increased on both sides—a silent, painful greeting. Both were glad to be out from under hypersleep and alive again.

Finally she whacked him across the face and their hands

parted. They laughed, young Dobermans at play. Drake was
the stronger but Vasquez was faster, Ripley decided as she
watched them. If they had to go down, she resolved to try
to keep them on either side of her. It would be the safest
place.

Bishop was moving quietly among the group, helping
with massages and a bottle of special postsleep fluid, acting
more like a valet than a ship's officer. He appeared older than
any of the troopers, including Lieutenant Gorman. As he
passed close to Ripley she noticed the alphanumeric code
tattooed across the back of his left hand. She stiffened in
recognition but said nothing.

"Hey," Private Frost said to someone out of Ripley's
view, "you take my towel?" Frost was as young as Hudson
but better-looking, or so he would insist to anyone who would
waste time listening. When it came time for bragging, the
two younger troopers usually came out about even. Hudson
tended to rely on volume while Frost hunted for the right
words.

Spunkmeyer was up near the head of the line and still
complaining. "I need some slack, man. How come they send
us straight back out like this? It ain't fair. We got some slack
comin', man."

Hicks murmured softly. "You just got three weeks. You
want to spend your whole life on slack time?"

"I mean breathing, not this frozen stuff. Three weeks in
the freezer ain't real off-time."

"Yeah, Top, what about it?" Dietrich wanted to know.

"You know it ain't up to me." Apone raised his voice
above the griping. "Awright, let's knock off the jawing. First
assembly's in fifteen. I want everybody looking like human
beings by then—most of you will have to fake it. Let's shag
it."

Hypersleep wear was stripped off and tossed into the
disposal unit. Easier to cremate the remains and provide fresh
new attire for the return journey than to try to recycle shorts

and tops that had clung to a body for several weeks. The line of lean, naked bodies moved into the shower. High-pressure water jets blasted away accumulated sweat and grime, set nerve endings tingling beneath scoured skin. Through the swirling steam Hudson, Vasquez, and Ferro watched Ripley dry off.

"Who's the freshmeat again?" Vasquez asked the question as she washed cleanser out of her hair.

"She's supposed to be some kinda consultant. Don't know much about her." The diminutive Ferro wiped at her belly, which was as flat and muscular as a steel plate, and exaggerated her expression and tone. "She saw an *alien* once. Or so the skipchat says."

"Whooah!" Hudson made a face. "I'm impressed."

Apone yelled back at them. He was already out in the drying room, toweling off his shoulders. They were as devoid of fat as those of troopers twenty years younger.

"Let's go, let's go. Buncha lazybutts'll run the recyclers dry. C'mon, cycle through. You got to get dirty before you can get clean."

Informal segregation was the order of the day in the mess room. It was automatic. There was no need for whispered words or little nameplates next to the glasses. Apone and his troopers requisitioned the large table while Ripley, Gorman, Burke, and Bishop sat at the other. Everyone nursed coffee, tea, spritz, or water while they waited for the ship's autochef to deal out eggs and ersatz bacon, toast and hash, condiments, and vitamin supplements.

You could identify each trooper by his or her uniform. No two were exactly alike. This was the result not of specialized identification insignia, but of individual taste. The *Sulaco* was no barracks and Acheron no parade ground. Occasionally Apone would have to chew someone out for a particularly egregious addition, like the time Crowe had showed up with a portrait of his latest girlfriend computer-

stenciled across the back of his armor. But for the most part
he let the troopers decorate their outfits as they liked.

"Hey, Top," Hudson chivvied, "what's the op?"

"Yeah." Frost blew bubbles in his tea. "All I know is I
get shipping orders and not time to say hello-goodbye to
Myrna."

"Myrna?" Private Wierzbowski raised a bushy eyebrow.
"I thought it was Leina?"

Frost looked momentarily uncertain. "I think Leina was
three months ago. Or six."

"It's a rescue mission." Apone sipped his coffee. "There's
some juicy colonists' daughters we gotta rescue."

Ferro made a show of looking disappointed. "Hell, that
lets me out."

"Says who?" Hudson leered at her. She threw sugar at
him.

Apone just listened and watched. No reason for him to
intervene. He could have quieted them down, could have
played it by the book. Instead he left it loose and fair, but
only because he knew that his people were the best. He'd
walk into a fight with any one of them watching his back
and not worry about what he couldn't see, knowing that
anything trying to sneak up on him would be taken care of
as efficiently as if he had eyes in the back of his head. Let
'em play, let 'em curse ECA and the corps and the Company
and him too. When the time came, the playing would stop,
and every one of them would be all business.

"Dumb colonists." Spunkmeyer looked to his plate as
food began to put in an appearance. After three weeks asleep
he was starving, but not so starving that he couldn't offer the
obligatory soldier's culinary comment. "What's this stuff supposed to be?"

"Eggs, dimwit," said Ferro.

"I know what an egg is, bubblebrain. I mean this soggy
flat yellow stuff on the side."

"Corn bread, I think." Wierzbowski fingered his portion

and added absently, "Hey, I wouldn't mind getting me some more a that Arcturan poontang. Remember that time?"

Hicks was sitting on his right side. The corporal glanced up briefly, then looked back to his plate. "Looks like that new lieutenant's too good to eat with us lowly grunts. Kissing up to the Company rep."

Wierzbowski stared past the corporal, not caring if anyone should happen to notice the direction of his gaze. "Yeah."

"Doesn't matter if he knows his job," said Crowe.

"The magic word." Frost hacked at his eggs. "We'll find out."

Perhaps it was Gorman's youth that bothered them, even though he was older than half the troopers. More likely it was his appearance: hair neat even after weeks in hypersleep, slack creases sharp and straight, boots gleaming like black metal. He looked too good.

As they ate and muttered and stared, Bishop took the empty seat next to Ripley. She rose pointedly and moved to the far side of the table. The ExO looked wounded.

"I'm sorry you feel that way about synthetics, Ripley."

She ignored him as she glared down at Burke, her tone accusing. "You never said anything about there being an android on board! Why not? Don't lie to me, either, Carter. I saw his tattoo outside the showers."

Burke appeared nonplussed. "Well, it didn't occur to me. I don't know why you're so upset. It's been Company policy for years to have a synthetic on board every transport. They don't need hypersleep, and it's a lot cheaper than hiring a human pilot to oversee the interstellar jumps. They won't go crazy working a longhaul solo. Nothing special about it."

"I prefer the term 'artificial person' myself," Bishop interjected softly. "Is there a problem? Perhaps it's something I can help with."

"I don't think so." Burke wiped egg from his lips. "A synthetic malfunctioned on her last trip out. Some deaths were involved."

"I'm shocked. Was it long ago?"

"Quite a while, in fact." Burke made the statement without going into specifics, for which Ripley was grateful.

"Must have been an older model, then."

"Hyperdine Systems 120-A/2."

Bending over backward to be conciliatory, Bishop turned to Ripley. "Well, that explains it. The old A/2s were always a bit twitchy. That could never happen now, not with the new implanted behavioral inhibitors. Impossible for me to harm or, by omission of action, allow to be harmed a human being. The inhibitors are factory-installed, along with the rest of my cerebral functions. No one can tamper with them. So you see, I'm quite harmless." He offered her a plate piled high with yellow rectangles. "More corn bread?"

The plate did not shatter when it struck the far wall as Ripley smacked it out of his hand. Corn bread crumbled as the plate settled to the floor.

"Just stay away from me, Bishop! You got that straight? You keep away from me."

Wierzbowski observed this byplay in silence, then shrugged and turned back to his food. "She don't like the corn bread, either."

Ripley's outburst sparked no more conversation than that as the troopers finished breakfast and retired to the ready room. Ranks of exotic weaponry lined the walls behind them. Some clustered their chairs and started an improvised game of dice. Tough to pick up a floating crap game after you've been unconscious for three weeks, but they tried nonetheless. They straightened lazily as Gorman and Burke entered, but snapped to when Apone barked at them.

"Tench-hut!" The men and women responded as one, arms vertical at their sides, eyes straight ahead, and focused only on what the sergeant might say to them next.

Gorman's eyes flicked over the line. If possible, the troopers were more motionless standing at attention than they

had been when frozen in hypersleep. He held them a moment
longer before speaking.

"At ease." The line flexed as muscles were relaxed. "I'm
sorry we didn't have time to brief you before we left Gateway,
but—"

"Sir?" said Hudson.

Annoyed, Gorman glanced toward the speaker. Couldn't
let him finish his first sentence before starting with the questions. Not that he'd expected anything else. He'd been warned
that this bunch might be like that.

"Yes, what is it, Hicks?"

The speaker nodded at the man standing next to him.
"Hudson, sir. He's Hicks."

"What's the question, soldier?"

"Is this going to be a stand-up fight, sir, or another bug-
hunt?"

"If you'd wait a moment, you might find some of your
questions anticipated, Hudson. I can understand your impa-
tience and curiosity. There's not a great deal to explain. All
we know is that there's still been no contact with the colony.
Executive Officer Bishop tried to rise Hadley the instant the
Sulaco hove within hailing distance of Acheron. He did not
obtain a response. The planetary deepspace satellite relay
checks out okay, so _that's_ not the reason for the lack of
contact. We don't know what it is yet."

"Any ideas?" Crowe asked.

"There is a possibility, just a possibility at this point,
mind, that a xenomorph may be involved."

"A whaat?" said Wierzbowski.

Hicks leaned toward him, whispered softly. "It's a bug-
hunt." Then louder, to the lieutenant, "So what are these
things, if they're there?"

Gorman nodded to Ripley, who stepped forward. Eleven
pairs of eyes locked on her like gun sights: alert, intent,
curious, and speculative. They were sizing her up, still unsure
whether to class her with Burke and Gorman or somewhere

else. They neither cared for her nor disliked her, because they didn't know her yet.

Fine. Leave it at that. She placed a handful of tiny recorder disks on the table before her.

"I've dictated what I know on these. There are some duplicates. You can read them in your rooms or in your suits."

"I'm a slow reader." Apone lightened up enough to smile slightly. "Tease us a bit."

"Yeah, let's have some previews." Spunkmeyer leaned back against enough explosive to blow a small hotel apart, snuggling back among the firing tubes and detonators.

"Okay. First off, it's important to understand the organism's life cycle. It's actually two creatures. The first form hatches from a spore, a sort of large egg, and attaches itself to its victim. Then it injects an embryo, detaches, and dies. It's essentially a walking reproductive organ. Then the—"

"Sounds like you, Hicks." Hudson grinned over at the older man, who responded with his usual tolerant smile.

Ripley didn't find it funny. She didn't find anything about the alien funny, but then, she'd seen it. The troopers still weren't convinced she was describing something that existed outside her imagination. She'd have to try to be patient with them. That wasn't going to be easy.

"The embryo, the second form, hosts in the victim's body for several hours. Gestating. Then it"—she had to swallow, fighting a sudden dryness in her throat—"emerges. Molts. Grows rapidly. The adult form advances quickly through a number of intermediate stages until it matures in the form of—"

This time it was Vasquez who interrupted. "That's all fine, but I only need to know one thing."

"Yes?"

"Where they are." She pointed her finger at an empty space between Ripley and the door, cocked her thumb, and blew away an imaginary intruder. Hoots and guffaws of approval came from her colleagues.

"Yo Vasquez!" As always, Drake delighted in his counterpart's demure bloodthirstiness. Her nickname was the Gamin Assassin. It was not misplaced.

She nodded brusquely. "Anytime. Anywhere."

"Somebody say 'alien'?" Hudson leaned back in his seat, idly fingering a weapon with an especially long and narrow barrel. "She thought they said 'illegal alien' and signed up."

"Fuck you." Vasquez threw the comtech a casual finger. He responded by mimicking her tone and attitude as closely as possible.

"Anytime. Anywhere."

Ripley's tone was as cold as the skin of the *Sulaco*. "Am I disturbing your conversation, Mr. Hudson? I know most of you are looking at this as just another typical police action. I can assure you it's more than that. I've seen this creature. I've seen what it can do. If you run into it, I can guarantee that you won't do so laughingly."

Hudson subsided, smirking. Ripley shifted her attention to Vasquez. "I hope it'll be as easy as you make it out to be, Private. I really do." Their eyes locked. Neither woman looked away.

Burke broke it up by stepping between them to address the assembled troops. "That's enough for a preview. I suggest all of you take the time to study the disks Ripley has been kind enough to prepare for you. They contain additional basic information, as well as some highly detailed speculative graphics put together by an advanced imaging computer. I believe you'll find them interesting. I promise they'll hold your attention." He relinquished the floor to Gorman. The lieutenant was brisk, sounding like a commander even if he didn't quite look like one.

"Thank you Mr. Burke, Ms. Ripley." His gaze roved over the indifferent faces of his squad. "Any questions?" A hand waved casually from the back of the group and he sighed resignedly. "Yes, Hudson?"

The comtech was examining his fingernails. "How do I get out of this outfit?"

Gorman scowled and forbore from offering the first thought that came to mind. He thanked Ripley again, and gratefully she took a seat.

"All right. I want this operation to go smoothly and by the numbers. I want full DCS and tactical data-base assimilation by oh-eight-thirty." A few groans rose from the group but nothing in the way of a strong protest. It was no less than what they expected.

"Ordnance loading, weapons strip and checkout, and dropship prep will have seven hours. I want everything and everybody ready to go on time. Let's hit it. You've had three weeks rest."

The *Sulaco* was a giant metallic seashell drifting in a black sea. Bluish lights flared soundlessly along the flanks of the unlovely hull as she settled into final orbit. On the bridge, Bishop regarded his instruments and readouts unblinkingly. Occasionally he would touch a switch or tap a flurry of commands into the system. For the most part all he had to do was observe while the ship's computers parked the vessel in the desired orbit. The automation that made interstellar navigation possible had reduced man to the status of a last-recourse backup system. Now synthetics like Bishop had replaced man. Exploration of the cosmos had become a chauffeured profession.

When the dials and gauges had lined up to his satisfaction, he leaned toward the nearest voice pickup. "Attention to the bridge. Bishop speaking. This concludes final intraorbital maneuvering operations. Geosynchronous insertion has been completed. I have adjusted artificial gravity to Acheron norm. Thank you for your cooperation. You may resume work."

In contrast to the peace and quiet that reigned throughout most of the ship, the cargo loading bay was swarming with activity. Spunkmeyer sat in the roll cage of a big powerloader, a machine that resembled a skeletal mechanical elephant and was much stronger. The waldo gloves in which his hands and feet were inserted picked up the PFC's movements and transferred them to the metal arms and legs of the machine, multiplying his carrying capacity by a factor of several thousand.

He slid the long, reinforced arms into a bulging ordnance rack and lifted out a rack of small tactical missiles. Working with the smooth, effortless movements of his external prosthesis, he swung the load up into the dropship's belly. Clicks and clangs sounded from within as the vessel accepted the offering and automatically secured the missiles in place. Spunkmeyer retreated in search of another load. The powerloader was battered and dirty with grease. Across its back the word *Caterpillar* was faintly visible.

Other troopers drove tow motors or ran loading arms. Occasionally they called to one another, but for the most part the loading and prep operation proceeded without conversation. Also without accident, the members of the squad meshed like the individual gears and wheels of some half-metal, half-organic machine. Despite the close quarters in which they found themselves, and the amount of dangerous machinery in constant motion, no one so much as scraped his neighbor. Hicks watched over it all, checking off one item after another on an electronic manifest, occasionally nodding to himself as one more necessary predrop procedure was satisfactorily completed.

In the armory Wierzbowski, Drake, and Vasquez were fieldstripping light weapons, their fingers moving with as much precision as the loading machines in the cargo bay. Tiny circuit boards were removed, checked, and blown clean of dust and lint before being reinserted into sleek metal and plastic sculptures of death.

Vasquez removed her heavy smartgun from its rack and locked it into a work stand and lovingly began to run it through the computer-assisted final checkout. The weapon was designed to be worn, not carried. It was equipped with an integral computer lock-and-fire, its own search-and-detection equipment, and was balanced on a precision gimbal that stabilized itself according to its operator's movements. It could do just about everything except pull its own trigger.

Vasquez smiled affectionately as she worked on it. It was a difficult child, a complex child, but it would protect her and her comrades and keep them safe from harm. She lavished more understanding and care on it than she did on any of her colleagues.

Drake understood completely. He also talked to his weapon, albeit silently. None of their fellow troopers found such behavior abnormal. Everyone knew that all Colonial Marines were slightly unbalanced and that smartgun operators were the strangest of the lot. They tended to treat their weapons as extensions of their own bodies. Unlike their colleagues, gun operation was their principal function. Drake and Vasquez didn't have to worry about mastering communications equipment, piloting a dropship, driving the armored personnel carrier, or even helping to load the ship for landing. All they were required to do was shoot at things. Death-dealing was their designated specialty.

Both of them loved their work.

Not everyone was as busy as the troopers. Burke had completed his few personal preparations for landing while

Gorman was able to leave the actual supervision of final prep to Apone. As they stood off to the side and watched, the Company representative spoke casually to the lieutenant.

"Still nothing from the colony?"

Gorman shook his head and noted something about the loading procedure that induced him to make a notation on his electronic pad. "Not even a background carrier wave. Dead on all channels."

"And we're sure about the relay satellite?"

"Bishop insists that he checked it out thoroughly and that it responded perfectly to every command. Says it gave him something to do while we were on final system approach. He ran a standard signal check along the relay back to Earth, and we should get a response in a few days. That'll be the final confirmation, but he felt sure enough of his own check to guarantee the system's performance."

"Then the problem's down on the surface somewhere."

Gorman nodded. "Like we've suspected all along."

Burke looked thoughtful. "What about local communications? Community video, operations to tractors, relays between the atmosphere processing stations, and the like?"

The lieutenant shook his head regretfully. "If anybody's talking to anybody else down there, they're doing it with smoke signals or mirrors. Except for the standard low-end hiss from the local sun, the electromagnetic spectrum's dead as lead."

The Company rep shrugged. "Well, we didn't expect to find anything else. Still, there was always hope."

"There still is. Maybe the colony's taken a mass vow of silence. Maybe all we'll run into is a collective pout."

"Why would they do something like that?"

"How should I know? Mass religious conversion or something else that demands radio silence."

"Yeah. Maybe." Burke wanted to believe Gorman. Gorman wanted to believe Burke. Neither man believed the other for a moment. Whatever had silenced the colony of

Acheron hadn't been a matter of choice. People liked to talk, colonists more than most. They wouldn't shut down all communications willingly.

Ripley had been watching the two men. Now she shifted her attention back to the ongoing process of loading and predrop prep. She'd seen military dropships on the newscasts, but this was the first time she'd stood close to one. It made her feel a little safer. Heavily armed and armored, it looked like a giant black wasp. As she looked on, a six-wheeled armored personnel carrier was being hoisted into the ship's belly. It was built like an iron ingot, low and squatty, unlovely in profile and purely functional.

Movement on her left made her stumble aside as Frost wheeled a rack of incomprehensible equipment toward her.

"Clear, please," the trooper said politely.

As she apologized and stepped away she was forced to retreat in another direction in order to get out of Hudson's way.

"Excuse me." He didn't look at her, concentrating on his lift load of supplies.

Cursing silently to herself, she hunted through the organized confusion until she found Apone. The NCO was chatting with Hicks, both of them studying the corporal's checklist as she approached. She kept quiet until the sergeant acknowledged her presence.

"Something?" he asked curiously.

"Yeah, there's something. I feel like a fifth wheel down here, and I'm sick of doing nothing."

Apone grinned. "We're all sick of doing nothing. What about it?"

"Is there anything I can do?"

He scratched the back of his head, eyeing her. "I don't know. *Is* there anything you can do?"

She turned and pointed. "I can drive that loader. I've got a class-two dock rating. My latest career move."

Apone glanced in the direction in which she was pointing. The *Sulaco*'s backup powerloader squatted dormant in its maintenance bay. His people were versatile, but they were soldiers first. Marines, not construction workers. An extra couple of hands would be welcome loading the heavy stuff, especially if they were fashioned of titanium alloy, as were the powerloader's.

"That's no toy." The skepticism in Apone's voice was matched by that on Hicks's face.

"That's all right," she replied crisply. "This isn't Christmas."

The sergeant pursed his lips. "Class-two, huh?"

By way of response, she spun on her heel and strode over to the loader, climbed the ladder, and settled into the seat beneath the safety cage. A quick inspection revealed that, as she'd suspected, the loader was little different from the ones she'd operated Portside on Earth. A slightly newer model, maybe. She jabbed at a succession of switches. Motors turned over. A basso whine emanated from the guts of the machine, rising to a steady hum.

Hands and feet slipped into waldo gloves. Like some paralyzed dinosaur suddenly shocked back to life, the loader rose on titanium pads. It boomed as she walked it over to the stack of cargo modules. Huge claws extended and dipped, slipping into lifting receptacles beneath the nearest container. She raised it from the top of the pile and swung it back toward the watching men. Her voice rose above the hum of the motors.

"Where you want it?"

Hicks glanced at his sergeant and cocked an eyebrow appreciatively.

Personal preparation proceeded at the same pace as dropship loading but with additional care. Something could go wrong with the APC, or the supplies crammed into it, or with communications or backup, but no soldier would allow anything to go wrong with his or her personal weaponry. Each of them was capable of fighting and winning a small war on his or her own.

First the armor was snapped together and checked for cracks or warps. Then the special combat boots, capable of resisting any combination of weather, corrosion, and teeth. Backpacks that would enable a fragile human being to survive for over a month in a hostile environment without any supplemental aid whatsoever. Harnesses to keep you from bouncing around during a rough drop or while the APC was grinding a path over difficult terrain. Helmets to protect your skull and visors to shield your eyes. Comsets for communicating with the dropship, with the APC, with whichever buddy happened to be guarding your rear.

Fingers flowed smoothly over fastenings and snaps. When everything was done and ready, when all had been checked out and operational, the whole procedure was run again from scratch. And when *that* was over, if you had a minute, you spent it checking out your neighbor's work.

Apone strode back and forth among his people, doing his own unobtrusive checking even though he knew it was unnecessary. He was, however, a firm believer in the for-want-of-a-nail school. Now was the time to spot the overlooked snap, the forgotten catch. Once things turned hairy, regrets were usually fatal.

"Let's move it, girls! On the ready-line. Let's go, let's go. You've slept long enough."

They formed up and headed for the dropship, chatting excitedly and shuffling along in twos and threes. Apone could have made it pretty if he'd wanted to, formed them up and called cadence, but his people weren't pretty, and he wasn't about to tell them how to walk. The sergeant was pleased to see that their new lieutenant had learned enough by now to keep his mouth shut. They filed into the ship muttering among themselves, no flags flying, no prerecorded bands tooting. Their anthem was a string of well-worn and familiar obscenities passed down from one to the next: defiant words from men and women ready to challenge death. Apone shared them. As all foot soldiers have known for thousands of years, there's nothing noble about dying. Only an irritating finality.

Once inside the dropship, they filed directly into the APC. The carrier would deploy the instant the shuttle craft touched down. It made for a rougher ride, but Colonial Marines do not expect coddling.

As soon as everyone was aboard and the dropship doors secured, a klaxon sounded, signaling depressurization of the *Sulaco*'s cargo bay. Service robots scurried for cover. Warning lights flashed.

The troopers sat in two rows opposite each other, a single aisle running between. Next to the soldiers in their hulking armor, Ripley felt small and vulnerable. In addition to her duty suit she wore only a flight jacket and a communications headset. No one offered her a gun.

Hudson was too juiced up to sit still. The adrenaline was flowing and his eyes were wide. He prowled the aisle, his movements predatory and exaggerated, a cat ready to pounce. As he paced, he kept up a steady stream of psychobabble, unavoidable in the confined space.

"I am *ready*, man. Ready to get it *on*. Check it out. I am the ultimate. State-of-the-art. You *do not* want to mess with me. Hey, Ripley." She glanced up at him, expressionless. "Don't worry, little lady. Me and my squad of ultimate killing machines will protect you. Check it out." He slapped the controls of the servocannon mounted in the overhead gun bay, careful not to hit any of the ready studs.

"Independently targeting particle-beam phalanx gun. Ain't she a cutey? *Vwap!* Fry half a city with this puppy. We got tactical smart missiles, phased-plasma pulse-rifles, RPGs. We got sonic ee-lectronic cannons, we got nukes no flukes, we got knives, sharp sticks—"

Hicks reached up, grabbed Hudson by his battle harness, and yanked him down into an empty seat. His voice was low but it carried.

"Save it."

"Sure, Hicks." Hudson sat back, suddenly docile.

Ripley nodded her thanks to the corporal. Young face, old eyes, she thought as she studied him. Seen more than he should have in his time. Probably more than he's wanted to. She didn't mind the quiet that followed Hudson's soliloquy. There was hysteria enough below. She didn't need to listen to any extra. The corporal leaned toward her.

"Don't mind Hudson. Don't mind any of 'em. They're all like that, but in a tight spot there're none better."

"If he can shoot his gun as well as he does his mouth, maybe it'll take my blood pressure down a notch."

Hicks grinned. "Don't worry on that score. Hudson's a comtech, but he's a close-combat specialist, just like everyone else."

"You too?"

He settled back in his seat: content, self-contained, ready. "I'm not here because I wanted to be a pastry chef."

Motors began to throb. The dropship lurched as it was lowered out of the cargo bay on its grapples.

"Hey," Frost muttered, "anybody check the locks on this coffin? If they're not tight, we're liable to bounce right out the bottom of the shuttle."

"Keep cool, sweets," said Dietrich. "Checked 'em out myself. We're secure. This six-wheeler goes nowhere until we kiss dirt." Frost looked relieved.

The dropship's engines rumbled to life. Stomachs lurched as they left the artificial gravity field of the *Sulaco* behind. They were free now, floating slowly away from the big transport. Soon they would be clear and the engines would fire fully. Legs and hands began to float in zero-gee, but their harnesses held them tight to their seats. The floor and walls of the APC quivered as the engines thundered. Gravity returned with a vengeance.

Burke looked like he was on a fishing cruiser off

Jamaica. He was grinning eagerly, anxious for the real adventure to begin. "Here we go!"

Ripley closed her eyes, then opened them almost immediately. Anything was better than staring at the black backsides of her lids. They were like tiny videoscreens alive with wild sparks and floating green blobs. Malign shapes appeared in the blobs. The taut, confident faces of Frost, Crowe, Apone, and Hicks made for more reassuring viewing.

Up in the cockpit, Spunkmeyer and Ferro studied readouts and worked controls. Gees built up within the APC as the dropship's speed increased. A few lips trembled. No one said a word as they plunged toward atmosphere.

Gray limbo below. The dark mantle of clouds that shrouded the surface of Acheron suddenly became something more than a pearlescent sheen to be admired from above. The atmosphere was dense and disturbed, boiling over dry deserts and lifeless rocks, rendering the landscape invisible to everything but sophisticated sensors and imaging equipment.

The dropship bounced through alien jet streams, shuddering and rocking. Ferro's voice sounded icy calm over the open intercom as she shouldered the streamlined craft through the dust-filled gale.

"Switching to DCS ranging. Visibility zero. A real picnic ground. What a bowl of crap."

"Two-four-oh." Spunkmeyer was too busy to respond in kind to her complaints. "Nominal to profile. Picking up some hull ionization."

Ferro glanced at a readout. "Bad?"

"Nothing the filters can't handle. Winds two hundred plus." A screen between them winked to life, displaying a topographic model of the terrain they were overflying. "Surface ranging on. What'd you expect, Ferro? Tropical beaches?" He nudged a trio of switches. "Starting to hit thermals. Vertical shift unpredictable. Lotta swirling."

"Got it." Ferro thumbed a button. "Nothing that ain't in

our programming. At least the weather hasn't changed down there." She eyed a readout. "Rough air ahead."

The pilot's voice sounded briskly over the APC's intercom system. "Ferro, here. You all read the profile on this dirtball. Summertime fun it ain't. Stand by for some chop."

Ripley's eyes flicked rapidly over her companions, crammed tightly together in the confines of the armored personnel carrier. Hicks lay slumped to one side, asleep in his seat harness. The bouncing seemed not to bother him in the slightest. Most of the other troopers sat quietly, staring straight ahead, their minds mulling over private thoughts. Hudson was talking steadily and silently to himself. His lips moved ceaselessly. Ripley didn't try to read them.

Burke was studying the interior layout of the APC with professional interest. Across from him Gorman sat with his eyes shut tight. His skin was pale, and the sweat stood out on his forehead and neck. His hands were in nonstop motion, rubbing the backs of his knees. Massaging away tenseness— or attempting to dry clamminess, she thought. Maybe it would help him to have someone to talk to.

"How many drops is this for you, Lieutenant?"

His eyes snapped open and he blinked at her. "Thirty-eight—simulated."

"How many *combat* drops?" Vasquez asked pointedly.

Gorman tried to reply as though it made no difference. A minor point, and what did it have to do with anything, anyway? "Well—two. Three, including this one."

Vasquez and Drake exchanged a glance, said nothing. They didn't have to. Their respective expressions were sufficiently eloquent. Ripley gave Burke an accusing look, and he responded with one of indifferent helplessness, as if to say, "Hey, I'm a civilian. Got no control over military assignments."

Which was pure bull, of course, but there was nothing to be gained by arguing about it now. Acheron lay beneath them, Earthside bureaucracy very far away indeed. She chewed her lower lip and tried not to let it bother her. Gorman seemed competent enough. Besides, in any actual confrontation or combat, Apone would run the show. Apone and Hicks.

Cockpit voices continued to reverberate over the intercom. Ferro managed to outgripe Spunkmeyer three to one. In between gripes and complaints they managed to fly the dropship.

"Turning on final approach," she was saying. "Coming around to a seven-zero-niner. Terminal guidance locked in."

"Always knew you were terminal," said Spunkmeyer. It was an old pilot's joke, and Ferro ignored it.

"Watch your screen. I can't fly this sucker and watch the terrain readouts too. Keep us off the mountains." A pause, then, "Where's the beacon?"

"Nothing on relay." Spunkmeyer's voice was calm. "Must've gone out along with communications."

"That's crazy and you know it. Beacons are automatic and individually powered."

"Okay. *You* find the beacon."

"I'll settle for somebody waving a lousy flag." Silence followed. None of the troopers appeared concerned. Ferro and Spunkmeyer had set them down softer than a baby's kiss in worse weather than Acheron's.

"Winds easing. Good kite-flying weather. We'll hold her steady up here for a while so you kids in back can play with your toys."

A flurry of motion as the troopers commenced final touchdown preparations. Gorman slipped out of his flight harness and headed up the aisle toward the APC's tactical operations center. Burke and Ripley followed, leaving the Marines to their work.

The three of them crowded into the bay. Gorman slid behind the control console while Burke took up a stance behind him so he could look over the lieutenant's shoulder. Ripley was pleased to see that there was nothing wrong with Gorman's mechanical skills. He looked relieved to have something to do. His fingers brought readouts and monitor screens to life like an organist extracting notes from stops and keys. Ferro's voice reached them from the cockpit, mildly triumphant.

"Finally got the beacons. Signal is hazy but distinct. And the clouds have cleared enough for us to get some visual. We can see Hadley."

Gorman spoke toward a pickup. "How's it look?"

"Just like the brochures," she said sardonically. "Vacation spot of the galaxy. Massive construction, dirty. A few lights on, so they've got power somewheres. Can't tell at this distance if they're regular or emergency. Not a lot of 'em. Maybe it's nap time. Give me two weeks in the Antarctic anytime."

"Spunkmeyer, your impressions?"

"Windy as all get out. They haven't been bombed. Structural integrity looks good, but that's from up here, looking through bad light. Sorry we're too busy to do a ground scan."

"We'll take care of that in person." Gorman turned his attention back to the multiple screens. The closer they came to setdown, the more confident he seemed to become. Maybe a fear of heights was his only weakness, Ripley mused. If that proved to be the case, she'd be able to relax.

In addition to the tactical screens there were two small ones for each soldier. All were name-labeled. The upper set relayed the view from the video cams built into the crown of each battle helmet. The lower provided individual bio readouts: EEG, EKG, respiratory rate, circulatory functioning, visual acuity, and so on. Enough information for whoever was monitoring the screens to build up a complete physiological profile of every trooper from the inside out.

Above and to the side of the double set of smaller screens were larger monitors that offered those riding inside the APC a complete wraparound view of the terrain outside. Gorman thumbed controls. Hidden telltales beeped and responded on cue.

"Looking good," he murmured to himself, as much as to his civilian observers. "Everybody on line." Ripley noted that the blood-pressure readouts held remarkably steady. And not one of the soldiers' heart rates rose above seventy-five.

One of the small video monitors displayed static instead of a clear view of the APC's interior. "Drake, check your camera," Gorman ordered. "I'm not getting a picture. Frost, show me Drake. Might be an external break."

The view on the screen next to Drake's shifted to reveal the helmeted face of the smartgun operator as he whacked himself on the side of the head with a battery pack. His screen snapped into focus instantly.

"That's better. Pan it around a bit."

Drake complied. "Learned that one in tech class," he informed the occupants of the operations bay. "Got to make sure you hit the left side only or it doesn't work."

"What happens if you hit the right side?" Ripley asked curiously.

"You overload the internal pressure control, the one that keeps your helmet on your head." She could see Drake smiling wolfishly into Frost's camera. "Your eyeballs implode and your brains explode."

"What brains?" Vasquez let out a snort. Drake promptly leaned forward and tried to smack the right side of her helmet with a battery pack.

Apone quieted them. He knew it didn't matter what was wrong with Drake's helmet, because the smartgun operator would abandon it the first chance he got. Likewise Vasquez. Drake would appear in his floppy cap and Vasquez in her red bandanna. Nonregulation battle headgear. Both claimed the helmets obstructed the movement of their gun sights, and if that was the way they felt about it, Apone wasn't about to argue with them. They could shave their skulls and fight bald-headed if they wished as long as they shot straight.

"Awright. Fire team A, gear up. Check your backup systems and your power packs. Anybody goes dead when we spread out is liable to end up that way. If some boogeyman doesn't kill you, I will. Let's move. Two minutes." He glanced to his right. "Somebody wake up Hicks."

A few guffaws sounded from the assembled troopers. Ripley had to smile as she let her gaze drop to the biomonitor with the corporal's name above it. The readings indicated a man overwhelmed with boredom. Apone's second in command was deep in REM sleep. Dreaming of balmier climes, no doubt. She wished she could relax like that. Once upon a time she'd been able to. Once this trip was over, maybe she'd be able to again.

The passenger compartment saw a new rush of activity as backpacks were donned and weapons presented. Vasquez and Drake assisted each other in buckling on their complex smartgun harnesses.

The forward-facing viewscreen gave those in the operations bay the same view as Ferro and Spunkmeyer. Directly ahead a metal volcano thrust its perfect cone into the clouds, belching hot gas into the sky. Audio pickups muted the atmosphere processor's thunder.

"How many of those are on Acheron?" Ripley asked Burke.

"That's one of thirty or so. I couldn't give you all the grid references. They're scattered all over the planet. Well, not scattered. Placed, for optimum injection into the atmosphere. Each is fully automated, and their output is controlled from Hadley Operations Central. Their production will be adjusted as the air here becomes more Earth-normal. Eventually they'll shut themselves down. Until that happens, they'll work around the clock for another twenty to thirty years. They're expensive and reliable. We manufacture them, by the way."

The ship was a drifting mote alongside the massive, rumbling tower. Ripley was impressed. Like everyone else whose work took them out into space, she'd heard about the big terraforming devices, but she'd never expected to see one in person.

Gorman nudged controls, swinging the main external imager around and down to reveal the silent roofs of the colony. "Hold at forty," he commanded Ferro via the console pickup. "Make a slow circle of the complex. I don't think we'll spot anything from up here, but that's the way the regs say to go, so that's how we'll do it."

"Can do," the pilot responded. "Hang on back there. Might bounce a little while we spiral in. This isn't an atmosphere flyer, remember. It's just a lousy dropship. Tight suborbital maneuvering ain't a highlight of its repertoire."

"Just do as you're told, Corporal."

"Yes, *sir*." Ferro added something else too low for her mike to unscramble. Ripley doubted that it was flattering.

They circled in over the town. Nothing moved among the buildings beneath them. The few lights they'd spotted from afar continued to burn. The atmosphere processor roared in the background.

"Everything looks intact," Burke commented. "Maybe some kind of plague has everyone on their backs."

"Maybe." To Gorman the colony structures looked like the wrecks of ancient freighters littering the ocean floor. "Okay," he said sharply to Apone, "let's do it."

Back in the passenger bay, the master sergeant rose from his seat and glared at his troops, hanging on to an overhead handgrip as the dropship rocked in Acheron's unceasing gale.

"Awright! You heard the lieutenant. I want a nice clean dispersal this time. Watch the suit in front of you. Anybody trips over anybody else's boots going out gets booted right back up to the ship."

"Is that a promise?" Crowe looked innocent.

"Hey, Crowe, you want your mommy?" Wierzbowski grinned at his colleague.

"Wish she were here," the private responded. "She'd wipe the floor with half you lot."

They filed toward the front lock, squeezing past operations. Vasquez gave Ripley a nudge as she strolled by. "You
staying in here?"

"You bet."

"Figures." The smartgun operator turned away, shifting
her attention to the back of Drake's head.

"Set down sixty meters this side of the main telemetry
mast." Gorman swiveled the imager's trakball control. Still
no sign of life below. "Immediate dust-off on my 'clear,' then
find a soft cloud and stay on station."

"Understood," said Ferro perfunctorily.

Apone was watching the chronometer built into his suit
sleeve. "Ten seconds, people. Look sharp!"

As the dropship descended to within a hundred and fifty
meters of the colony landing pad, its exterior lights flashed
on automatically, the powerful beams penetrating a surprising
distance into the gloom. The tarmac was damp and freckled
with wind-blown garbage, none of which was large enough
to upset Ferro's carefully timed touchdown. Hydraulic legs
absorbed the shock of contact as tons of metal settled to
ground. Seconds later the APC roared out of the cargo bay
and away from the compact vessel. Having barely made contact with the surface of Acheron, the dropship's engines thundered, and it crawled back up into the dark sky.

Nothing materialized out of the muck to challenge or
confront the personnel carrier as it rumbled up to the first of
the silent colony buildings. Spray and mud flew from beneath
its solid, armored wheels. It swerved sharply left so that the
crew door would face the town's main entrance. Before the
door was half open, Hudson had piled out and hit the ground
running. His companions were right behind him. They spread
out fast, to cover as much ground as possible without losing
sight of one another.

Apone's attention was riveted to the screen of his visor's
image intensifier as he scanned the buildings surrounding
them. The scanner's internal computer magnified the avail-

able light and cleaned up the view as much as it could, resulting in a bright picture that was still luridly tinted and full of contrast. It was enough.

Colony architecture tended to the functional. Beautification of surroundings would come later, when the wind wouldn't ruin all such efforts no matter how modest. Wind whipped trash between the buildings—that detritus that was too heavy to blow away. A chunk of metal rocked on an uneven base, banging mindlessly against a nearby wall, any echo subsumed by the wind. A few neonic lights flickered unsteadily. Gorman's voice sounded crisply over everyone's suit communicator.

"First squad up, on line. Hicks, get your people in a cordon between the entrance and the APC. Watch your rear. Vasquez, take point. Let's move."

A line of troopers advanced on the main entrylock. No one expected a greeting committee to meet them, any more than they expected to cycle the lock and stroll in without difficulty, but it was still something of a shock to encounter the pair of heavy-duty tractors that were parked nose-to-nose in front of the big door, barring any entry. It implied a conscious effort on the part of those inside to keep something outside.

Vasquez reached the silent machines first and paused to peer inside the operator's cab of the nearest. The controls had been ripped out and strewn around the interior. Impassive, she squeezed between the earthmovers, her tone phlegmatic as she reported back.

"Looks like somebody took a crowbar to the instrumentation." She reached the main doorway and nodded to her right, where Drake flanked her. Apone arrived, scanned the barrier, and moved to the external door controls. His fingers tried every combination. None of the telltale lights came alive.

"Busted?" Drake inquired.

"Sealed. There's a difference. Hudson, get up here. We need a bypass."

No funny cracks now as the comtech, all business, put his gun aside and bent to examine the door panel. "Standard stuff," he said in less than a minute. Using a tool taken from his work belt, he pried away the protective weather facing and studied the wiring. "Take two puffs, Sarge." His fingers deft and deliberate in their movements, despite the wind and cold, he began patching around the ruined circuitry. Apone and the others waited and watched.

"First squad," the sergeant snapped into his suit pickup, "assemble on me at the main lock."

A sign creaked and groaned overhead where it had broken loose from its moorings. The wind howled around them, buffeting nerves more than bodies. Hudson made a connection. Two indicator lights flickered fitfully. Moaning against the dust that had accumulated in its guide rail, the big door slid back on its tracks, traveling in fits and starts, in sync with the blinking lights. Halfway open it jammed. It was more than enough.

Apone motioned Vasquez forward. The muzzle of her smartgun preceding her, she stepped inside. Her companions followed as Gorman's voice crackled in their headsets.

"Second team, move up. Flanking positions, close quarters. How's it look, Sergeant?"

Apone's eyes scanned the interior of the silent structure. "Clean so far, sir. Nobody home yet."

"Right. Second team, keep watching behind you as you advance." The lieutenant spared a moment to glance up and behind him. "You okay, Ripley?"

She was abruptly aware that she was breathing too fast, as though she'd just finished running a marathon instead of having been standing in one place. She nodded curtly, angry at herself, angry at Gorman for his concern. He returned his attention to the console.

Vasquez and Apone strode down the wide, deserted cor-

ridor. A few lights burned blue overhead. Emergency illumination, already beginning to weaken. No telling how long
the batteries had been burning. The wind accompanied them
partway in, whistling down the metal concourse. Pools of
water stained the floor. Farther along, rain dripped through
blast holes in the ceiling. Apone tilted his head back so that
his helmet camera would simultaneously record the evidence
of the firefight and transmit it back to the APC.

"Pulse-rifles," he murmured, explaining the cause of the
ragged holes. "Somebody's a wild shot."

In the operations bay, Ripley glanced sharply at Burke.
"People confined to bed don't run around firing pulse-rifles
inside their habitat. People with inoperative communications
equipment don't go around firing off pulse-rifles. Something
else makes them do things like that." Burke simply shrugged
and turned to watch the screens.

Apone made a face at the blast holes. "Messy." It was
a professional opinion, not an aesthetic one. The master sergeant couldn't abide sloppy work. Of course, these were only
colonists, he reminded himself. Engineers, structural tech-
nicians, service classifications. No soldiers. Maybe one or
two cops. No need for soldiers—until now. And why now?
The wind taunted him. He searched the corridor ahead, seek-
ing answers and finding only darkness.

"Move out."

Vasquez resumed her advance, more machinelike in her
movements than any robot. Her smartgun cannon shifted
slowly from left to right and back again, covering every inch
ahead every few seconds. Her eyes were downcast, intent on
the gun's tracking monitor instead of the floor underfoot.
Footsteps echoed around and behind her, but ahead it was
silent.

Gorman tapped a finger alongside a large red button.
"Quarter and search by twos. Second team, move inside.
Hicks, take the upper level. Use your motion trackers. Any-
body sees *anything* moving, sing out."

Someone ventured a couple of lines a capella from Thor's storm-calling song at the end of *Das Rheingold*. It sounded like Hudson, but Ripley couldn't be sure, and no one owned up to the chorus. She tried to watch all the individual camera monitors simultaneously. Every dark corner inside the building was a gateway to Hell, every shadow a lethal threat. She had to fight to keep her breathing steady.

Hicks led his squad up a deserted stairwell to the town's second level. The corridor was a mirror image of the one directly beneath, maybe a little narrower but just as empty. It did offer one benefit: They were pretty well out of the wind.

Standing in the middle of a knot of troops, he unlimbered a small metal box with a glass face. It had delicate insides and, like most marine equipment, a heavily armored exterior. He aimed it down the hallway and adjusted the controls. A couple of LEDs lit up brightly. The gauges stayed motionless. He panned it slowly from right to left.

"Nothing," he reported. "No movement, no signs of life."

"Move out" was Gorman's disappointed response.

Hicks held the scanner out in front of him while his squad covered him, front, back, and sideways. They passed rooms and offices. Some of the doors stood ajar, others shut tight. The interiors were similar and devoid of surprises.

The farther they went, the more blatant became the evidence of struggle. Furniture was overturned and papers scattered about. Irreplaceable computer storage disks had been trampled underfoot. Personal possessions, shipped at great cost over interstellar distances, had been thrown thoughtlessly aside, smashed and broken. Priceless books of real paper floated soddenly in puddles of water that had leaked from frozen pipes and holes in the ceiling.

"Looks like my room in college." Burke was trying to be funny. He failed.

Several of the rooms Hicks's squad passed had not just

been turned upside down; they'd been burned. Black streaks seared walls of metal and composite. In several offices the triple-paned safety-glass windows had been blown out. Rain and wind gusted through the gaps. Hicks stepped inside one office to lift a half-eaten doughnut from a listing table. A nearby coffee cup overflowed with rainwater. The dark grounds lay scattered across the floor, floating like water mites in the puddles.

Apone's people systematically searched the lower level, moving in pairs that functioned as single organisms. They went through the colonists' modest, compact living quarters one apartment at a time. There wasn't much to see. Hudson kept his eyes on his scanner as he prowled alongside Vasquez, looking up only long enough to take note of a particular stain on one wall. He didn't need sophisticated electronic analyzers to tell him what it was: dried blood. Everyone in the APC saw it too. No one said anything.

Hudson's tracker let out a beep, the sound explosively loud in the empty corridor. Vasquez whirled, her gun ready. Tracker and smartgun operator exchanged a glance. Hudson nodded, then walked slowly toward a half-open door that was splintered partway off its frame. Holes produced by pulse-rifle rounds peppered the remnants of the door and the walls framing it.

As the comtech eased out of the way, Vasquez sidled up close to the ruined barrier and kicked it in. She came as close as possible to firing without actually unleashing a stream of destruction on the room's interior.

Dangling from a length of flex conduit, a junction box swung back and forth like a pendulum, driven by the wind that poured in through a broken window. The heavy metal box clacked against the rails of a child's bunk bed as it swung.

Vasquez uttered a guttural sound. "Motion detectors. I hate 'em." They both turned back to the hallway.

Ripley was watching the view provided by Hicks's monitor. Suddenly she leaned forward. "Wait! Tell him to—"

Abruptly aware that only Burke and Gorman could hear her, she hurried to plug in her headset jack, patching herself into the intersuit communications net. "Hicks, this is Ripley. I saw something on your screen. Back up." He complied, and the picture on his monitor retreated. "That's it. Now swing left. There!"

The two men who shared the operations bay with her watched as the image provided by the corporal's camera panned until it stabilized on a section of wall full of holes and oddly shaped gouges and depressions. Ripley went cold. She knew what had caused the irregular pattern of destruction.

Hicks ran a glove over the battered metal. "You seeing this okay? Looks melted."

"Not melted," Ripley corrected him. "Corroded."

Burke looked over at her, raised an eyebrow. "Hmm. Acid for blood."

"Looks like somebody bagged them one of Ripley's bad guys here." Hicks sounded less impressed than the Company rep.

Hudson had been making his own inspection of a room on the lower level. Now he beckoned to his companions to join him. "Hey, if you like that, you're gonna love this." Ripley and her companions shifted their attention to the view being relayed back to the APC by the voluble private's camera.

He was looking down. His feet framed a gaping hole. As he leaned forward over the edge they could see another hole directly below the first and beyond, dimly illuminated by his helmet light, a section of the maintenance level. Pipes, conduits, wiring—all had been eaten away by the action of some ferocious liquid.

Apone examined the view, turned away. "Second squad, talk to me. What's your status?"

Hicks's voice replied. "Just finished our sweep. There's nobody home."

The master sergeant nodded to himself, spoke to the

occupants of the distant APC. "The place is dead, sir. Dead and deserted. All's quiet on the Hadley front. Whatever happened here, we missed it."

"Late for the party again." Drake kicked a lump of corroded metal aside.

Gorman leaned back and looked thoughtful. "All right. The area's secured. Let's go in and see what their computer can tell us. First team, head for Operations. You know where that is, Sergeant?"

Apone nudged a sleeve switch. A small map of the Hadley colony appeared on the inside of his helmet visor. "That tall structure we saw coming in. It's not far, sir. We're on our way."

"Good. Hudson, when you get there, see if you can bring their CPU on-line. Nothing fancy. We don't want to use it; we just want to talk to it. Hicks, we're coming in. Meet me at the south lock by the uplink tower. Gorman out."

"Out is right." Hudson would have spat save for the fact that no suitable target presented itself. "He's coming in. I feel safer already."

Vasquez made sure her suit mike was off before agreeing.

The powerful arc lights mounted on the front of the APC illuminated the stained, wind-scoured walls of the colony buildings as the armored vehicle trundled down the main service street. They passed a couple of smaller vehicles parked in a shielded area. The APC's gleaming metal wheels threw up sheets of dirty water as it rumbled through oversize potholes. Internal shocks absorbed the impact. Wind-blown rain lashed the headlights.

In the driver's compartment, Bishop and Wierzbowski worked smoothly side by side, man and synthetic functioning in perfect harmony. Each respected the other's abilities. Both knew, for example, that Wierzbowski could ignore any advice Bishop gave. Both also knew that the human would probably take it. Wierzbowski squinted through the narrow driver's port and pointed.

"Over there, I think."

Bishop checked the flashing, brightly colored map on the screen between them. "That has to be it. There's no other lock in this area." He leaned on the wheel, and the heavy machine swung toward a cavernous opening in the wall nearby.

"Yeah, there's Hicks."

Apone's second in command emerged from the open lock as the armored personnel carrier ground to a halt. He watched while the crew door cycled and slid aside. A suited Gorman was first down the ramp, followed closely by Burke, Bishop, and Wierzbowski. Burke looked back, searching for the tank's remaining occupant, only to see her hesitate in the portal. She wasn't looking at him. Her attention was focused on the dark entrance leading deep into the colony.

"Ripley?"

Her eyes lowered to meet his. By way of reply, she shook her head sharply from side to side.

"The area's secured." Burke tried to sound understanding. "You heard Apone."

Another negative gesture. Hudson's voice sounded in their headsets.

"Sir, the colony CPU is on-line."

"Good work, Hudson," said the lieutenant. "Those of you in Operations, stand by. We'll be there soon." He nodded to his companions. "Let's go."

VI

In person the devastation looked much worse than it had on the APC's monitors.

"Looks like your company can write off its share of *this* colony," he murmured to Burke.

"The buildings are mostly intact." The company rep didn't sound concerned. "The rest's insured."

"Yeah? What about the colonists?" Ripley asked him.

"We don't know what's happened to them yet." He sounded slightly irritated by the question.

It was chilly inside the complex. Internal control had failed along with the power, and in any case, the blown-out windows and gaping holes in the walls would have overloaded the equipment quickly, anyway. Ripley found that she was sweating despite her environment suit's best efforts to keep her comfortable. Her eyes were as active as any trooper's as she checked out every hole in the walls and floor, every shadowed corner.

This was where it had all begun. This was the place where *it* had come from. The alien. There was no doubt in her mind what had happened here. An alien like the one that had caused the destruction of the *Nostromo* and the deaths of all her shipmates had gotten loose in Hadley Colony.

Hicks noticed her nervousness as she scanned the ravaged hallway and the fire-gutted offices and storage rooms. Wordlessly he motioned to Wierzbowski. The trooper nodded

85

imperceptibly, adjusted his stride so that he fell into position
on Ripley's right. Hicks slowed down until he was flanking
her on the left. Together they formed a protective cordon
around her. She noticed the shift and glanced at the corporal.
He winked, or at least she thought he might have. It was too
fast for her to be certain. Might just have been blinking at
something in his eye. Even in the corridor there was enough
of a breeze to blow sand and soot around.

Frost emerged from the side corridor just ahead. He
beckoned to the new arrivals, speaking to Gorman but looking
at Hicks.

"Sir, you should check this out."

"What is it, Frost?" Gorman was in a hurry to rendezvous
with Apone. But the soldier was insistent.

"Easier to show you, sir."

"Right. It's up this way?" The lieutenant gestured down
the corridor. Frost nodded and turned up into darkness, the
others following.

He led them into a wing that was completely without
power. Their suit lights revealed scenes of destruction worse
than anything yet encountered. Ripley found that she was
trembling. The APC, safe, solid, heavily armed, and not far
off, loomed large in her thoughts. If she ran hard, she'd be
back there in a few minutes. And alone once again. No matter
how secure the personnel carrier was, she knew she was safer
here, surrounded by the soldiers. She kept telling herself that
as they advanced.

Frost was gesturing. "Right ahead here, sir."

The corridor was blocked. Someone had erected a makeshift barricade of welded pipes and steel plate, extra door
panels, ceiling sheathing, and composite flooring. Acid holes
and gashes scarred the hastily raised barrier. The metal had
been torn and twisted by hideously powerful forces. Just to
the right of where Frost was standing the barricade had been
ripped open like an old soup can. They squeezed through the
narrow opening one at a time.

Lights played over the devastation beyond. "Anybody know where we are?" Gorman asked.

Burke studied an illuminated company map. "Medical wing. We're in the right section, and it has the right look."

They fanned out, the lights from their suits illuminating overturned tables and cabinets, broken chairs and expensive surgical equipment. Smaller medical instruments littered the floor like steel confetti. Additional tables and furniture had been piled, bolted, and welded to the inside of the barricade that once had sealed the wing off from the rest of the complex. Black streaks showed where untended fire had flamed, and the walls were pockmarked with holes from pulse-rifle fire and acid.

Despite the absence of lights, the wing wasn't completely energy-dead. A few isolated instruments and control boards glowed softly with emergency power. Wierzbowski ran a gloved hand over a hole in the wall the size of a basketball.

"Last stand. They threw up that barricade and holed up in here."

"Makes sense." Gorman kicked an empty plastic bottle aside. It went clattering across the floor. "Medical would have the longest-lasting emergency power supply plus its own stock of supplies. This is where I'd come also. No bodies?"

Frost was sweeping the far end of the wing with his light. "I didn't see any when I came in here, sir, and I don't see any now. Looks like it was a fight."

"Don't see any of your bad guys, either, Ripley." Wierzbowski looked up and around. "Hey, Ripley?" His finger tensed on the pulse-rifle's trigger. "Where's Ripley?"

"Over here."

The sound of her voice led them into a second room. Burke examined their new surroundings briefly before pronouncing identification. "Medical lab. Looks pretty clean. I don't think the fight got this far. I think they lost it in the outer room."

Wierzbowski's eyes roved the emergency-lit chamber until they found what had attracted Ripley's attention. He muttered something under his breath and walked toward her. So did the others.

At the far side of the lab seven transparent cylinders glowed with violet light. Combined with the fluid, they contained the light served to preserve the organic material within. All seven cylinders were in use.

"It's a still. Somebody makes booze here," Gorman said. Nobody laughed.

"Stasis tubes. Standard equipment for a colony med lab this size." Burke approached the glass cylinders.

Seven tubes for seven specimens. Each cylinder held something that looked like a severed hand equipped with too many fingers. The bodies to which the long fingers were attached were flattened and encased in a material like beige leather, thin and translucent. Pseudo-gills drifted lazily in the stasis suspension fluid. There were no visible organs of sight or hearing. A long tail hung from the back of each abomination, trailing freely in the liquid. A couple of the creatures held their tails coiled tightly against their undersides.

Burke spoke to Ripley without taking his eyes off the specimens. "Are these the same as the one you described in your report?" She nodded without speaking.

Fascinated, the Company rep moved toward one cylinder, leaning forward until his face was almost touching the special glass.

"Watch it, Burke," Ripley warned him.

As she concluded the warning the creature imprisoned in the tube lunged sharply, slamming against the inner lining of the cylinder. Burke jumped back, startled. From the ventral portion of the flattened handlike body a thin, fleshy projection had emerged. It looked like a tapered section of intestine as it slithered tonguelike over the tube's interior. Eventually it retracted, curling up inside a protective sheath between the gill-like structures. Legs and tail contracted into a resting position.

Hicks glanced emotionlessly at Burke. "It likes you."

The Company rep didn't reply as he moved down the line, inspecting each of the cylinders in turn. As he passed a tube he would press his hand against the smooth exterior. Only one of the remaining six specimens reacted to his presence. The others drifted aimlessly in the suspension fluid, their fingers and tails floating freely.

"These are dead," he said when he'd finished with the last tube. "There's just two alive. Unless there's a different state they go into, but I doubt it. See, the dead ones have a completely different color. Faded, like."

A file folder rested atop each cylinder. By exerting every ounce of self-control she possessed, Ripley was able to remove the file from the top of a tube containing a live facehugger. Retreating quickly, she opened the folder and began reading with the aid of her suit light. In addition to the printed material the file was overflowing with charts and sonographs. There were a couple of nuclear magnetic resonance image plates, which attempted to show something of the creatures' internal structure. They were badly blurred. All of the lengthy computer printouts had copious notes scribbled freehand in the margins. A physician's handwriting, she decided. They were mostly illegible.

"Anything interesting?" Burke was leaning around the stasis cylinder whose file she was perusing, studying the creature it contained from every possible angle.

"Probably a great deal, but most of it's too technical for me." She tapped the file. "Report of the examining physician. Doctor named Ling."

"Chester O. Ling." Burke tapped the tube with a fingernail. This time the creature inside failed to respond. "There were three doctors stationed at Hadley. Ling was a surgeon, I believe. What's he have to say about this little prize here?"

"Removed surgically before embryo implantation could be completed. Standard surgical procedures useless."

"Wonder why?" Gorman was as interested in the specimen as the rest of them but not to the point of taking his eyes off the rest of the room.

"Body fluids dissolved the instruments as they were applied. They had to use surgical lasers to both remove and cauterize the specimen. It was attached to somebody named Marachuk, John L." She glanced up at Burke, who shook his head.

"Doesn't ring a bell. Not an administrator or one of the higher-ups. Must've been a tractor driver or roustabout."

She looked back down at the report. "He died during the procedure. They killed him getting it off."

Hicks walked over to have a look at the report, peering over Ripley's shoulder. He didn't have the chance to read it. His motion tracker emitted an unexpected and startlingly loud beep.

The four soldiers spun, checking first the entrance to the lab, moving on to squint at dark corners. Hicks aimed the tracker back toward the barricade.

"Behind us." He gestured toward the corridor they'd just left.

"One of us?" Without thinking, Ripley moved closer to the corporal.

"No way of telling. This baby isn't a precision instrument. She's made to take a lot of abuse from dumb grunts like me and still keep on working, but she doesn't render judgments."

Gorman addressed his headset pickup. "Apone, we're up in medical and we've got something. Where are your people?" He gave his visor map a quick scan. "Anybody in D-Block?"

"Negative." All of them could hear the sergeant's filtered reply. "We're all over in Operations, as ordered. You want some company?"

"Not yet. We'll keep you posted." He nudged the aural pickup away from his mouth. "Let's go, Vasquez."

She nodded tersely and swung the smartgun into the ready position on its support arm. It locked in place with an authoritative click. She and Hicks started off in the direction of the signal source while Frost and Wierzbowski brought up the rear.

The corporal led them back out into the main corridor and turned right, into a stainless-steel labyrinth. "Getting stronger. Definitely not mechanical." He held the tracker firmly in one hand, cradled his rifle with the other. "Irregular movement. Where the heck are we, anyway?"

Burke surveyed their surroundings. "Kitchen. We'll be in among the food-processing equipment if we keep going this way."

Ripley had slowed until she fell behind Wierzbowski and Frost. Realizing suddenly that there was nothing behind her but darkness, she hurried to catch up to her companions.

Burke's appraisal was confirmed as they advanced and their lights began to bounce off the shiny surfaces of bulky machinery: freezers, cookers, defrosters, and sterilizers. Hicks ignored it all, intent on his tracker.

"It's moving again."

Vasquez's gaze was cold as she scanned her environment. Plenty of cover in here. Her fingers caressed the smartgun's controls. A long preparation table loomed in their path.

"Which way?"

Hicks hesitated briefly, then nodded toward a complicated array of machinery designed to process freeze-dried meats and vegetables. The soldiers advanced on it, their tread a deliberate, solemn march. Wierzbowski stumbled over a metal canister and angrily booted it aside, sending it clanging off into the shadows. He kept his balance and his aplomb, but Ripley half climbed the nearest wall.

The corporal's tracker was beeping steadily now, almost humming. The hum rose to a sharp whine. A pile of stockpots

suddenly came crashing down off to their right, and a dim
shape was faintly glimpsed moving through the shadows behind the preparation counters.

Vasquez pivoted smoothly, her finger already contracting
on the trigger. At the same instant Hick's rifle slammed the
heavier barrel upward. Tracer fire ripped into the ceiling,
sending droplets of molten metal flying. She whirled and
screamed at him.

Ignoring her, he hurried forward into her line of fire and
aimed his bright-light under a row of metal cabinets. He
stayed like that for what seemed a short eternity before beck-
oning for Ripley to join him. Her legs wouldn't work, and
her feet seemed frozen to the floor. Hicks gestured again,
more urgently this time, and she found herself moving forward in a daze.

He was bending over, trying to work his light beneath
a high storage locker. She crouched down next to him.

Pinned against the wall by his light like a butterfly on
a mounting pin was a tiny, terrified figure. Filthy and staring,
the little girl cowered away from the intruders. In one hand
she held a plastic food packet that had been half gnawed.
The other clutched tight the head of a large doll, holding it
by its hair. Of the remainder of the plastic body there was
no sign. The child was as emaciated as she was dirty, the
skin taut around her small face. She looked far more fragile
than the doll's head she carried. Her blond hair was tangled
and matted, a garland of steel wool framing her face.

Ripley tried but couldn't hear her breathing.

The girl blinked against the light, the brief gesture sufficient to jump-start Ripley's mind. She extended a hand
toward the waif slowly, fingers closed, and smiled at her.

"Come on out," she said soothingly. "It's all right. There's
nothing to be afraid of here." She tried to reach farther behind
the cabinet.

The girl retreated from the extending fingers, backing
away and trembling visibly. She had the look of a rabbit

paralyzed by oncoming headlights. Ripley's fingers almost reached her. She opened her hand, intending to gently caress the torn blouse.

Like a shot, the girl bolted to her right, scuttling along beneath the cabinetry with incredible agility. Ripley dove forward, scrambling on elbows and knees as she fought to keep the child in view. Outside the cabinets Hicks crabbed frantically sideways until a small gap appeared between two storage lockers. He snapped out a hand, and his fingers locked around a tiny ankle. An instant later he drew it back.

"Ow! Watch it, she bites."

Ripley reached for the other retreating foot and missed. A second later the girl reached a ventilation duct whose grille had been kicked out. Before Hicks or anyone else could make another grab for her, she'd scrambled inside, wriggling like a fish. Hicks didn't even try to follow. He wouldn't have fit through the narrow opening stark naked, much less clad in his bulky armor.

Ripley dove without thinking, squirming into the duct with her arms held out in front of her, moving with thighs and arms. Her hips barely cleared the opening. The girl was just ahead of her, still moving. As Ripley followed, her breathing loud in the confined tunnel, the child slammed a metal hatch in place ahead of her. With a lunge Ripley reached the barrier and shoved it open before it could be latched from the other side. She cursed as she banged her forehead against the metal overhead.

Shining her light ahead, she forgot the pain. The girl was backed against the far end of a small spherical chamber, one of the colony's ventilation system's pressure-relief bubbles. She was not alone.

Surrounding her were wadded-up blankets and pillows mixed with a haphazard collection of toys, stuffed animals, dolls, cheap jewelry, illustrated books, and empty food packets. There was even a battery-operated disk player muffled by cut-up pillows. The entire array was the result of the girl's foraging through the complex. She'd hauled it back to this place by herself, furnishing her private hideaway according to her own childish plan.

It was more like a nest than a room, Ripley decided.

Somehow this child had survived. Somehow she had coped with and adapted to her devastated environment when all the adults had succumbed. As Ripley struggled with the import of what she was seeing, the girl continued to edge around the back wall. She was heading for another hatch. If the conduit it barred was no bigger in diameter than the cover protecting it, the girl would be out of their grasp. Ripley saw that she could never enter it.

The child turned and dove, and Ripley timed her own lunge to coincide. She managed to get both arms around the girl, locking her in a bear hug. Finding herself trapped, the girl went into a frenzy, kicking and hitting and trying to use her teeth. It was not only frightening, it was horrifying: because, as she fought, the child stayed dead silent. The only noise in the confined space as she struggled in Ripley's grasp was her frantic breathing, and even that was eerily subdued. Only once in her life had Ripley had to try to control someone small who'd fought with similar ferocity, and that was Jones, when she'd had to take him to the vet.

She talked to the child as she kept clear of slashing feet and elbows and small sharp teeth. "It's okay, it's okay. It's over, you're going to be all right now. It's okay, you're safe."

Finally the girl ran out of strength, slowing down like a failing motor. She went completely limp in Ripley's arms, almost catatonic, and allowed herself to be rocked back and forth. It was hard to look at the child's face, to meet her traumatized, vacant stare. Lips white and trembling, eyes darting wildly and seeing nothing, she tried to bury herself in the adult's chest, shrinking back from a dark nightmare world only she could see.

Ripley kept rocking the girl back and forth, back and forth, cooing to her in a steady, reassuring voice. As she whispered, she let her gaze roam the chamber until it fell on something lying on the top of the pile of scavanged goods. It was a framed solido of the girl, unmistakable and yet so different. The child in the picture was dressed up and smiling, her hair neat and recently shampooed, a bright ribbon shining in the blond tresses. Her clothing was immaculate and her skin scrubbed pink. The words beneath the picture were embossed in gold:

FIRST-GRADE CITIZENSHIP AWARD
REBECCA JORDEN

"Ripley. Ripley?" Hicks voice, echoing down the air shaft. "You okay in there?"

"Yes." Aware they might not have heard her, she raised her voice. "I'm okay. We're both okay. We're coming out now."

The girl did not resist as Ripley retraced her crawl feet first, dragging the child by the ankles.

VII

The girl sat huddled against the back of the chair, hugging her knees to her chest. She looked neither right nor left, nor at any of the adults regarding her curiously. Her attention was focused on a distant point in space. A biomonitor cuff had been strapped to her left arm. Dietrich had been forced to modify it so that it would fit properly around the child's shrunken arm.

Gorman sat nearby while the medtech studied the information the cuff was providing. "What's her name again?"

Dietrich made a notation on an electronic caduceus pad. "What?"

"Her name. We got a name, didn't we?"

The medtech nodded absently, absorbed by the readouts. "Rebecca, I think."

"Right." The lieutenant put on his best smile and leaned forward, resting his hands on his knees. "Now think, Rebecca. Concentrate. You have to try to help us so that we can help you. That's what we're here for, to help you. I want you to take your time and tell us what you remember. Anything at all. Try to start from the beginning."

The girl didn't move, nor did her expression change. She was unresponsive but not comatose, silent but not mute. A disappointed Gorman sat back and glanced briefly to his left as Ripley entered carrying a steaming coffee mug.

"Where are your parents? You have to try to—"

"Gorman! Give it a rest, would you?"

The lieutenant started to respond sharply. His reply faded to a resigned nod. He rose, shaking his head. "Total brainlock. Tried everything I could think of except yelling at her, and I'm not about to do that. It could send her over the edge. If she isn't already."

"She isn't." Dietrich turned off her portable diagnostic equipment and gently removed the sensor cuff from the girl's unresisting arm. "Physically she's okay. Borderline malnutrition, but I don't think there's any permanent damage. The wonder of it is that she's alive at all, scrounging unprocessed food packets and freeze-dried powder." She looked at Ripley. "You see any vitamin packs in there?"

"I didn't have time for sight-seeing, and she didn't offer to show me around." She nodded toward the girl.

"Right. Well, she must know about supplements because

she's not showing any signs of critical deficiencies. Smart little thing."

"How is she mentally?" Ripley sipped at her coffee, staring at the waif in the chair. The child's skin was like parchment over the backs of her hands.

"I can't tell for sure, but her motor responses are good. I think it's too early to call it brainlock. I'd say she's on hold."

"Call it anything you want." Gorman rose and headed for the exit. "Whatever it is, we're wasting our time trying to talk to her." He strode out of the side room and back into Operations to join Burke and Bishop in staring at the colony's central computer terminal. Dietrich headed off in another direction.

For a while Ripley watched the three men, who were intent on the terminals Hudson had resurrected, then knelt alongside the girl. Gently she brushed the child's unkempt hair back out of her eyes. She might have been combing a statue for all the response she elicited. Still smiling, she proffered the steaming cup she was holding.

"Here, try this. If you're not hungry, you must be thirsty. I'll bet it gets cold in that vent bubble, what with the heat off and everything." She moved the cup around, letting the air carry the warm, aromatic smell of the contents to the girl's nostrils. "It's just a little instant hot chocolate. Don't you like chocolate?" When the girl didn't react, Ripley wrapped the small hands around the cup, bending the fingers toward each other. Then she tilted hands and cup upward.

Dietrich was correct about the child's motor responses. She drank mechanically and without watching what she was doing. Cocoa spilled down her chin, but most of it went down the small throat and stayed down. Ripley felt vindicated.

Not wanting to overwhelm an obviously shrunken stomach, she pulled the cup away when it was still half full. "There, wasn't that nice? You can have some more in a minute. I don't know what you've been eating and drinking, and we don't want to make you sick by giving you too much rich stuff too quickly." She pushed at the blond tresses again.

"Poor thing. You don't talk much, do you? That's okay by me. You feel like keeping quiet, you keep quiet. I'm kind of the same way. I've found that most people do a lot of talking and they wind up not saying very much. Especially adults when they're talking to children. It's kind of like they enjoy talking at you but not to you. They want you to listen to them all the time, but they don't want to listen to you. I think that's pretty stupid. Just because you're small doesn't mean you don't have some important things to say." She set the cup aside and dabbed at the brown-stained chin with a cloth. It was easy to feel the ridge of unfinished bone beneath the tightly drawn skin.

"Uh-oh." She grinned broadly. "I made a clean spot here. Now I've gone and done it. Guess I'll just have to do the whole thing. Otherwise nothing will match."

From an open supply packet she withdrew a squeeze bottle full of sterilized water and used it to soak the cloth she was holding. Then she applied the makeshift scrubber firmly to the girl's face, wiping away dirt and accumulated grime in addition to the remaining cocoa spots. Throughout the operation the child sat quietly. But the bright blue eyes shifted and seemed to focus on Ripley for the first time.

She felt a surge of excitement and fought to suppress it. "Hard to believe there's a little girl under all this." She made a show of examining the cloth's surface. "Enough dirt there to file a mining claim on." Bending over, she stared appraisingly at the newly revealed face. "Definitely a little girl. And a pretty one, at that."

She looked away just long enough to assure herself that no one from Operations was about to barge in. Any interruption at this critical moment might undo everything that she'd worked so hard to accomplish with the aid of a little hot chocolate and clean water.

No need to worry. Everyone in Operations was still clus-

tered around the main terminal. Hudson was seated at the
console fingering controls while the others looked on.

A three-dimensional abstract of the colony drifted across
the main screen, lazy geometric outlines tumbling from left
to right, then bottom to top, as Hudson manipulated the program. The comtech was neither playing nor showing off; he
was hunting something. No rude comments spilled from his
lips now, no casual profanity filled the air. It was work time.
If he cursed at all, it was to himself. The computer knew all
the answers. Finding the right questions was an agonizingly
slow process.

Burke had been inspecting other equipment. Now he
shifted his position for a better view as he whispered to
Gorman.

"What's he scanning for?"

"PDTs. Personal data transmitters. Every colonist has
one surgically implanted as soon as they arrive."

"I know what a PDT is," Burke replied mildly. "The
Company manufactures them. I just don't see any point in
running a PDT scan. Surely if there was anyone else left alive
in the complex, we'd have found them by now. Or they'd
have found us."

"Not necessarily." Gorman's reply was polite without
being deferential. Technically Burke was along on the expedition as an observer for the Company, to look after its
financial interests. His employer was paying for this little
holiday excursion in tandem with the colonial administration,
but what authority he had was largely unwritten. He could
give advice but not orders. This was a military expedition,
and Gorman was in charge. On paper Burke was his equal.
The reality was very different.

"Someone could be alive but unable to move. Injured,
or maybe trapped inside a damaged building. Sure the scan's
a long shot, but procedure demands it. We have to run the

check." He turned to the comtech. "Everything functioning properly, Hudson?"

"If there's anyone alive within a couple of kilometers of base central, we'll read it out here." He tapped the screen. "So far I've got zip except for the kid."

Wierzbowski offered a comment from the far side of the room. "Don't PDTs keep broadcasting if the owner dies?"

"Not these new ones." Dietrich was sorting through her instruments. "They're partly powered by the body's own electrical field. If the owner fades out, so does the signal. A stiff's electrical capacitance is nil. That's the only drawback to using the body as a battery."

"No kidding?" Hudson spared the comely medtech a glance. "How can you tell if somebody's AC or DC?"

"No problem in your case, Hudson." She snapped her medical satchel shut. "Clear case of insufficient current."

It was easier to find another clean cloth than to try to scrub out the first one. Ripley was working on the girl's small hands now, excavating dirt from between the fingers and beneath the nails. Pink skin emerged from behind a mask of dark grime. As she cleaned, she kept up a steady stream of reassuring chatter.

"I don't know how you managed to stay alive with everybody else gone away, but you're one brave kid, Rebecca."

A sound new to Ripley's ears, barely audible. "N-newt."

Ripley tensed and looked away so her excitement wouldn't show. She kept moving the washcloth as she leaned closer. "I'm sorry, kid, I didn't hear you. Sometimes my hearing's not so good. What did you say?"

"Newt. My n-name's Newt. That's what everybody calls me. Nobody calls me Rebecca except my brother."

Ripley was finishing off the second hand. If she didn't respond, the girl might lapse back into silence. At the same time she had to be careful not to say anything that might upset her. Keep it casual and don't ask any questions.

"Well, Newt it is, then. My name's Ripley—and people call me Ripley. You can call me anything you like, though." When no reply was forthcoming from the girl, Ripley lifted the small hand she'd just finished cleaning and gave it a formal shake.

"Pleased to meet you, Newt." She pointed at the disembodied doll head that the girl still clutched fiercely in one hand. "And who is that? Does she have a name? I bet she does. Every doll has a name. When I was your age, I had lots of dolls, and every one of them had a name. Otherwise, how can you tell them apart?"

Newt glanced down at the plastic sphere with its vacant, glassy eyes. "Casey. She's my only friend."

"What about me?"

The girl looked at her so sharply that Ripley was taken aback. The assurance in Newt's eyes bespoke a hardness that was anything but childish. Her tone was flat, neutral.

"I don't want you for a friend."

Ripley tried to conceal her surprise. "Why not?"

"Because you'll be gone soon, like the others. Like everybody." She gazed down at the doll head. "Casey's okay. She'll stay with me. But you'll go away. You'll be dead and you'll leave me alone."

There was no anger in that childish declamation, no sense of accusation or betrayal. It was delivered coolly and with complete assurance, as though the event had already occurred. It was not a prediction, but rather a statement of fact soon to take place. It chilled Ripley's blood and frightened her more than anything that had happened since the dropship had departed the safety of the orbiting _Sulaco_.

"Oh, Newt. Your mom and dad went away like that, didn't they? You just don't want to talk about it." The girl nodded, eyes downcast, staring at her knees. Her fingers were white around the doll head. "They'd be here if they could, honey," Ripley told her solemnly. "I know they would."

"They're dead. That's why they can't come see me any-

more. They're dead like everybody else." This delivered with
a cold certainty that was terrifying to see in so small a child.

"Maybe not. How can you be sure?"

Newt raised her eyes and stared straight at Ripley. Small
children do not look adults in the eye like that, but Newt was
a child in stature only. "I'm sure. They're dead. They're dead,
and soon you'll be dead, and then Casey and I'll be alone
again."

Ripley didn't look away and she didn't smile. She knew
this girl could see straight through anything remotely phony.
"Newt. Look at me, Newt. I'm not going away. I'm not going
to leave you and I'm *not* going to be dead. I promise. I'm
going to stay around. I'll be with you as long as you want
me to."

The girl's eyes remained downcast. Ripley could see her
struggling with herself, wanting to believe what she'd just
heard, trying to believe. After a while she looked up again.

"You promise?"

"Cross my heart." Ripley performed the childish gesture.

"And hope to die?"

Now Ripley did smile, grimly. "And hope to die."

Girl and woman regarded one another. Newt's eyes began to brim, and her lower lip to tremble. Slowly the tension
fled from her small body, and the indifferent mask she'd
pulled across her face was replaced by something much more
natural: the look of a frightened child. She threw both arms
around Ripley's neck and began to sob. Ripley could feel the
tears streaming down the newly washed cheeks, soaking her
own neck. She ignored them, rocking the girl back and forth
in her arms, whispering soothing nothings to her.

She closed her own eyes against the tears and the fear
and lingering sensation of death that permeated Hadley Operations Central and hoped that the promise she'd just made
could be kept.

The breakthrough with the girl was matched by another
in Operations as Hudson let out a triumphant whoop. "Hah!

Stop your grinnin' and drop your linen! Found 'em. Give old Hudson a decent machine and he'll turn up your money, your secrets, and 'your long-lost cousin Jed." He rewarded the control console with an affectionate whack. "This baby's been battered, but she can still play ball."

Gorman leaned over the comtech's shoulder. "What kind of shape are they in?"

"Unknown. These colonial PDTs are long on signal and short on details. But it looks like all of them."

"Where?"

"Over at the atmosphere processing station." Hudson studied the schematic. "Sublevel C under the south part of the complex." He tapped the screen. "This charmer's a sweetheart when it comes to location."

Everyone in Operations had clustered around the comtech for a look at the monitor. Hudson froze the colony scan and enlarged one portion. In the center of the processing station's schematic a cluster of glowing blue dots pulsed like deep-sea crustaceans.

Hicks grunted as he stared at the screen. "Looks like a town meeting."

"Wonder why they all went over there?" Dietrich mused aloud. "I thought we'd decided that this was where they made their last stand?"

"Maybe they were able to make a break for it and secure themselves in a better place." Gorman turned away, brisk and professional. "Remember, the processing station still has full power. That'd be worth a lot. Let's saddle up and find out."

"Awright, let's go, girls." Apone was slipping his pack over his shoulders. Operations became a hive of activity. "They ain't payin' us by the hour." He glanced at Hudson. "How do we get over there?"

The comtech adjusted the screen, reducing the magnification. An overview of the colony appeared on the monitor. "There's one small service corridor. It's a pretty good hike, Sarge."

Apone looked to Gorman, waiting for orders. "I don't
know about you, Sergeant," the lieutenant told him, "but I'm
not fond of long, narrow corridors. And I'd like for everyone
to be fresh when we arrive. I'd also like to have the APC's
armament backing us up when we go in there."

"My thoughts exactly, sir." The sergeant looked relieved.
He'd been ready to suggest and argue and was glad that neither
was going to be necessary. A couple of the troops nodded
and looked satisfied. Gorman might be inexperienced in the
field, but at least he wasn't a fool.

Hicks yelled back toward the small ready room. "Hey,
Ripley, we're going for a ride in the country. You coming?"

"We're both coming." A few looks of surprise greeted
her as she led the girl out of the back room. "This is Newt.
Newt, these are my friends. They're your friends too."

The girl simply nodded, unwilling to extend that privilege beyond Ripley as yet. A couple of the soldiers nodded
to the child as they shouldered their equipment. Burke smiled
encouragingly at her. Gorman looked surprised.

Newt looked up at her live friend, still clutching the
disembodied doll head tightly in her right hand. "Where are
we going?"

"To a safe place. Soon."

Newt almost smiled.

The atmosphere in the APC during the ride from colony
Operations to the processing station was more subdued than
it had been when they'd first roared out of the dropship. The
universal devastation; the hollow, wounded buildings; and the
unmistakable evidence of hard fighting had put a damper on
the Marines' initial high spirits.

It was clear that the cause of the colony's interrupted
communications with Earth had nothing to do with its relay
satellite or base instrumentation. It had to do with Ripley's
critter. The colonists had ceased communicating because
something had compelled them to do so. If Ripley was to be
believed, that something was still hanging around. Undoubt-

edly the little girl was a storehouse of information on the
subject, but no one tried to press questions on her. Dietrich's
orders. The child's recovery was still too fragile to jeopardize
with traumatizing inquiries. So as they rode along in the APC
they had to fill in the gaps in Ripley's library disks with their
imaginations. Soldiers have active imaginations.

Wierzbowski drove the personnel carrier across the twilight landscape, traversing a causeway that connected the rest
of the colony complex to the atmosphere-processing station
a kilometer away. Wind tore at the massive vehicle but could
not sway it. The APC was designed for comfortable travel
in winds up to three hundred kph. A typical Acheronian gale
didn't bother it. Behind it, the dropship had settled to ground
at the landing field, awaiting the soldiers' return. Ahead, the
conical tower of the massive processing unit glowed with a
spectral light as it continued with its business of terraforming
Acheron's inhospitable atmosphere.

Ripley and Newt sat side by side just aft of the driver's
cab. Wierzbowski kept his attention on his driving. Within
the comparative safety of the heavily armored vehicle the girl
gradually grew more voluble. Though there were at least a
dozen questions Ripley badly wanted to ask her, she just sat
patiently and listened, letting her charge ramble on. Occasionally Newt would offer the answer to an unasked question,
anyway. Like now.

"I was best at the game." She hugged the doll head and
stared at the opposite wall. "I knew the whole maze."

"The 'maze'?" Ripley thought back to where they'd found
her. "You mean the air-duct system?"

"Yeah, you know," she replied proudly. "And not just
the air ducts. I could even get into tunnels that were full of
wires and stuff. In the walls, under the floor. I could get into
anywhere. I was the _ace._ I could hide better than anybody.
They all said I was cheating because I was smaller than
everybody else, but it wasn't 'cause I was smaller. I was just

smarter, that's all. And I've got a real good memory. I could remember anyplace I'd been before."

"You're really something, ace." The girl looked pleased. Ripley's gaze shifted forward. Through the windshield the processing station loomed directly ahead.

It was an unbeautiful structure, strictly utilitarian in design. Its multitude of pipes and chambers and conduits had been scoured and pitted by decades of wind-blown rock and sand. It was as efficient as it was ugly. Working around the clock for years on end, it and its sister stations scattered around the planet would break down the components of Acheron's atmosphere, scrub them clean, add to them, and eventually produce a pleasant biosphere equipped with a balmy, homelike climate. A great deal of beauty to spring forth from so much ugliness.

The monolithic metal mass towered over the armored personnel carrier as Wierzbowski braked to a stop across from the main entryway. Led by Hicks and Apone, the waiting troopers deployed in front of the oversize door. Up close to the complex, the *thrum* of heavy machinery filled their ears, rising above the steady whistle of the wind. The well-built machinery continued to do its job even in the absence of its human masters.

Hudson was first to the entrance and ran his fingers over the door controls like a locksmith casing his next crack.

"Surprise, chiluns. Everything works." He thumbed a single button, and the heavy barrier slid aside to reveal an interior walkway. Off to the right a concrete ramp led downward.

"Which way, sir?" Apone inquired.

"Take the ramp," Gorman instructed them from inside the APC. "There'll be another at the bottom. Take it down to C-level."

"Check." The sergeant gestured at his troops. "Drake, take point. The rest of you follow by twos. Let's go."

Hudson hesitated at the control panel. "What about the door?"

"There's nobody here. Leave it open."

They started down the broad ramp into the guts of the station. Light filtered down from above, slanting through floors and catwalks fashioned of steel mesh, bending around conduits ranked side by side like organ pipes. They had their suit lights switched on, anyway. Machinery pounded steadily around them as they descended.

The multiple views provided by their suit cameras bounced and swayed as they walked, making viewing difficult for those watching the monitors inside the APC. Eventually the floor leveled out and the images steadied. Multiple lenses revealed a floor overflowing with heavy cylinders and conduits, stacks of plastic crates, and tall metal bottles.

"B-level." Gorman addressed the operations bay pickup. "They're on the next one down. Try to take it a little slower. It's hard to make anything out when you're moving fast on a downslope."

Dietrich turned to Frost. "Maybe he wants us to fly? That way the picture wouldn't bounce."

"How about if I carry you instead?" Hudson called back to her.

"How about if I throw you over the railing?" she responded. "Picture would be steady that way, too, until you hit bottom."

"Shut up back there," Apone growled as they swung around a turn in the descending rampway. Hudson and the rest obliged.

In the Operations bay Ripley peered over Gorman's right shoulder, and Burke around the other, while Newt tried to squeeze in from behind. Despite all the video wizardry the lieutenant could command, none of the individual suit cameras provided a clear picture of what the troops were seeing.

"Try the low end gain," Burke suggested.

"I did that first thing, Mr. Burke. There's an awful lot of interference down there. The deeper they go, the more junk their signals have to get through, and those suit units don't put out much power. What's an atmosphere-processing station's interior built out of, anyway?"

"Carbon-fiber composites and silica blends up top wherever possible, for strength and lightness. A lot of metallic glass in the partitions. Foundations and sublevels don't have to be so fancy. Concrete and steel floors with a lot of titanium alloy thrown in."

Gorman was unable to contain his frustration as he fiddled futilely with his instruments. "If the emergency power was out and the station shut down, I'd be getting clearer reception, but then they'd be advancing with nothing but suit lights to guide them. It's a trade-off." He shook his head as he studied the blurred images and leaned toward the pickup.

"We're not making that out too well ahead of you. What is it?"

Static garbled Hudson's voice as well as the view provided by his camera. "You tell me. I only work here."

The lieutenant looked back at Burke. "Your people build that?"

The Company rep leaned toward the row of monitors, squinting at the dim images being relayed back from the bowels of the atmosphere-processing station.

"Hell, no."

"Then you don't know what it is?"

"I've never seen anything like it in my life."

"Could the colonists have added it?"

Burke continued to stare, finally shook his head. "If they did, they improvised it. That didn't come out of any station construction manual."

Something had been added to the latticework of pipes and conduits that crisscrossed the lowest level of the processing station. There was no question that it was the result of design and purpose, not some unknown industrial accident.

Visibly damp and lustrous in spots, the peculiar material that had been used to construct the addition resembled a solidified liquid resin or glue. In places light penetrated the material to a depth of several centimeters, revealing a complex internal structure. At other locations the substance was opaque. What little color it displayed was muted: greens and grays, and here and there a touch of some darker green.

Intricate chambers ranged in size from half a meter in diameter to a dozen meters across, all interconnected by strips of fragile-looking webwork that on closer inspection turned out to be about as fragile as steel cable. Tunnels led off deeper into the maze while peculiar conical pits dead-ended in the floor. So precisely did the added material blend with the existing machinery that it was difficult to tell where human handiwork ended and something of an entirely different nature began. In places the addition almost mimicked existing station equipment, though whether it was imitation with a purpose or merely blind duplication, no one could tell.

The whole gleaming complex extended as far back into C-level as the trooper's cameras could penetrate. Although it filled every available empty space, the epoxylike incrustation did not appear to have in any way impaired the functioning of the station. It continued to rumble on, having its way with Acheron's air, unaffected by the heteromorphic chambering that filled much of its lower level.

Of them all, only Ripley had some idea of what the troopers had stumbled across, and she was momentarily too numb with horrid fascination to explain. She could only stare and remember.

Gorman happened to glance back long enough to catch the expression on her face. "What is it?"

"I don't know."

"You know something, which is more than any of the rest of us. Come on, Ripley. Give. Right now I'd pay a hundred credits for an informed guess."

"I really don't know. I think I've seen something like it

once before, but I'm not sure. It's different, somehow. More elaborate and—"

"Let me know when your brain starts working again." Disappointed, the lieutenant turned back to the mike. "Proceed with your advance, Sergeant."

The troopers resumed their march, their suit lights shining on the vitreous walls surrounding them. The deeper they went into the maze, the more it took on the appearance of having been grown or secreted rather than built. The labyrinth looked like the interior of a gigantic organ or bone. Not a human organ, not a human bone.

Whatever else its purpose, the addition served to concentrate waste heat from the processor's fusion plant. Steam from dripping water formed puddles on the floor and hissed around them. Factory respiration.

"It's opening up a little just ahead." Hicks panned his camera around. The troop was entering a large, domed chamber. The walls abruptly changed in character and appearance. It was a testimony to their training that not one of the troopers broke down on the spot.

Ripley muttered, "Oh, God." Burke mumbled a shocked curse.

Cameras and suit lights illuminated the chamber. Instead of the smooth, curving walls they'd passed earlier, these were rough and uneven. They formed a rugged bas-relief composed of detritus gathered from the town: furniture, wiring, solid-and fluid-state components, bits of broken machinery, personal effects, torn clothing, human bones and skulls, all fused together with that omnipresent, translucent, epoxylike resin.

Hudson reached out to run a gloved hand along one wall, casually caressing a cluster of human ribs. He picked at the resinous ooze, barely scratching it.

"Ever see anything like this stuff before?"

"Not me." Hicks would have spat if he'd had room. "I'm not a chemist."

Dietrich was expected to render an opinion and did so.

"Looks like some kind of secreted glue. Your bad guys spit this stuff out or what, Ripley?"

"I—I don't know how its manufactured, but I've seen it before, on a much smaller scale."

Gorman pursed his lips, analysis taking over from the initial shock. "Looks like they ripped apart the colony for building materials." He indicated the view offered by Hicks's screen. "There's a whole stack of blank storage disks imbedded there."

"And portable power cells." Burke gestured toward another of the individual monitors. "Expensive stuff. Tore it all apart."

"And the colonists," Ripley pointed out, "when they were done with them." She turned to look down at the somber-visaged little girl standing next to her.

"Newt, you'd better go sit up front. Go on." She nodded and obediently headed for the driver's cab.

The steam on C-level intensified as the troops moved still deeper into the chamber. It was accompanied by a corresponding increase in temperature.

"Hotter'n a furnace in here," Frost grumbled.

"Yeah," Hudson agreed sarcastically, "but it's a *dry* heat."

Ripley looked to her left. Burke and Gorman stayed intent on the videoscreens. To the lieutenant's left was a small monitor that showed a graphic readout of the station's ground plan.

"They're right under the primary heat exchangers."

"Yeah." A fascinated Burke was unable to take his eyes off the view being relayed by Apone's camera. "Maybe the organisms like the heat. That's why they built—"

"That's not what I mean. Gorman, if your people have to use their weapons in there, they'll rupture the cooling system."

Burke abruptly realized what Ripley was driving at. "She's right."

"So?" asked the lieutenant.

"So," she continued, "that releases the freon and/or the water that's been condensed out of the air for cooling purposes."

"Fine." He tapped the screens. "It'll cool everybody off."

"It'll do more than cool them off."

"For instance?"

"Fusion containment shuts down."

"So? *So*?" Why didn't she get to the point? Didn't the woman realize that he was trying to direct a search-and-clear expedition here?

"We're talking thermonuclear explosion."

That made Gorman sit back and think. He weighed his options. His decision was made easier by the fact that he didn't have any. "Apone, collect rifle magazines from everybody. We can't have any firing in there."

Apone wasn't the only one who overheard the order. The troopers eyed one another with a combination of disbelief and dismay.

"Is he crazy?" Wierzbowski clutched his rifle protectively to his ribs, as if daring Gorman to come down and disarm it personally.

Hudson all but growled. "What're we supposed to use, man? Harsh language?" He spoke into his headset. "Hey, Lieutenant, you want maybe we should try judo? What if they ain't got any arms?"

"They've got arms," Ripley assured him tightly.

"You're not going in naked, Hudson," Gorman told him. "You've got other weapons you can use."

"Maybe that wouldn't be such a bad idea," Dietrich muttered.

"What, using alternates?" Wierzbowski muttered.

"No. Hudson going in naked. No living thing could stand the shock."

"Screw you, Dietrich," the comtech shot back.

"Not a chance." With a sigh the medtech yanked the fully charged magazine from her rifle.

"Flame units only." Gorman's tone was no-nonsense. "I want all rifles slung."

"You heard the lieutenant." Apone began circulating among them, collecting magazines. "Pull 'em out."

One by one the rifles were rendered harmless. Vasquez turned over the power packs for her smartgun with great reluctance. Three of the troopers carried portable incinerator units in addition to their penetration weapons. These were unlimbered, warmed up, and checked. Unnoticed by Apone or any of her colleagues, Vasquez slipped a spare power cell from the back of her pants and slipped it into her smartgun. As soon as the sergeant's eyes and all suit cameras were off them, Drake did likewise. The two smartgun operators exchanged a grim wink.

Hicks had no one to wink at and no smartgun to jimmy with. What he did have was a cylindrical sheath attached to the inner lining of his battle harness. Unzipping his torso armor, he opened the sheath to reveal the gunmetal-gray twin barrels of an antique pump twelve-gauge shotgun with a sawed-off butt stock. As Hudson looked on with professional interest the corporal resealed his armor, clicked back the stock of the well-maintained relic, and chambered a round.

"Where'd you get that, Hicks? When I saw that bulge, I thought you were smuggling liquor, except that'd be out of character for you. Steal it from a museum?"

"Been in my family for a long time. Cute, isn't it?"

"Some family. Can it do anything?"

Hicks showed him a single shell. "Not your standard military-issue high-velocity armor-piercing round, but you don't want it going off in your face, either." He kept his voice down. "I always keep this handy. For close encounters. I don't think it'll penetrate anything far enough to set off any mushrooms."

"Yeah, real cute." Hudson favored the sawed-off with a last admiring look. "You're a traditionalist, Hicks."

The corporal smiled thinly. "It's my tender nature."

Apone's voice carried back to them from just ahead. "Let's move. Hicks, since you seem to like it back there, you take rear guard."

"My pleasure, Sarge." The corporal rested the old shotgun against his right shoulder, balancing it easily with one hand, his finger light on the heavy trigger. Hudson grinned appreciatively, gave Hicks the high sign, and jogged forward to take up his assigned position near the point.

The air was thick, and their lights were diffused by the roiling steam. Hudson felt as though they were advancing through a steel-and-plastic jungle.

Gorman's voice echoed in his headset. "Any movement?" The lieutenant sounded faint and far away, even though the comtech knew he was only a couple of levels above and just outside the entrance to the processing station. He kept his eyes on his tracker as he advanced.

"Hudson here, sir. Nothing so far. Zip. The only thing moving around down here is the air."

He turned a corner and glanced up from the miniature readouts. What he saw made him forget the tracker, forget his rifle, forget everything.

Another encrusted wall lay directly in front of them. It was marred by bulges and ripples and had been sculpted by some unknown, inhuman hand, a teratogenic version of Rodin's *Gates of Hell*. Here were the missing colonists, entombed alive in the same epoxylike resin that had been used to construct the latticework and tunnels, chambers and pits, and had transformed the lowest level of the processing station into something out of a xenopsychotic nightmare.

Each had been cocooned in the wall without regard for human comfort. Arms and legs had been grotesquely twisted, broken when necessary in order to make the unfortunate victim fit properly into the alien scheme and design. Heads lolled at unnatural angles. Many of the bodies had been reduced to desiccated lumps of bone from which the flesh and skin had decayed. Others had been cleaned to the naked bone. They were the fortunate ones who had been granted the gift of death. Every corpse had one thing in common, no matter where it was situated or how it had been placed in the wall: the rib cages had been bent outward, as though the sternum had exploded from behind.

The troopers moved slowly into the embryo chamber. Their expressions were grim. No one said anything. There wasn't one among them who hadn't laughed at death, but this was worse than death. This was obscene.

Dietrich approached the still-intact figure of a woman. The body was ghostly white, drained. The eyelids fluttered and opened as the woman sensed movement, a presence, something. Madness dwelt within. The figure spoke in a hollow, sepulchral voice, a whisper conjured up out of desperation. Trying to hear, Dietrich leaned closer.

"Please—kill me."

Wide-eyed, the medtech stumbled back. Within the safety of the APC Ripley could only stare helplessly, biting down hard on the knuckles of her left hand. She knew what was coming, knew what prompted the woman's ultimate request, just as she knew that neither she nor anyone else could do anything except comply. The sound of somebody retching came over the Operations bay speakers. Nobody made jokes about that, either.

The woman imprisoned in the wall began to convulse. Somewhere she summoned up the energy to scream, a steady, sawing shriek of mindless agony. Ripley took a step toward the nearest mike, wanting to warn the troopers of what was coming but unable to make her throat work.

It wasn't necessary. They'd studied the research disks she'd prepared for them.

"Flamethrower!" Apone snapped. "Move!"

Frost handed his incinerator to the sergeant, stepped

aside. As Apone took possession, the woman's chest erupted in a spray of blood. From the cavity thus formed, a small fanged skull emerged, hissing viciously.

Apone's finger jerked the trigger of the flamethrower. The two other soldiers who carried similar devices imitated his action. Heat and light filled the chamber, searing the wall and obliterating the screaming horror it contained. Cocoons and their contents melted and ran like translucent taffy. A deafening screeching echoed in their ears as they worked the fire over the entire end of the room. What wasn't carbonized by the intense heat melted. The wall puddled and ran, pooling around their boots like molten plastic. But it didn't smell like plastic. It gave off a thick, organic stench.

Everyone in the chamber was intent on the wall and the flamethrowers. No one saw a section of another wall twitch.

The alien had been lying dormant, prone in a pocket that blended in perfectly with the rest of the room. Slowly it emerged from its resting niche. Smoke from burning cocoons and other organic matter billowed roofward, reducing visibility in the chamber to near zero.

Something made Hudson glance briefly at his tracker. His pupils expanded, and he whirled to shout a warning. "Movement! I've got movement."

"Position?" inquired Apone sharply.

"Can't lock up. It's too tight in here, and there's too many other bodies."

An edge crept into the master sergeant's voice. "Don't tell me that. Talk to me, Hudson. Where is it?"

The comtech struggled to refine the tracker's information. That was the trouble with these field units: They were tough but imprecise.

"Uh, seems to be in front _and_ behind."

In the Operations bay of the APC, Gorman frantically adjusted gain and sharpness controls on individual monitors. "We can't see anything back here, Apone. What's going on?"

Ripley knew what was going on. Knew what was coming. She could sense it, even if they couldn't see it, like a wave rushing a black sand beach at night. She found her voice and the mike simultaneously.

"Pull your team out, Gorman. Get them out of there _now_."

The lieutenant spared her an irritated glare. "Don't give me orders, lady. I know what I'm doing."

"Maybe, but you don't know what's being _done_."

Down on C-level the walls and ceiling of the alien chamber were coming to life. Biomechanical fingers extended talons that could tear metal. Slime-lubricated jaws began to flex, pistoning silently as their owners awoke. Uncertain movements were glimpsed dimly through smoke and steam by the nervous human intruders.

Apone found himself starting to back up. "Go to infrared. Look sharp, people!" Visors were snapped into place. On their smooth, transparent insides images began to materialize, nightmare silhouettes moving in ghostly silence through the drifting mist.

"Multiple signals," Hudson declared, "all around. Closing from all directions."

Dietrich's nerves snapped, and she whirled to retreat. As she turned, something tall and immensely powerful loomed above the smoke to wrap long arms around her. Limbs like metal bars locked across her chest and contracted. The med-tech screamed, and her finger tensed reflexively on the trigger of her flamethrower. A jet of flame engulfed Frost, turning him into a blindly stumbling bipedal torch. His shriek echoed through everyone's headset.

Apone pivoted, unable to see anything in the dense atmosphere and poor light but able to hear entirely too much. The heat from the cooling exchangers on the level above distorted the imaging ability of the troopers' infrared visors.

In the APC, Gorman could only stare as Frost's monitor went to black. At the same time his bioreadouts flattened, hills and valleys signifying life being replaced by grim, straight lines. On the remaining monitor screens, images and outlines bobbed and panned confusedly. Blasts of glowing napalm from the remaining operative flamethrowers combined to overload the light-sensing ability of suit cameras, flaring what images they did provide.

In the midst of chaos and confusion Vasquez and Drake found each other. High-tech harpy nodded knowingly to new-wave neanderthal as she slammed her sequestered magazine back in place.

"Let's rock," she said curtly.

Standing back to back, they opened up simultaneously with their smartguns, laying down two arcs of fire like welders sealing the skin of a spaceship. In the confined chamber the din from the two heavy weapons was overpowering. To the operators of the smartguns the thunder was a Bach fugue and Grimoire stanthisizer all rolled into one.

Gorman's voice echoed in their ears, barely audible over the roar of battle. "Who's firing? I ordered a hold on heavy fire!"

Vasquez reached up just long enough to rip away her headset, her eyes and attention riveted on the smartgun's targeting screen. Feet, hands, eyes, and body became exten-sions of the weapon, all dancing and spinning in unison. Thunder, lightning, smoke, and screams filled the chamber, a little slice of Armageddon on C-level. A great calmness flowed through her.

Surely Heaven couldn't be any better than this.

Ripley flinched as another scream reverberated through the Operations bay speakers. Wierzbowski's suit camera crumbled, followed by the immediate flattening of his bio-monitors. Her fingers clenched, the nails digging into the palms. She'd liked Wierzbowski.

What was she doing here, anyway? Why wasn't she back home, poor and unlicensed, but safe in her little apartment, surrounded by Jones and ordinary people and common sense? Why had she voluntarily sought the company of night-mares? Out of altruism? Because she'd suspected all along what had been responsible for the break in communications between Acheron and Earth? Or because she wanted a lousy flight certificate back?

Down in the depths of the processing station, frantic, panicky voices ran into one another on the single personal communications frequency. Headset components sorted sense from the babble. She recognized Hudson's above everyone else's. The comtech's unsophisticated pragmatism shone through the breakdown in tactics.

"Let's get out of here!"

She heard Hicks yelling at someone else. The corporal sounded more frustrated than anything else. "Not that tunnel, the other one!"

"You sure?" Crowe's picture swung crazily as he ducked something unseen, the view provided by his suit camera a wild blur full of smoke, haze, and biomechanical silhouettes. "Watch it—behind you. Move, will you!"

Gorman's hands slowed. Something besides button-pushing was required now, and Ripley could see from the ashen expression that had come over the lieutenant's face that he didn't have it.

"Get them out of there!" she screamed at him. "Do it *now!*"

"Shut up." He was gulping air like a grouper, studying his readouts. Everything was unraveling, his careful plan of advance coming apart on the remaining monitors too fast for him to think it through. Too fast. "Just shut up!"

The groan of metal being ripped apart sounded over Crowe's headset pickup as his telemetry went black. Gorman stuttered something incomprehensible, trying to keep control of himself even as he was losing control of the situation.

"Uh, Apone, I want you to lay down a suppressing fire with the incinerators and fall back by squads to the APC. Over."

The sergeant's distant reply was distorted by static, the roar of the flamethrowers, and the rapid fire stutter of the smartguns.

"Say again? All after incinerators?"

"I said . . ." Gorman repeated his instructions. It didn't matter if anyone heard them. The men and women trapped in the cocoon chamber had time only to react, not to listen.

Only Apone fiddled with his headset, trying to make sense of the garbled orders. Gorman's voice was distorted beyond recognition. The headsets were designed to operate and deliver a clear signal under any conditions, including under water, but there was something happening here that hadn't been anticipated by the communications equipment designers, something that couldn't have been foreseen by anyone because it hadn't been encountered before.

Someone screamed behind the sergeant. Forget Gorman. He switched the headset over to straight intersuit frequency. "Dietrich? Crowe? Sound off! Wierzbowski, where are you?"

Movement to his left. He whirled and came within a millimeter of blowing Hudson's head off. The comtech's eyes were wild. He was teetering on the edge of sanity and barely recognized the sergeant. No bold assertions now; all false bravado fled. He was terrified out of his skin and made no effort to conceal the fact.

"We're getting juked! We're gonna die in here!"

Apone passed him a rifle magazine. The comtech slapped it home, trying to look every which way at once. "Feel better?" Apone asked him.

"Yeah, right. Right!" Gratefully the comtech chambered a pulse-rifle round. "Forget the heat exchanger." He sensed movement, turned, and fired. The slight recoil imparted by the weapon traveled up his arm to restore a little of his lost confidence.

Off to their right, Vasquez was laying down an uninterrupted field of fire, destroying everything not human that came within a meter of her—be it dead, alive, or part of the processing plant's machinery. She looked out of control. Apone knew better. If she was out of control, they'd all be dead by now.

Hicks ran toward her. Pivoting smoothly, she let loose a long burst from the heavy weapon. The corporal ducked as the smartgun's barrel swung toward his face, stumbling clear as the nightmarish figure stalking him was catapulted backward by Vasquez's blast. Biomechanical fingers had been centimeters from his neck.

Within the APC, Apone's monitor suddenly spun crazily and went dark. Gorman stared at it, as though by doing so, he could will it back to life, along with the man it represented.

"I told them to fall back." His tone was distant, disbelieving. "They must not have heard the order."

Ripley shoved her face into his, saw the dazed, baffled expression. "They're cut off in there! _Do_ something!"

He looked up at her slowly. His lips worked, but the mumble they produced was unintelligible. He was shaking his head slightly.

No help from that quarter. The lieutenant was out of it. Burke had backed up against the opposite wall, as though by putting distance between himself and the images on the remaining active monitors he could somehow remove himself from the battle that was raging in the bowels of the processing station.

There was only one thing that would do the surviving soldiers any good now, and that was some kind of immediate help. Gorman wasn't going to do anything about it, and Burke couldn't. So that left Jones's favorite human.

If the cat had been present and capable of taking action on Ripley's behalf, she knew what he would have done: turned the armored personnel carrier around and driven that sucker at top speed for the landing field. Piled into the dropship, lifted back to the *Sulaco*, slipped into hypersleep, and *gone home*. Not likely anyone in colonial administration would dispute her report this time. Not with a shell-shocked Gorman and half-comatose Burke to back her up. Not with the recordings automatically stored by the APC's computer taken directly from the soldier's suit cameras to flash in the faces of those smug, content Company representatives.

Get out, go home, get *away*, the voice inside her skull screamed at her. You've got the proof you came for. The colony's kaput, one survivor, the others dead or worse than dead. Go back to Earth and come back with an army next time, not a platoon. Atmosphere fliers for air cover. Heavy weapons. Level the place if they have to, but let 'em do it without you.

There was only one problem with that comforting line of reasoning. Leaving now would mean abandoning Vasquez and Hudson and Hicks and everyone else still alive down in C-level to the tender ministrations of the aliens. If they were lucky, they would die. If they were not, they'd end up cemented into a cocoon wall as replacement for the still-living host colonists they'd mercifully carbonized.

She couldn't do that and live with it. She'd see their faces and hear their screams every time she rested her head on a pillow. If she fled, she'd be swapping the immediate nightmare for hundreds later on. A bad trade. One more time the numbers were against her.

She was terrified of what she had to do, but the anger that had been building inside her at Gorman's ineffectiveness

and at the Company for sending her out here with an inexperienced field officer and less than a dozen troops (to save
money, no doubt) helped drive her past the paralyzed lieutenant toward the APC's cockpit.

The sole survivor of Hadley Colony awaited her with a
solemn stare.

"Newt, get in the back and put your seat belt on."

"You're going after the others, aren't you?"

She paused as she was strapping herself into the driver's
chair. "I have to. There are still people alive down there, and
they need help. You understand that, don't you?"

The girl nodded. She understood completely. As Ripley
clicked home the latches on the driver's harness, the girl raced
back down the aisle.

The warm glow of instruments set in the hold mode
greeted Ripley as she turned to the controls. Gorman and
Burke might be incapable of reaction, but no such psycho-
logical restraints inhibited the APC's movements. She started
slapping switches and buttons, grateful now for the time spent
during the past year operating all sorts of heavy loading and
transport equipment out in Portside. The oversize turbo-
charged engine raced reassuringly, and the personnel carrier
shook, eager to move out.

The vibration from the engine was enough to shock
Gorman back to the real world. He leaned back in his chair
and shouted forward. "Ripley, what are you doing?"

Easy to ignore him, more important to concentrate on
the controls. She slammed the massive vehicle into gear.
Drive wheels spun on damp ground as the APC lurched toward the gaping entrance to the station.

Smoke was pouring out of the complex. The big armored
wheels skidded slightly on the damp pavement as she wrenched
the machine sideways and sent it hurtling down the wide,
descending rampway. The ramp accommodated the APC with
room to spare. It had been designed to admit big earthmovers
and service vehicles. Colonial construction was typically

overbuilt. Even so, the roadway was depressed by the weight
of the APC's armor, but no cracks appeared in its wake as
Ripley sent it racing downward. Her hands hammered the
controls of the independently powered wheels as she took out
some of her anger on the uncomplaining plastic.

Mist and haze obscured the view provided by the external
monitors. She switched to automatic navigation, and the APC
kept itself from crashing into the enclosing walls, ranging
lasers reading the distance between wheels and obstacles twenty
times a second and reporting back to the vehicle's central
computer. She maintained speed, knowing that the machine
wouldn't let her crash.

Gorman stopped staring at the dimly seen walls rushing
by on the Operations bay screens, released his suit harness,
and stumbled forward, bouncing off the walls as Ripley sent
the APC careening wildly around tight corners.

"What are you doing?"

"What's it look like I'm doing?" She didn't turn to face
him, absorbed in controlling the carrier.

He put a hand on her shoulder. "Turn around! That's an
order!"

"You can't give me orders, Gorman. I'm a civilian,
remember?"

"This is a military expedition under military control. As
commanding officer, I am ordering you to turn this vehicle
around!"

She gritted her teeth, attention focused on the forward
viewscreens. "Go sit on a grenade, Gorman. I'm busy."

He reached down and tried to pull her out of the chair.
Burke got both arms around him and pulled him off. She
would have thanked the Company rep, but she didn't have
the time.

They reached C-level and the big wheels screamed as
she sent the APC into a mad turn, simultaneously switching
off the automatic navigation system and the ranging lasers.
The engine revved as they rumbled forward, tearing away

pipes and conduits, equipment modules, and chunks of alien encrustation. She glanced at the control console until she located the external instrumentation she wanted: strobe beacon, siren, running lights. She wiped the entire panel with the palm of her right hand.

The exterior of the APC came alive with sodium-arc lights, infrared homing beacons, spinning locater flashers, and the piercing whine of the battle siren. The individual suit monitors were all back in the Operations bay, but she didn't need to see them, zeroing in on the flash of weapons fire just ahead. The lights and roar came from beyond a thick wall of translucent alien resin, the material eerily distributing the light from the guns throughout its substance, giving the cocoon chamber the appearance of a dome pulsing from within.

She nudged the accelerator. The APC smashed through the curving wall like an iron ingot shot from a cannon. Fragments of resin and biomechanical mortar went flying. Huge chunks were crushed beneath the armored wheels. She wrenched on the wheel, and the personnel carrier pivoted neatly. The rear of the powerful machine swung around and brought down another section of alien wall.

Hicks appeared out of the smoke. He was firing back the way he'd come, holding the big pulse-rifle in one hand while supporting a limping Hudson with the other. Adrenaline, muscle, and determination were all that kept the two men going. Ripley looked away from the windshield and back down the APC's central aisle.

"Burke, they're coming!"

A faint reply as he hollered back toward the cockpit: "I'm on my way! Hang on."

The Company rep stumbled to the crew access door, fumbled with unfamiliar controls until the armored hatch cycled wide. Following in Hicks's and Hudson's footsteps, the two smartgun operators materialized out of the dense mist. They were retreating with precision, side by side, firing and covering the retreat as they fell back on the personnel carrier.

As Ripley looked on, Drake's gun went empty. Automatically he snapped the release buckles on the smartgun harness. It sloughed away like an old skin. Before it hit the ground, he'd pulled a flamethrower from his back and had brought it into play. The hollow *whoosh* of napalm mixed with the deep-throated chatter of Vasquez's still operative smartgun.

Hicks reached the APC, put his weapon aside, and all but threw the injured Hudson through the opening. Then he tossed his pulse-rifle after the comtech and cleared the hatch in two strides. Vasquez was still firing as the corporal got both hands under her arms and heaved, pulling her in after him. At the same time she saw a dark, towering silhouette lunge toward Drake from behind, and she changed her field of fire as Hicks was dumping her onto the APC's deck.

A flash of contact lit up an inhuman, frozen grin as the smartgun shells tore apart the alien's thorax. Bright yellow body fluid sprayed in all directions. It splashed across Drake's face and chest. Smoke rose from the staggering body of the smartgun operator as the acid chewed rapidly through flesh and bone. His muscles spasmed, and his flamethrower fired as he toppled backward.

Vasquez and Hicks rolled as a gout of flame slashed through the open crew door, setting portions of the APC's flammable interior ablaze. As Drake fell, Hicks charged the hatch and started to cycle the door. Moving on hands and knees, Vasquez lunged wildly at the opening. The corporal had to leave the controls to grab her. It was a struggle to keep her from plunging outside.

"Drake!" She was screaming, not calm and controlled anymore. "He's down!"

It took all of Hicks's superior size and strength to wrench her around to face him. "He's gone! Forget it, Vasquez. He's gone."

She stared up at him, irrational, her face streaked with soot and grime. "No. No, he's not! He's ..."

Hicks looked back at the APC's other occupants. "Get

her away from here. We've got to get this door closed."
Hudson nodded. Together he and Burke dragged the dazed
smartgun operator away from the entry hatch. The corporal
looked toward the cockpit and raised what was left of his
voice. "Let's go! We're clear back here."

"Going!" Ripley jammed on the controls and nailed the
accelerator. The armored personnel carrier roared and shuddered as she sent it racing backward up the ramp.

A storage rack broke free, burying Hudson beneath a
pile of equipment. Cursing and flailing, he threw the stuff
aside, indifferent to whether it was marked EMERGENCY RA-
TIONS or EXPLOSIVES.

Hicks turned his attention back to the door, fumbled with
the controls. It was nearly shut when two sets of long claws
suddenly appeared to slam into the metal flange like a pair
of power hammers. From her seat Newt let out a primordial
child's scream. The saber-tooth, the giant bear, the boogeyman was at the entrance to the cave, and this time she had
no place to hide.

Vasquez stumbled to her feet and joined Hicks and Burke
in leaning on the door. Despite their combined efforts, the
metal barrier was slowly being wrenched open from the outside. Locks and seals groaned in protest.

Hicks managed to find enough wind to yell at the still
numbed Gorman. "Get on the door!"

The lieutenant heard him and reacted. Reacted by backing away and shaking his head, his eyes wide. Hicks muttered
a curse and jammed his shoulder against the latching lever.
This freed one hand to pull out the sawed-off twelve-gauge
just as a nightmare alien head wedged its way through the
opening. Outer jaws parted to reveal the pistonlike inner
throat and penetrating teeth. As slime-covered fangs swung
toward him, Hicks jammed the muzzle of the shotgun between
the gaping demon jaws and pulled the trigger. The explosion
of the ancient projectile weapon echoed through the personnel
carrier as the shattered skull fell backward, fountaining acid

blood. The spray immediately began to eat into the door and deck.

Hicks and Vasquez fell aside, but some of the droplets struck Hudson on the arm. Smoke rose from skin as hissing flesh dissolved. The comtech operator let out a howl and stumbled into the empty seats.

Hicks and Burke slammed the hatch shut and locked it.

Like a runaway comet, the APC rumbled backward up the ramp and slammed into a mass of conduit. Ripley worked on the wheels, spinning the oversize metal rims and ripping free. Sparks showered over the vehicle. In the crew quarters behind her, everyone seemed to be yelling simultaneously. Extinguishers were unbolted and brought into play on the internal fire. Newt stayed out of the way, sitting silently in her seat as panicky adults ran to and fro around her. She was breathing hard but steadily, eyes alert, watching. None of what was happening was new to her. She'd been through it all before.

Something made a soft metallic thump as it landed on the roof.

Gorman had retreated into a corner to the left of the aisle. He was staring blankly at his frantic companions. Consequently he did not see the small gun hatch, against which he was leaning, begin to vibrate. But he felt it when the hatch cover was ripped from its seals. He started to turn, not nearly fast enough, and was snatched through the opening.

There was something at the tip of the alien's tail, something silver-sharp and superfast. It whipped around one leg to bury itself in the lieutenant's shoulder. He screamed. Hicks threw himself into the crew bay fire-control chair and clutched the controls, jabbing contact points and switches with his other hand as the seat motor hummed and swung him around. Brightly colored telltales came to life on the board, adding no cheer to the beleaguered APC's interior but bringing a smile to the corporal's face.

In response to his actions servomotors whirred and a

small turret came to life on the personnel carrier's roof. It spun in a half circle. The alien holding Gorman two-thirds of the way out of the vehicle turned sharply in the direction of the new sound just as twin guns fired in its direction. The heavy shells blew it right off the top of the machine, the impact knocking it clear before the acid in its body began to spill.

Burke dragged the unconscious Gorman back inside while Vasquez hunted for something to plug the opening with.

Trailing fire and smoke, the APC tore up the ramp. Ripley wrestled with the controls as the big vehicle slewed sideways, broadsiding a control room outbuilding. Office furniture and splintered sections of wall exploded in all directions, forming a wake of plastic and composite fiber behind the retreating machine.

Almost clear now, almost out. Another minute or two, and if nothing broke down, they'd be free of the station's confines. Free to...

An alien arm arced down right in front of her face to smash the shatterproof windshield. Glistening, slime-coated jaws lunged inside. Ripley threw up both arms to shield her face and leaned away. Once before, she'd been this close to perdition. In the shuttle *Narcissus*, secure in its pilot's seat, luring another alien close so that she could blow it out the airlock. But there was no airlock here, no comforting atmosphere suit enclosing her, no tricks left to pull, and no time to think of any.

She tried to crush the brakes underfoot. The big wheels locked up at high speed, screeching over the sound of the chaos outside. She felt herself being thrown forward, her head flying toward those gaping jaws. But her seat harness checked her motion and kept her in the chair.

No such restraints secured the alien. Leaning over the windshield, it was clinging awkwardly to the edge of the roof, and not even its inhuman strength could prevent it from being thrown forward. As soon as it landed on the ground

she threw the personnel carrier back in gear. It didn't even
bump as it trundled over the skeletal body, crushing it beneath
its massive weight. Acid squirted over armored wheels, but
the APC's forward movement carried it clear before more
than a few inconsequential pits had been eaten in the spinning
disks. Their movement was not affected.

Darkness ahead. Clean, welcoming darkness. Not a blank
falling over her mind but the darkness of a dimly lit world:
the surface of Acheron, framed by the walls of the station.
A moment later they were through, rumbling over the connecting causeway toward the landing field.

A noise like bolts dropped in a food processor was coming from the rear of the APC. Occasionally a louder clunk
could be heard. It was a sound beyond the soothing effects
of lubrication, beyond repair. She fiddled with controls and
tried to adjust the noise out of existence, but like her recurring
nightmares, it refused early dismissal.

Hicks came forward and, gently but firmly, eased her
fingers off the accelerator control. Her face was as white as
her knuckles. She blinked, glanced back up at him.

"It's okay," he assured her, "we're clear. They're all
behind us. I don't think fighting out in the open suits them.
Ease up. We're not going much further in this hunk of junk,
anyway."

The grinding noise was overpowering as they slowed.
She listened intently as she brought the big vehicle to a halt.

"Don't ask me for an analysis. I'm an operator, not a
mechanic."

Hicks cocked an ear in the direction of the metallic
gargling. "Sounds like a blown transaxle. Maybe two. You're
just grinding metal. Actually I'm surprised that the underside
of this baby isn't lying back on B-level somewhere. They
build these things tough."

"Not tough enough." That was Burke's voice, filtering
up to them from somewhere in the passenger compartment.

"Nobody expected to have to face anything like these

creatures. Ever." Hicks leaned toward the console and rotated an exterior viewer. The APC looked terrible on the outside, a smoking, acid-scarred hulk. It was supposed to be invulnerable. Now it was scrap.

Ripley spun her seat, glanced at the empty one next to her, and then turned to stare down the aisle that led back through the personnel carrier.

"Newt. Where's Newt?"

A tug on her pants leg. Not hard, so she didn't jump. Newt was squeezed into the tiny space between the driver's seat and the APC's armored bulkhead. She was trembling and terrified but alert. No catatonia this time, no withdrawal from reality. No reason for an extreme reaction, Ripley knew. Doubtless the girl had been witness to much worse when the aliens had overwhelmed the colony.

Had she been watching the Operations bay monitors when the soldiers had initially penetrated the alien cocoon chamber? Had she seen the face of the woman who had whispered in agony to Dietrich? What if the woman had been...?

But she couldn't have been. If that had been Newt's mother, the girl would be beyond catatonia by now. Gone, withdrawn, and unreachable, perhaps forever.

"You okay?" Sometimes inanities had to be asked. Besides, she wanted, needed, to hear the child respond.

Newt did so with a thumbs-up gesture, still employing selective silence as a defense mechanism. Ripley didn't push her to talk. Keeping quiet while everyone around her was being killed had kept her alive.

"I have to check on the others," she told the upturned face. "Will you be all right?"

A nod this time, accompanied by a shy little smile that made Ripley swallow hard. She tried to conceal what she was feeling inside, because this wasn't the time or place to break down. They could do that when they were safely back aboard the *Sulaco*.

"Good. I'll be right back. If you get tired of staying under there, you can come back and join the rest of us, okay?" The smile widened slightly and was followed by a more vigorous nod, but the girl stayed put. She still trusted her own instincts more than she trusted any adult. Ripley wasn't offended. She unbuckled herself and headed back down the aisle.

Hudson was standing off to one side inspecting his arm. The fact that he still had an arm showed that he'd only been lightly misted by the alien acid. He was reliving the last twenty minutes of his life, replaying every second over and over in his mind and not believing what he saw there. She could hear him muttering to himself.

"—I don't believe it. It didn't happen. It didn't happen, man."

Burke tried to have a look at the injured comtech's arm, more curious than sympathetic. Hudson jerked away from the Company rep.

"I'm all right. Leave it!"

Burke pursed his lips, wanting to see but not willing to push. "Better let somebody take a look at it. Can't tell what the side effects are. Might be toxic."

"Yeah? And if it is, I suppose you're going to check stores and break out an antidote in a couple of minutes, right? Dietrich's the medtech." He swallowed and his anger faded. "Was our medtech. Stinking bugs."

Hicks was bending over the motionless Gorman, checking for a pulse. Ripley joined him.

"Anything?" she asked tightly.

"Heartbeat's slow but steady. He's breathing the same way. It's the same with the rest of his vital signs: slowed down but regular. He's alive. If I didn't know better, I'd say he was sleeping, but it ain't sleep. I think he's paralyzed."

Vasquez pushed both of them aside and grabbed the unconscious lieutenant by his collar. She was too furious to cry. "He's dead is what he is!" She hauled the upper half of

Gorman's body upright with one hand and drew back the other in a fist, screaming in his face.

"Wake up, *pendejo*! Wake up. I'm gonna kill you, you useless waste!"

Hicks inserted his bulk between her and the frozen lieutenant. Same soft voice employed, but with a slight edge to it now. Same hard eyes staring into the smartgun operator's face.

"Hold it. Hold it. Back off—right now."

Their eyes locked. Vasquez continued to hold Gorman half off the deck. Something basic cut its way through her fury. Marine—she was a Marine, and Marines live by basics. The basics in this case were simple. Apone was gone and therefore Hicks was in charge.

"It ain't worth bruising my knuckles," she finally muttered. She released the lieutenant's collar, and his head bounced off the deck as she turned away, still cursing to herself. Ripley didn't doubt for an instant that if Hicks hadn't intervened, the smartgun operator would have beaten the unconscious Gorman to a pulp.

With Vasquez out of the way Ripley bent over the paralyzed officer and opened his tunic. The bloodless purple puncture wound that marred his shoulder had already sealed itself.

"Looks like it stung him or something. Interesting. I didn't know they could do that."

"Hey!"

The excited shout made Hicks and her turn toward the Operations bay. Hudson was in there. He'd been staring morosely at the biomonitors and videoscreens, and something had caught his eye. Now he beckoned to his remaining companions.

"Look. Crowe and Dietrich aren't dead, man." He gestured at the bio readouts, swallowed uneasily. "They must be like Gorman. Their signs are real low, but they ain't dead...."
His voice trailed off, along with his initial excitement.

If they weren't dead and they were like Hudson, that meant— The comtech started to shake with a mixture of anger and sorrow. He was standing on the thin edge of hysteria. They all were. It clung to them like a psychic leech, hanging on the fringes of their sanity, threatening to invade and take over the instant anyone let down his mental guard.

Ripley knew what those soporific bioreadouts meant. She tried to explain, but she couldn't meet Hudson's eyes as she did so.

"You can't help them."

"Hey, but if they're still alive—"

"Forget it. Right now they're being cocooned, just like those others. Like the colonists you found in the wall when you went in there. You can't do a damn thing for them. Nobody can. That's the way it is. Just be glad you're here talking about them instead of down there with them. If Dietrich was here, she'd know she couldn't do anything to help you."

The comtech seemed to sag in on himself. "This ain't happening."

Ripley turned away from him. As she did so, her gaze met Vasquez's. It would have been easy for her to say "I told you so" to the smartgunner. It also would have been superfluous. That one look communicated everything the two women needed to say.

This time it was Vasquez who turned away.

IX

In the colony medical lab Bishop stood hunched over an ocular probe. Beneath the lens was a stretched slice of one of the dead facehugger parasites, extracted from the specimen in the nearest stasis cylinder. Even in death the biopsied creature looked threatening, lying on its back on the dissection table. The clutching legs looked poised to grab any face that bent too close, the powerful tail ready to propel the creature clear across the room in a single pistoning leap.

The internal structure was as fascinating as the functional exterior, and Bishop was glued to the probe's eyepiece. By combining the probe's resolving power with the versatility of his own artificial eye, he was able to see a great deal that the colonists might have missed.

One of the questions that particularly intrigued him, and which he was anxious to answer, involved the definite possibility of an alien parasite attempting to attach itself to a synthetic like himself. His insides were radically different from those of a purely biological human being. Would a parasite be able to detect the differences before it sprang? If not and it attempted to utilize a synthetic as a host, what might be the probable results of such an enforced union? Would it simply drop off and go searching for another body, or would it mindlessly insert the embryonic seed it carried into an artificial host? If so, would the embryo be able to grow or would it be the more surprised of the couple as it struggled to mature within a body devoid of flesh and blood?

Could a robot be parasitized?

Something made a noise near the doorway. Bishop looked up long enough to see the dropship crew chief roll a pallet full of equipment and supplies into the lab.

"Where you want this stuff?"

"Over there." Bishop gestured. "By the end of the bench will do nicely."

Spunkmeyer began unloading the shipping pallet. "Need anything else?"

Bishop waved vaguely without taking his gaze from the probe.

"Right. I'll be back in the ship. Buzz me if you need anything."

Another wave. Spunkmeyer shrugged and turned to leave.

Bishop was a funny sort of bird, the crew chief mused as he wheeled his hand truck down the empty corridors and back out onto the landing tarmac. Funny sort of hybird, he thought, correcting himself and smiling at the pun. He whistled cheerfully as he snugged his collar higher up around his neck. The wind wasn't blowing too badly, but it was still chilly outside without a full environment suit. Concentrating on a tune also helped to keep his mind off the disaster that had befallen the expedition.

Crowe, Dietrich, old Apone—all gone. Hard to believe, as Hudson kept mumbling over and over to himself. Hard to believe and a shame. He'd known them all; they'd flown together on a number of missions. Though he couldn't say he knew any of them intimately.

He shrugged, even though there was no one around to see the gesture. Death was something they were all used to, an acquaintance each of them fully expected to encounter prior to retirement. Crowe and Dietrich had early appointments, that was all. Nothing to be done about it. But Hicks and the rest had made it out okay. They'd finish their studies and cleanup here and be out by tomorrow. That was the plan. A little more study, make a few last recordings, and get out of there. He knew he wasn't the only one looking forward to the moment when the dropship would heave mass and head back to the good ol' *Sulaco*.

His thoughts went back to Bishop again. Maybe there'd been some sort of subtle improvement in the new model synthetics, or maybe it was just Bishop himself, but he found that he rather liked the android. Everybody said that the artificial-intelligence boys had been working hard to improve personality programming for years, even adding a bit of randomness to each new model as it walked off the assembly line. Sure, that was it—Bishop was an individual. You could tell him from another synthetic just by talking to him. And it didn't hurt to have one quiet, courteous companion among all the boastful loudmouths.

As he rolled the hand truck to the top of the dropship's loading ramp, he slipped. Catching his balance, he bent to examine the damp spot. Since there was no depression in which rainwater could pool up, he thought he must have busted a container of Bishop's precious preserving fluid, but there was no tickling, lingering odor of formaldehyde. The shiny stuff clinging to the metal ramp looked more like a thick slime or gel.

He shrugged and straightened. He couldn't remember busting a bottle containing anything like that, and as long as nobody asked him about it, there was no point in worrying. No time for worrying, either. Too much to do so they could get ready to leave.

The wind beat at him. Lousy atmosphere, and yet it was a lot milder than what it had been before the atmosphere processors had started work here. "Unbreathable," the pre-sleep briefing had said. Pulling the hand truck in behind him, he hit the switch to retract the ramp and close the door.

Vasquez was pacing the length of the APC. Inactivity in what was still a combat situation was a foreign sensation to her. She wanted a gun in her hands and something to shoot at. She knew the situation called for careful analysis, and it frustrated her because she wasn't the analytical type. Her methods were direct, final, and didn't involve any talk. But she was smart enough to realize that this wasn't your standard operation anymore. Standard operating procedure had been chewed up and spit out by the enemy. Knowing this failed to calm her, however. She wanted to kill something.

Occasionally her fingers would flex as though they were still gripping the controls of her smartgun. Watching her would have made Ripley nervous if she wasn't already as tense as it was possible to be without snapping like the overwound mainspring of an ancient timepiece.

It got to the point where Vasquez knew she could say something or start tearing her hair out. "All right, we can't blow them up. We can't go down there as a squad; we can't even go back down in the APC because they'll take us apart like a can full of peas. Why not roll some canisters of CN-20 down there? Nerve gas the whole nest? We've got enough on the dropship to make the whole colony uninhabitable."

Hudson was pleading with his eyes, glancing at each of them in turn. "Look man, let's just bug out and call it even, okay?" He glanced at the woman standing next to him. "I'm with Ripley. Let 'em make the whole colony into a playpen if they want to, but we get out now and come back with a warship."

Vasquez stared at him out of slitted eyes. "Getting queasy, Hudson?"

"Queasy!" He straightened a little in reaction to the implicit challenge. "We're in over our heads here. Nobody said we'd run into anything like this. I'll be the first one to volunteer to come back, but when I do, I want the right kind of equipment to deal with the problem. This ain't like mob control, Vasquez. You try kicking some butts here and they'll eat your leg right off."

Ripley looked at the smartgun operator. "The nerve gas won't work, anyway. How do we know if it'll affect their biochemistry? Maybe they'll just snort the stuff. The way these things are built, nerve gas might just give them a pleasant high. I blew one of them out an airlock with an emergency grapple stuck in its gut, and all it did was slow it down. I had to fry it with my ship's engines." She leaned back against the wall.

"I say we take off and nuke the entire site from orbit and the whole high plateau where we originally found the ship that brought them here. It's the only way to be sure."

"Now hold on a second." Having been silent during the ongoing discussion, Burke abruptly came to life. "I'm not authorizing that kind of action. That's about as extreme as you can get."

"You don't think the situation's extreme?" growled Hudson. He toyed with the bandage on his acid-scarred arm and glared hard at the Company representative.

"Of course it's extreme."

"Then why won't you authorize the use of nukes?" Ripley pressed him. "You lose the colony and one processing station, but you've still got ninety-five percent of your terraforming capability unimpaired and operational on the rest of the planet. So why the hesitation?"

Sensing the challenge in her tone, the Company rep backpedaled flawlessly into a conciliatory mode.

"Well, I mean, I know this is an emotional moment. I'm as upset as anybody else. But that doesn't mean we have to resort to snap judgments. We have to move cautiously here. Let's think before we throw out the baby with the bathwater."

"The baby's dead, Burke, in case you haven't noticed." Ripley refused to be swayed.

"All I'm saying," he argued, "is that it's time to look at the whole situation, if you know what I mean."

She crossed her arms over her chest. "No, Burke, what do you mean?"

He thought fast. "First of all, this installation has a substantial monetary value attached to it. We're talking about an entire colony setup here. Never mind the replacement cost. The investment in transportation alone is enormous, and the process of terraforming Acheron is just starting to show some real progress. It's true that the other atmosphere-processing stations function automatically, but they still require regular maintenance and supervision. Without the means to house and service an appropriate staff locally, that would mean keeping several transports in orbit as floating hotels for the necessary personnel. That involves an ongoing cost you can't begin to imagine."

"They can bill me," she told him unsmilingly. "I got a tab running. What else?"

"For another thing, this is clearly an important species we're dealing with here. We can't just arbitrarily exterminate those who've found their way to this world. The loss to science would be incalculable. We might never encounter them again."

"Yeah, and that'd be just too bad." She uncrossed her arms. "Aren't you forgetting something, Burke? You told me that if we encountered a hostile life-form here, we'd take care of it and forget the scientific concerns. That's why I never liked dealing with administrators: you guys all have selective memories."

"It just isn't the way to handle things," he protested.

"Forget it!"

"Yeah, forget it." Vasquez echoed Ripley's sentiments as well as her words. "Watch us."

"Maybe you haven't been keeping up on current events," Hudson put in, "but we just got fragged, pal."

"Look, Burke." Clearly Ripley was not pleased. "We had an agreement. I think I've proved my case, made my point, whatever you want to call it. We came here for confirmation of my story and to find out what caused the break in communications between Acheron and Earth. You got your confirmation, the Company's got its explanation, and I've got my vindication. Now it's time to get away from here."

"I know, I know." He put an arm over her shoulders, careful not to make it look as if he were being familiar, and turned her away from the others as he lowered his voice. "But we're dealing with changing scenarios here. You have to be ready to put aside the first reaction that comes to mind, put aside your natural emotions, and know how to take advantage. We've survived here; now we've got to be ready to survive back on Earth."

"What are you getting at, Burke?"

Either he didn't notice the chill in her eyes or else he chose not to react to it. "What I'm trying to say is that this thing is *major*, Ripley. I mean, really major. We've never encountered anything like these creatures before, and we might never have the chance to do so again. Their strength and their resourcefulness is unbelievable. You don't just annihilate something like that, not with the kind of potential they imply. You back off until you learn how to handle them, sure, but you don't just blow them away."

"Wanna bet?"

"You're not thinking rationally. Now, I understand what you're going through. Don't think that I don't. But you've got to put all that aside and look at the larger picture. What's done is done. We can't help the colonists, and we can't do anything for Crowe and Apone and the others, but we can help ourselves. We can learn about these things and make use of them, turn them to our advantage, master them."

"You don't master something like these aliens. You get out of their way; and if the opportunity presents itself, you blow them to atoms. Don't talk to me about 'surviving' back on Earth."

He took a deep breath. "Come on, Ripley. These aliens are special in ways we haven't begun to understand. Unique-

ness is one thing the cosmos is stingy with. They need to be
studied, carefully and under the right conditions, so that we
can learn from them. All that went wrong here was that the
colonists started studying them without the proper equipment.
They didn't know what to expect. We do."

"Do we? Look what happened to Apone and the rest."

"They didn't know what they were up against, and they
went in a little overconfident. They got caught in a tight spot.
That's a mistake we won't make again."

"You can bet on that."

"What happened here is tragic, sure, but it won't be
repeated. When we come back, we'll be properly equipped.
That acid can't eat through everything. We'll take a sample
back somehow, have it analyzed in company labs. They'll
develop a defense, a shield. And we'll figure out a way to
immobilize the mature form so it can be manipulated and
used. Sure, the aliens are strong, but they're not omnipotent.
They're tough but they're not invulnerable. They can be killed
by hand weapons as small as pulse-rifles and flamethrowers.
That's one thing this expedition *has* proved. You proved it
yourself," he added in a tone of admiration she didn't believe
for an instant.

"I'm telling you, Ripley, this is an opportunity few people are given. We can't blow it on an emotional spur-of-the-
moment decision. I didn't think you were the type to throw
away the chance of a lifetime for something as abstract as a
little revenge."

"It doesn't have anything to do with revenge," she told
him evenly. "It has to do with survival. Ours."

"You're still not hearing me." He dropped his voice to
a whisper. "See, since you're the representative of the company that discovered this species, your percentage of the
eventual profits to be derived from the study and concomitant
exploitation of them will naturally be some serious money.
The fact that the Company once prosecuted you and then had
the decision of the prosecuting board overturned doesn't enter

into it. Everybody knows that you're the sole survivor of the crew that first encountered these creatures. The law requires that you receive an appropriate royalty. You're going to be richer than you dreamed possible, Ripley."

She stared silently at him for a long time, as though she were observing an entirely new species of alien just encountered. A particularly loathsome variety at that.

"You son of a. . . ."

He backed off, his expression hardening. The false sense of camaraderie he'd tried to promote was sloughed off like a mask. "I'm sorry you feel that way. Don't make me pull rank, Ripley."

"What rank? We've been through all this before." She nodded down the aisle. "I believe Corporal Hicks has authority here."

Burke started to laugh at her. Then he saw that she was serious. "You're kidding. What is this, a joke? *Corporal* Hicks? Since when was a corporal in charge of anything except his own boots?"

"This operation is under military jurisdiction," she reminded him quietly. "That's the way the *Sulaco*'s dispatch orders read. Maybe you didn't bother to read them. I did. That's the way Colonial Administration worded it. You and I, Burke, we're just observers. We're just along for the ride. Apone's dead and Gorman might as well be. Hicks is next in the chain of command." She peered past the stunned Company rep. "Right?"

Hicks's reply was matter-of-fact. "Looks that way."

Burke's careful corporate self-control was beginning to slip. "Look, this is a multimillion credit operation. He can't make that kind of decision. Corporals don't authorize nukes. He's just a grunt." Second thoughts and a hasty glance in the soldier's direction prompted Burke to add a polite, "No offense."

"None taken." Hicks's response was cool and correct.

He spoke to his headset pickup. "Ferro, you been copying all of this?"

"Standing by" came the dropship pilot's reply over their speakers.

"Prepare for dust-off. We're gonna need an immediate evac."

"Figured as much from what we heard over here. Tough."

"You don't know the half of it." Hicks's expression was unchanged as he regarded the tight-lipped Burke. "You're right about one thing. You can't make a decision like this on the spur of the moment."

Burke relaxed slightly. "That's more like it. So what are we going to do?"

"Think it over, like you said we should." The corporal closed his eyes for about five seconds. "Okay, I've thought it over. What I think is that we'll take off and nuke the site from orbit. It's the only way to be *sure*."

He winked. The color drained from the Company rep's face. He took an angry step in Hicks's direction before realizing that what he was thinking of doing bore no relation to reality. Instead he had to settle for expressing his outrage verbally.

"This is absurd! You seriously can't be thinking of dropping a nuclear device on the colony site."

"Just a little one," Hicks assured him calmly, "but big enough." He put his hands together, smiled and pushed them apart. "*Whoosh*."

"I'm telling you for the last time that you don't have the authority to do something like—"

His tirade was interrupted by a loud *clack*: the sound of a pulse-rifle being activated. Vasquez cradled the powerful weapon beneath her right arm. It wasn't pointed in Burke's direction, but then it wasn't exactly aimed away from him, either. Her expression was blank. He knew it wouldn't change if she decided to put a pulse-shell through his chest, either.

End of discussion. He sat down heavily in one of the empty seats that lined the wall.

"You're all crazy," he muttered. "You know that."

"Man," Vasquez told him softly, "why else would anyone join the Colonial Marines?" She glanced over at the corporal. "Tell me something, Hicks: Does that mean I can plead insanity for shooting this *mierda*? If I can, I might as well shoot that sorry excuse for a lieutenant while I'm at it. Don't want to waste a good defense."

"Nobody's shooting anybody," the corporal informed her firmly. "We're getting out of here."

Ripley met his eyes, nodded once, then turned and sat down. She put a reassuring arm around the only conscious nonparticipant in the discussion. Newt leaned against her shoulder.

"We're going home, honey," she told the girl.

Now that their course of action had been determined, Hicks took a moment to check out the interior of the APC. Between the fire damage and the holes eaten by alien acid, it was clearly a write-off.

"Let's get together what we can carry. Hudson, give me a hand with the lieutenant."

The comtech eyed the paralyzed form of his commanding officer with undisguised distaste. "How about we just sit him up in Operations and strap him to the chair? He'll feel right at home."

"No sell. He's still alive, and we've got to get him out of here."

"Yeah, I know, I know. Just don't keep reminding me."

"Ripley, you keep an eye on the child. She's sort of taken to you, anyway."

"The feeling's mutual." She clasped Newt tightly to her.

"Vasquez, can you cover us until the dropship touches down?"

She smiled at him, showing perfect teeth. "Can pigs fly?" She tapped the stock of the pulse-rifle.

The corporal turned to face the landing team's last human member. "You coming?"

"Don't be funny," Burke grumbled.

"I won't. Not here. This isn't a funny place." He switched on his headset pickup. "Bishop, you found anything out?"

The synthetic's voice filled the passenger bay. "Not much. The equipment here is colonial-style basic. I've gone about as far as I can go with the tools available."

"It doesn't matter. We're getting out. Pack it up and meet us on the tarmac. Can you make it okay? I don't want to abandon the APC until the dropship's on final approach."

"No problem. It's been quiet back here."

"Okay. Don't take anything you can't carry easily. Move it."

The dropship rose from its place on the concrete pad, fighting the wind as it lifted. Under Ferro's steady hand it hovered, pivoted in midair, and began to move over the colony toward the stalled APC.

"Got you on visual. Wind's let up a little. I'll set her down as close as I can," Ferro informed them.

"Roger." Hicks turned to his companions. "Ready?" Everyone nodded except Burke, who looked sour but said nothing. "Then let's get out of here." He cycled the door.

Wind and rain poured in as the ramp extended. They filed rapidly out of the vehicle. The dropship was already in plain sight, edging toward them. Searchlights blazed from its flanks and belly. One illuminated a single human shape striding through the mist toward them.

"Bishop!" Vasquez waved. "Long time no see."

He called across to her. "Didn't work out so good, huh?"

"It stank." She spat downwind. "Tell you all about it sometime."

"Later. After hypersleep. After we've put this place far behind us."

She nodded, the only one of the waiting group whose attention was not monopolized by the approaching dropship.

Her dark eyes continuously scanned the landscape around the personnel carrier. Nearby, Ripley waited, gripping Newt's small hand tightly. Hudson and Hicks carried the still-unconscious Gorman between them.

"Hold it there," Ferro instructed them. "Give me a little room. I don't want to come down on top of you." She thumped her headset pickup. "It'd be nice if I had a little help up here, Spunkmeyer. Get off the pot."

The compartment door slid aside behind her. She glanced back over her shoulder, angry and not bothering to hide the fact. "It's about time. Where the . . .?"

Her eyes widened, and the rest of the accusation trailed away.

It wasn't Spunkmeyer.

The alien barely fit through the opening. Outer jaws flared to reveal the inner set of teeth. There was a blur of movement and an explosive, organic *whoosh*. Ferro barely had time to scream as she was slammed backward into the control console.

From below, the would-be refugees watched in dismay as the dropship veered wildly to port. Its main engines roared to life, and it accelerated even as it lost altitude. Ripley grabbed Newt and sprinted toward the nearest building.

"*Run!*"

The dropship clipped a rock formation at the edge of the causeway, slewed left, and struck a basalt ridge. It tumbled, turning completely on its back like a dying dragonfly, struck the tarmac, and exploded. Sections and compartments began to break away from the mainframe, some of them already afire. The body of the ship arced into the air once more, bouncing off the unyielding stone, fire blazing from it engines and superstructure.

Part of an engine module slammed into the APC, setting off its armament. The personnel carrier blew itself to bits as shells and fuel exploded inside it. A flaming Catherine wheel, the remains of the dropship skipped past and rolled into the outskirts of the atmosphere processing station. A tremendous fireball lit the dark sky of Acheron. It faded rapidly.

Emerging from concealment, the stunned survivors stared at the debris in disbelief as their superior firepower and hopes of getting off the planet were simultaneously reduced to charred metal and ash.

"Well that's *great*!" said a near hysterical Hudson. "That's just great, man. *Now* what are we supposed to do? We're in some real fine shape now."

"Are you finished?" Hicks stared hard at the comtech until Hudson looked abashed. Then he glanced at Ripley. "You okay?"

She nodded and tried to hide her real feelings as she looked down at Newt. She could have spared herself the effort. It was impossible to hide anything from the child. Newt looked calm enough. She was breathing hard, true, but it was from the effort of racing for cover, not from fear. The girl shrugged, sounding remarkably grown-up.

"I guess we're not leaving, right?"

Ripley bit her lip. "I'm sorry, Newt."

"You don't have to be sorry. It wasn't your fault." She stared silently at the flaming wreckage of the dropship.

Hudson was kicking aside rocks, bits of metal, anything smaller than his boot. "Just tell me what we're supposed to do now. What're we gonna do *now*?"

Burke looked annoyed. "Maybe we could build a fire and sing songs."

Hudson took a step toward the Company rep, and Hicks had to intervene.

"We should get back." Everyone turned to look down at Newt, who was still staring at the burning dropship. "We should get back 'cause it'll be dark soon. *They* come mostly at night. Mostly."

"All right." Hicks nodded in the direction of the ruined APC. It was mostly metal and composites and shouldn't burn much longer. "The fire's about had it. Let's see what we can find."

"Scrap metal," suggested Burke.

"And maybe something more. You coming?"

The Company rep rose from where he'd been sitting. "I'm sure not staying here."

"Up to you." The corporal turned to their synthetic. "Bishop, see if you can make Operations livable. What I mean is, make sure it's . . . clear."

The android responded with a gentle smile. "Take point? I know what that means. I'm expendable, of course."

"Nobody's expendable." Hicks started across the tarmac toward the smoking APC. "Let's move it."

Day on Acheron was dim twilight; night was darker than the farthest reaches of interstellar space, because not even the stars shone through its dense atmosphere to soften the barren surface with twinkling light. The wind howled around the battered metal buildings of Hadley town, whistling down corridors and rattling broken doors. Sand pattered against cracked windows, a perpetual snare-drum roll. Not a comforting sound to be heard. Inside, everyone waited for the nightmare to come.

Emergency power was sufficient to light Operations and its immediate environs but not much else. There the weary and demoralized survivors gathered to consider their options. Vasquez and Hudson had made one final run to the hulk that was the armored personnel carrier. Now they set down their prize, a large, scorched, dented packing case. Several similar cases were stacked nearby.

Hicks glanced at the case and tried not to sound too disappointed. He knew what the answer to his question would be but asked it, anyhow. Maybe he was wrong.

"Any ammo?" Vasquez shook her head and slumped into an office chair.

"Everything was stored in the airspace between the APC's walls. It all went up when it caught fire." She pulled off her sweat-soaked bandanna and wiped a forearm across her hairline. "Man, what I wouldn't give for some soap and a hot shower."

Hicks turned toward the table on which reposed their entire weapons inventory.

"This is it, then. Everything we could salvage." His gaze examined the stock, wishing he could triple it by looking at it. "We've got four pulse-rifles with about fifty rounds each. Not so good. About fifteen M-40 grenades and two flamethrowers less than half full—one damaged. And we've got four of these robot-sentry units with their scanners and display relays intact." He approached the stack of packing cases and broke the seal on the nearest. Ripley joined him in inspecting the contents.

Stabilized in packing foam was a squat automatic weapon. Secured in a separate set of boxes next to it was matching video and movement-sensor instrumentation.

"Looks pretty efficient," she commented.

"They are." Hicks shut the case. "Without them I'd say we might as well cut our wrists right now. With them, well, our chances are better than none, anyway. Trouble is we need about a hundred like this one and ten times the ammunition. But I'm grateful for small favors." He rapped his knuckles on the hard plastic case. "If these hadn't been packed like this, they would've gone blooey with the rest of the APC."

"What makes you think we stand a chance, anyway?" Hudson said.

Ripley ignored him. "How long after we're declared overdue can we expect a rescue?"

Hicks looked thoughtful. He'd been too absorbed with the problems of their immediate survival to think about the possibility of help from outside.

"We should have filed a mission update yesterday. Call it about seventeen days from tonight."

The comtech whirled and stomped off, waving his arms disconsolately. "Man, we're not going to make it seventeen *hours*. Those things are going to come in here just like they did before, man. They're going to come in here and get us long before anyone from Earth comes poking around to see what's left of us. And they're gonna find us, too, all sucked out and blown dry like those poor colonists we cremated down on C-level. Like Dietrich and Crowe, man." He started to sob.

Ripley indicated the silently watching Newt. *"She* survived longer than that with no weapons and no training. The colonists didn't know what hit them. We know what to expect, and we've got more than wrenches and hammers to fight back with. We don't have to clean them out. All we have to do is survive for a couple of weeks. Just keep them away from us and stay alive."

Hudson laughed bitterly. "Yeah, no sweat. Just stay alive. Dietrich and Crowe are alive too."

"We're here, we've got some armaments, and we know what's coming. So you'd better just start dealing with it. Just deal with it, Hudson. Because we need you and I'm tired of your comments." He gaped at her, but she wasn't through.

"Now get on that central terminal and call up some kind of floor-plan file. Construction blueprints, maintenance schematics, anything that shows the layout of this place. I want to see air ducts, electrical access tunnels, subbasements, water pipes: every possible way into this wing of the colony. I want to see the guts of this building, Hudson. If they can't reach us, they can't hurt us. They haven't ripped through these walls yet, so maybe that means they can't. This is colony Operations. We're in the most solid structure on the planet, excepting maybe the big atmosphere-processing stations. We're up off the ground, and they haven't shown any signs of being able to climb a sheer wall."

Hudson hesitated, then straightened slightly, relieved to have something to concentrate on. Hicks nodded his approval to Ripley.

"Aye-firmative," the comtech told her, a little of his

cockiness restored. With it came a dram of confidence. "I'm on it. You want to know where every plug is in this dump, I'll find it." He headed for the vacant computer console. Hicks turned to the synthetic.

"You want a job or have you already got something in mind?"

Bishop looked uncertain. This was part of his social programming. An android could never be actually uncertain. "If you require me for something specific . . ." Hicks shook his head. "In that case I'll be in Medical. I'd like to continue my research. Perhaps I may stumble across something that will prove useful to us."

"Fine," Ripley told him. "You do that." She was watching him closely. If Bishop was conscious of this excessive scrutiny, he gave no sign of it as he turned and headed for the lab.

Once Hudson had something to work on, he moved fast. Before long, Ripley, Hicks, and Burke were clustered around the comtech, peering past him at the large flat video display. It illuminated a complex series of charts and mechanical drawings. Newt hopped from one foot to the other, trying to see around the adults' bulk.

Ripley tapped the screen. "This service tunnel has to be what they're using to move back and forth."

Hudson studied the readout. "Yeah, right. It runs from

the processing station right into the colony maintenance sub-level, here." He traced the route with a fingertip. "That's how they slipped in and surprised the colonists. That's the way I'd come too."

"All right. There's a fire door at this end. This first thing we do is put one of the remote sentries in the tunnel and seal that door."

"That won't stop them." Hicks's gaze roved over the plans. "Once they've been stopped in the service tunnel, they'll find another way in. We gotta figure on them getting into the complex eventually."

"That's right. So we put up welded barricades at these intersections"—she pointed to the schematic as she spoke—"and seal these ducts here, and here. Then they can only come at us from these two corridors, and we create a free field of fire for the other two sentry units, here." She tapped the location, her nail clicking on the hard surface of the illuminated screen. "Of course, they can always tear the roof off, but I think that'd take them a while. By then our relief should arrive, and we'll be out of here."

"We'd better be," Hicks muttered. He studied the layout of Operations intently. "Otherwise this looks outstanding. Seal the fire door in the tunnel, weld the corridors shut, then all we need is a deck of cards to pass the time." He straightened and eyed his companions. "All right, let's move like we got a purpose."

Hudson half snapped to attention. "Aye-firmative."

Next to him Newt copied the gesture and the inflection. "Aye-firmative." The comtech looked down at her and smiled before he caught himself. Hopefully no one noticed the transient grin. It would ruin his reputation as an incorrigible hardcase.

Hudson grunted as he set the second heavy sentry gun onto its recoil-absorbing tripod. The weapon was squat, ugly, unencumbered by sights or triggers. Vasquez locked the weapon in place, then snapped on the connectors that led from the firing mechanism to the attached motion sensor. When she was certain the comtech was out of the way, she nudged a single switch marked ACTIVATE. A small green light came to life atop the gun. On the small diagnostic readout set flush in the side, READY flashed yellow, then red.

Both troopers stepped clear. Vasquez picked up a battered wastebasket that had rolled into the corridor and shouted toward the weapon's aural pickup. "Testing!" Then she threw the empty metal container out into the middle of the corridor.

Both guns swiveled and let loose before the basket hit the floor, reducing the container to dime-size shrapnel. Hudson whooped with delight.

"Take that, suckers!" He lowered his voice as he turned to Vasquez, his eyes rolling. "Oh, give me a home, where the firepower roams, and the deer and the antelope get shot to hamburger."

"You always were the sensitive type," Vasquez told him.

"I know. It shows in my face." Turning, he put a shoulder against the fire door. "Give me a hand with this."

Vasquez helped him roll the heavy steel barrier into place. Then she unpacked the high-intensity portable welding torch she'd brought with her and snapped it alight. Blue flame roared from the muzzle. She turned a dial on the handle, refining the acetylene finger.

"Give me some room, man, or I'm liable to seal your foot to your boot." Hudson complied, stepping back to watch her. He began to pace, staring down the empty serviceway and listening. He fingered the controls of his headset nervously.

"Hudson here."

Hicks responded instantly. "How're you two doing? We're working on the big air duct you located in the plans."

"A and B sentries are in place and activated. Looks good. Nothing comes up this tunnel they can't pick out." Vasquez's torch hissed nearby. "We're sealing the fire door right now."

"Roger. When you're through, get yourselves back up here."

"Hey, you think I want a ticket for loitering?"

Hicks smiled to himself. That sounded more like the old Hudson. He nudged the tiny mike away from his lips and adjusted the thick metal plate he was carrying so that it covered the duct opening. Ripley nodded at him and shoved her plate in place. He unlimbered a duplicate of Vasquez's welder and began sealing the plate to the floor.

Behind him, Burke and Newt worked busily, stacking containers of medicine and food in a corner. The aliens hadn't touched the colony's food supplies. More importantly the water-distillation system was still functioning. Since it was self-pressurized, no power was needed to draw it from the taps. They wouldn't starve or go thirsty.

When he'd sealed down two-thirds of the plate, Hicks set the welder aside and extracted a small bracelet from a belt pouch. He flicked a tiny switch set flush with the metal, and a minuscule LED came to life as he handed the circlet to Ripley.

"What is it?"

"Emergency beeper. Military version of the PDTs the colonists had surgically implanted. Doesn't have the range they do, and you wear it outside instead of inside your body, but the idea's the same. With that on I can locate you anywhere near the complex on this." He tapped the miniature tracker that was built into his battle harness.

She studied it curiously. "I don't need this."

"Hey, it's just a precaution. You know."

She regarded him quizzically for a moment, then shrugged and slipped the bracelet over her wrist. "Thanks. You wearing one?"

He smiled and looked away. "Only got one tracker." He tapped his harness. "I know where I am. What's next?"

She forgot all about the bracelet as she consulted the hard-copy printout of Hudson's schematic.

Something very strange happened while they worked. They were too busy to notice, and it was left to Newt to point it out.

The wind had died. Stopped utterly. In the unAcheronic stillness outside the colony, a diffuse mist swirled and roiled uncertainly. In two visits to Acheron this was the first time Ripley hadn't heard the wind. It was disquieting.

The absence of wind reduced outside visibility from poor to nonexistent. Fog swirled around Operations, giving the world beyond the triple-paned windows the look of being under water. Nothing moved.

In the service tunnel that connected the buildings of the colony to the processing station and each other, a pair of robot guns sat silently, their motion scanners alert and humming. C gun surveyed the empty corridor, its ARMED light flashing green. Through a hole in the ceiling at the far end of the passageway, fog swirled in. Water condensed on bare metal walls and dripped to the floor. The gun did not fire on the falling drops. It was smarter, more selective than that, able to distinguish between harmless natural phenomena and inimical movement. The water made no attempt to advance, and so the weapon held its fire, waiting patiently for something to kill.

Newt had carried boxes until she'd worn herself out. Ripley carried her from Operations into the medical wing, the small head resting wearily on the woman's shoulder. Occasionally she would try to say something, and Ripley would reply as though she understood. She was hunting for a place where the child could rest quietly and in comparative safety.

The operating theater was located at the far end of the medical section. Much of its complex equipment sat in recesses in the walls while the rest hung from the ceiling at the tips of extensible arms. A large globe containing lights and additional surgical instrumentation dominated the ceiling. Cabinets and equipment not fastened down had been shoved into a corner to provide room for several folding metal cots.

This was where they would sleep. This was where they would retreat to if the aliens breached the outer defenses. The inner redoubt. The keep. The operating room was sealed tighter and had thicker walls than any other part of the colony complex, or so the schematics Hudson had called forth insisted. It looked a lot like an oversize, high-tech vault. If they had to shoot themselves in order to keep from falling alive into the aliens' hands, this was where any future rescuers would find the bodies.

But for now it was a safe haven, snug and quiet. Gently Ripley lowered the girl to the nearest cot, smiling down at the upturned face.

"Now you just lie there and have a nap. I have to go help the others, but I'll come in every chance I get to check on you. You deserve a rest. You're exhausted."

Newt stared up at her. "I don't want to sleep."

"You have to, Newt. Everybody has to sometime. You'll feel better after you've had a rest."

"But I have scary dreams."

It struck a familiar chord in Ripley, but she managed to feign cheerfulness. "Everybody has bad dreams, Newt."

The girl snuggled deeper into the padded cot. "Not like mine."

Don't bet on it, child, she thought. Aloud she said, "I'll bet Casey doesn't have bad dreams." She disengaged the doll head from the girl's small fingers and made a show of peering inside. "Just as I thought: Nothing bad in there. Maybe you could try to be like Casey. Pretend there's nothing in here." She tapped the girl's forehead, and Newt smiled back.

"You mean, try to make it all empty-like?"

"Yes, empty-like. Like Casey." She caressed the delicate face, brushing hair back from Newt's forehead. "If you do that, I'll bet you'll be able to sleep without having any bad dreams."

She closed the doll head's unblinking eyes and handed it back to its owner. Newt took it, rolling her own eyes as if to say, "Don't pull that five-year-old stuff on me, lady. I'm six."

"Ripley, she doesn't have bad dreams, because she's just a piece of plastic."

"Oh. Sorry, Newt. Well, then, maybe you could pretend you're like her that way. Just made of plastic."

The girl almost smiled. Almost. "I'll try."

"Good girl. Maybe I'll try it myself."

Newt pulled Casey close up to her neck, looking thoughtful. "My mommy always said there were no such things as monsters. No real ones. But there *are*."

Ripley continued to brush isolated strands of blond hair back from the pale forehead. "Yes, there are, aren't there?"

"They're as real as you and me. They're not make-believe, and they didn't come out of a book. They're really real, not fake-real like the ones I used to watch on the video. Why do they tell little kids things like that, things that aren't true?" There was a faint tinge of betrayal in her voice.

No lying to this child, Ripley knew. Not that she had the slightest intention of doing so. Newt had experienced too much reality to be fooled by a simple fib. Ripley instinctively sensed that to lie to this girl would be to lose her trust forever.

"Well, some kids can't handle it like you can. The truth, I mean. They're too scared, or their grown-ups think they'll be too scared. Grown-ups have a way of always underestimating little kids' ability to handle the truth. So they try to make things easier for them by making things up."

"About the monsters. Did one of those things grow inside mommy?"

Ripley found some blankets and began pulling them up around the small body, tucking them tightly around narrow ribs. "I don't know, Newt. Neither does anybody else. That's the truth. I don't think anybody will ever know."

The girl considered. "Isn't that how babies come? I mean, people babies. They grow inside you?"

A chill went down Ripley's spine. "No, not like that,

not like that at all. It's different with people, honey. The way it gets started is different, and the way the baby comes is different. With people the baby and the mother work together. With these aliens the—"

"I understand," Newt said, interrupting. "Did you ever have a baby?"

"Yes." She pushed the blanket up under the child's chin. "Just once. A little girl."

"Where is she? Back on Earth?"

"No. She's gone."

"You mean, dead."

It wasn't a question. Ripley nodded slowly, trying to remember a small female thing not unlike Newt running and playing, a miracle with dark curls bouncing around her face. Trying to reconcile that memory with the picture of an older woman briefly glimpsed, child and mature lady linked together through time overspent in the stasis of hypersleep. The child's father was a more distant memory still. So much of a life lost and forgotten. Youthful love marred by a lack of common sense, a brief flare of happiness smothered by reality. Divorce. Hypersleep. Time.

She turned away from the bed and reached for a portable space heater. While it wasn't uncomfortable in the operating theater, it would be more comfortable with the heater on. It looked like a slab of plastic, but when she thumbed the "on" switch, it emitted a whirr and a faint glow as its integral warming elements came to life. As the heat spread, the operating room became a little less sterile, a shade cozier. Newt blinked sleepily.

"Ripley, I was thinking. Maybe I could do you a favor and fill in for her. Your little girl, I mean. Nothing permanent. Just for a while. You can try it, and if you don't like it, it's okay. I'll understand. No big deal. Whattaya think?"

It took what little remained of Ripley's determination and self-control not to break down in front of the child. She settled for hugging her tightly. She also knew that neither of them might see the light of another dawn. That she might have to turn Newt's face away during a very possible apocalyptic last moment and put the muzzle of a pulse-rifle to those blond tresses.

"I think it's not the worst idea I've heard all day. Let's talk about it later, okay?"

"Okay." A shy, hopeful smile.

Ripley switched off the room light and started to rise. A small hand grabbed her arm with desperate force.

"Don't go! Please."

With great reluctance Ripley disengaged her arm from Newt's grip. "It'll be all right. I'll be in the other room, right next door. I'm not going to go anywhere else. And don't forget that that's there." She indicated the miniature video pickup that was imbedded over the doorway. "You know what that is, don't you?" A small nod in the darkness.

"Uh-huh. It's a securcam."

"That's right. See, the green light's on. Mr. Hicks and Mr. Hudson checked out all the securcams in this area to make sure all of them were operating properly. It's watching you, and I'll be watching its monitor over in the other room. I'll be able to see you just as clearly in there as I can when I'm right here."

When Newt still seemed to hesitate, Ripley unsnapped the tracer bracelet Hicks had given her. She slipped it around the girl's smaller wrist, cinching it tight.

"Here. This is for luck. It'll help me keep an eye on you too. Now go to sleep—and don't dream. Okay?"

"I'll try." The sound of a small body sliding down between clean sheets.

Ripley watched in the dim light from the instruments on standby as the girl turned onto her side, hugging the doll head and gazing through half-lidded eyes at the steadily glowing function light imbedded in the bracelet. The space heater hummed comfortingly as she backed out of the room.

Other half-opened eyes were twitching erratically back

and forth. They were the only visible evidence that Lieutenant Gorman was still alive. It was an improvement of sorts. One step further from complete paralysis.

Ripley leaned over the table on which the lieutenant was lying, studying the eye movements and wondering if he could recognize her. "How is he? I see he's got his eyes open."

"That might be enough to wear him out." Bishop looked up from a nearby workbench. He was surrounded by instruments and shining medical equipment. The light of the single high-intensity lamp he was working with threw his features into sharp relief, giving his face a macabre cast.

"Is he in pain?"

"Not according to his bioreadouts. They're hardly conclusive, of course. I'm sure he'll let us know as soon as he regains the use of his larynx. By the way, I've isolated the poison. Interesting stuff. It's a muscle-specific neurotoxin. Affects only the nonvital parts of the system; leaves respiratory and circulatory functions unimpaired. I wonder if the creatures instinctively adjust the dosage for different kinds of potential hosts?"

"I'll ask one of them first chance I get." As she stared, one eyelid rose all the way before fluttering back down again. "Either that was an involuntary twitch or else he winked at me. Is he getting better?"

Bishop nodded. "The toxin seems to be metabolizing. It's powerful, but the body appears capable of breaking it down. It's starting to show up in his urine. Amazing mechanism, the human body. Adaptable. If he continues to flush the poison at a constant rate, he should wake up soon."

"Let me get this straight. The aliens paralyzed the colonists they didn't kill, carried them over to the processing station, and cocooned them to serve as hosts for more of those." She pointed into the back room where the stasis cylinders held the remaining facehugger specimens.

"Which would mean lots of those parasites, right? One

for each colonist. Over a hundred, at least, assuming a mortality rate during the final fight of about a third."

"Yes, that follows," Bishop readily agreed.

"But these things, the parasitic facehugger form, come from eggs. So where are all the eggs coming from? When the guy who first found the alien ship reported back to us, he said there were a lot of eggs inside, but he never said how many, and nobody else ever went in after him to look. And not all those eggs may have been viable.

"The thing is, judging from the way the colony here was overwhelmed, I don't think the first aliens had time to haul eggs from that ship back here. That means they had to come from somewhere else."

"That is the question of the hour." Bishop swiveled his chair to face her. "I have been pondering it ceaselessly since the true nature of the disaster here first became apparent to us."

"Any ideas, bright or otherwise?"

"Without additional solid evidence it is nothing more than a supposition."

"Go ahead and suppose, then."

"We could assume a parallel to certain insect forms who have a hivelike organization. An ant or termite colony, for example, is ruled by a single female, a queen, who is the source of new eggs."

Ripley frowned. Interstellar navigation to entomology was a mental jump she wasn't prepared to make. "Don't insect queens come from eggs also?"

The synthetic nodded. "Absolutely."

"What if there was no queen egg aboard the ship that brought these things here?"

"There's no such thing in a social insect society as a 'queen egg,' until the workers decide to create one. Ants, bees, termites, all employ essentially the same method. They select an ordinary egg and feed the pupa developing inside a special food high in certain nutrients. Among bees, for example, it is called royal jelly. The chemicals in the jelly act to change the composition of the maturing pupa so that what eventually emerges is an adult queen and not another worker. Theoretically any egg can be used to hatch a queen. Why the insects choose the particular eggs they do is something we still do not know."

"You're saying that one of those things lays *all* the eggs?"

"Well, not exactly like one we're familiar with. Only if the insect analogy holds up. Assuming it does, there could be other similarities. An alien queen analogous to an ant or termite queen could be much larger physically than the aliens we have so far encountered. A termite queen's abdomen is so bloated with eggs that she can't move by herself at all. She is fed and tended by workers, mated to drones, and defended by highly specialized warriors. She is also quite harmless. On the other hand, a queen bee is far more dangerous than any worker bee because she can sting many times. She is the center of their lives, quite literally the mother of their society.

"In one respect, at least, we are fortunate that the analogy does not hold up. Ants and bees develop from eggs directly to larvae, pupae, and adults. Each alien embryo requires a live host in which to mature. Otherwise Acheron would be covered with them by now."

"Funny, but that doesn't reassure me a whole lot. These things are a lot bigger than any ant or termite. Could they be intelligent? Could this hypothetical queen? That's something we never could decide on back on the *Nostromo*. We were too busy trying to keep from getting killed. Not much time for speculation."

"It's hard to say." Bishop looked thoughtful. "There is one thing worth considering, though."

"What's that?"

"It may have been nothing more than blind instinct, attraction to the heat or whatever, but she did choose, assuming she exists, to incubate her eggs in the one spot in the colony where we couldn't destroy her without destroying ourselves. Beneath the heat exchangers at the processing plant. If that site was chosen from instinct, it means that they may be no brighter than your average termite. If, on the other hand, it was selected on the basis of intelligence, well, then I think we're in very deep trouble indeed.

"That's *if* there's any reality to these suppositions at all. Despite the distance involved, the eggs these aliens hatched from might have been brought down here by the first ones to emerge. There might be no queen involved at all, no complex alien society. Whether by intelligence or instinct, though, we have seen that they cooperate. That's something we don't have to speculate on. We've seen them in action."

Ripley stood there and considered the ramifications of Bishop's analysis. None of them were encouraging, nor had she expected any to be. She nodded toward the stasis cylinders.

"I want those specimens destroyed as soon as you're done with them. You understand?"

The android glanced toward the two live facehuggers pulsing malevolently in their tubular prisons. He looked unhappy. "Mr. Burke gave instructions that they were to be kept alive in stasis for return to the Company laboratories. He was very specific."

The wonder of it was that she went for the intercom instead of the nearest weapon. "Burke!"

A faint whisper of static failed to mar his reply. "Yes? That's you, isn't it, Ripley?"

"You bet it's me! Where are you?"

"Scavenging while there's still time. I thought I might learn something on my own, since I just seem to be in everybody's way up there."

"Meet me in the lab."

"Now? But I'm still—"

"Now!" She closed the connection and glared at the inoffensive Bishop. "You come with me." Obediently he put his work aside and rose to follow her. That was all she was after; to make sure that he'd obey an order if she gave it. It meant he wasn't completely under Burke's sway, Company machine or no Company machine. "Never mind, forget it."

"I shall be happy to accompany you if that is what you wish."

"That's all right. I've decided to handle it on my own. You continue with your research. That's more important than anything else."

He nodded, looking puzzled, and resumed his seat.

Burke was waiting for her outside the entrance to the lab. His expression was bland. "This better be important. I think I was onto something, and we may not have much time left."

"You may not have _any_ time left." He started to protest, and she cut him off with a gesture. "No, in there." She gestured at the operating theater. It was soundproofed inside, and she could scream at him to her heart's content without drawing everyone else's attention. Burke ought to be grateful for her thoughtfulness. If Vasquez overheard what the Company representative had been planning, she wouldn't waste time arguing with him. She'd put a bullet through him on the spot.

"Bishop tells me you have intentions of taking the live parasites home in your pocket. That true?"

He didn't try to deny it. "They're harmless in stasis."

"Those suckers aren't harmless unless they're dead. Don't you understand that yet? I want them killed as soon as Bishop's gotten everything out of them he can."

"Be reasonable, Ripley." A ghost of the old, self-assured corporate smile stole over Burke's face. "Those specimens are worth millions to the Bioweapons Division of the Company. Okay, so we nuke the colony. I'm outvoted on that one. But not on this. Two lousy specimens, Ripley. How much trouble could they cause while secured in stasis? And if you're worried about something happening when we get them back to Earthside labs, don't. We have people who know how to handle things like these."

"Nobody knows how to handle 'things like these.' Nobody's ever encountered anything like them. You think it'd be dangerous for some germs to get loose from a weapons lab? Try to imagine what would happen if just one of those parasites got loose in a major city, with its thousands of kilometers of sewers and pipes and glass-fiber channels to hide in."

"They're not going to get loose. Nothing can break a stasis field."

"No sale, Burke. There's too much we don't know about these monsters. It's too risky."

"Come on, I know you're smarter than this." He was trying to mollify and persuade her at the same time. "If we play it right, we can both come out of this heroes. Set up for life."

"Is that the way you really see it?" She eyed him askance. "Carter Burke, alien smasher? Didn't what happened in C-level of the processing station make any impression on you at all?"

"They went in unprepared and overconfident." Burke's tone was flat, unemotional. "They got caught in tight quarters where they couldn't use the proper tactics and weapons. If they'd all used their pulse-rifles and kept their heads and managed to get out without shooting up the heat exchangers, they'd all be here now and we'd be on our way back to the *Sulaco* instead of holed up in Operations like a bunch of frightened rabbits. Sending them in like that was Gorman's decision, not mine. And besides, those were adult aliens they were fighting, not parasites."

"I didn't hear you object loudly when strategy was being discussed."

"Who would've listened to me? Don't you remember what Hicks said? What you said? Gorman wouldn't have been any different." His tone turned sarcastic. "This is a *military* expedition."

"Forget the whole idea, Burke. You couldn't pull it off even if I let you. Just try getting a dangerous organism past ICC quarantine. Section 22350 of the Commerce Code."

"You've been doing your homework. That's what the code says, all right. But you're forgetting one thing. The code's nothing but words on paper. Paper never stopped a determined man. If I have five minutes alone with the customs inspector on duty when we turn through Gateway Station, we'll get them through. Leave that end of it to me. The ICC can't impound something they don't know anything about."

"But they *will* know about it, Burke."

"How? First they'll want to talk to us, then they'll make us walk through a detection tunnel. Big deal. By the time the relief team gets around to inspecting our luggage, I'll have made the necessary arrangements with ship's personnel to set up the stasis tubes somewhere down near the engine or waste-products recycling. We'll pick them up and slip them off the relief ship the same way. Everyone'll be so busy shooting questions at us, they'll have no time for checking cargo.

"Besides, everyone will know we found a devastated colony and that we got out as fast as we could. No one will be looking for us to smuggle anything back in. The Company will back me up on this, Ripley, especially when they see what we've brought them. They'll take good care of you, too, if that's what you're worrying about."

"I'm sure they'll back you up," she said. "I don't doubt that for an instant. Any outfit that would send less than a dozen soldiers out here with an inexperienced goofball like Gorman in charge after hearing my story is capable of anything."

"You worry too much."

"Sorry. I like living. I don't like the idea of waking up some morning with an alien monstrosity exploding out of my chest."

"That's not going to happen."

"You bet it isn't. Because if you try taking those ugly little teratoids out of here, I'll tell everyone on the rescue ship what you're up to. This time I think people will listen to me. Not that it would ever get that far. All I have to do is tell Vasquez, or Hicks, or Hudson what you have in mind. They won't wait around for a directive, and they'll use more than angry words. So you might as well give it up, Burke." She nodded in the direction of the cylinders. "You're not getting them out of this lab, much less off the surface of this planet."

"Suppose I can convince the others?"

"You can't, but supposing for a minute that you could, how would you go about convincing them that you're not responsible for the deaths of the one hundred and fifty-seven colonists here?"

Burke's combativeness drained away and he turned pale. "Now wait a second. What are you talking about?"

"You heard me. The colonists. All those poor, unsuspecting good Company people. Like Newt's family. You said I'd been doing my homework, remember? *You* sent them to that ship, to check out the alien derelict. I just checked it out in the colony log. It's as intact as the plans Hudson called up. Would make interesting reading in court. 'Company Directive Six Twelve Nine, dated five thirteen seventy-nine. Proceed to inspect possible electromagnetic emission at coordinates—but I'm not telling you anything you don't already know, am I? Signed Burke, Carter J.'" She was trembling with anger. It was all spilling out of her at once, the frustration and fury at the incompetence and greed that had brought her back to this world of horror.

"You sent them out there, and you didn't even warn them, Burke. You sat through the inquest. You heard my story. Even if you didn't believe everything, you must have believed enough of it to want the coordinates checked out. You must have thought there was something to it or you wouldn't have gone to the trouble of having anyone go out there to look around. Out to the alien ship. You might not have believed, but you suspected. You wondered. Fine. Have it checked out. But checked out carefully by a fully equipped team, not some independent prospector. And warn them of what you suspected. Why didn't you warn them, Burke?"

"Warn them about what?" he protested. He'd heard only her words, hadn't sensed the moral outrage in her voice. That in itself explained a great deal. She was coming to understand Carter J. Burke quite well.

"Look, maybe the thing didn't even exist, right? Maybe there wasn't much to it. All we had to go on was your story, which was a bit much to take at face value."

"Was it? The *Narcissus*'s recorder was tampered with, Burke. Remember me telling the board of inquiry about that? You wouldn't happen to know what happened to the recorder, would you?"

He ignored the question. "What do you think would've happened if I'd stuck my neck out and made it into a major security situation?"

"I don't know," she said tightly. "Enlighten me."

"Colonial Administration would've stepped in. That means government officials looking over your shoulder at every turn, paperwork coming out your ears, no freedom of movement at all. Inspectors crawling all over the place looking for an excuse to shut you down and take over in the name of the almighty public interest. No exclusive development rights, nothing. The fact that your story turned out to be right is as much a surprise to me as everyone else." He shrugged, his manner as blasé as ever. "It was a bad call, that's all."

Something finally snapped inside Ripley. Surprising both of them, she grabbed him by the collar and slammed him against the wall.

"*Bad call*? These people are *dead*, Burke! One hundred and fifty-seven of them less one kid, all dead because of your 'bad call.' That's not counting Apone and the others torn

apart or paralyzed over there." She jerked her head in the
direction of the processing station.

"Well, they're going to nail your hide to the shed, and
I'll be standing there helping to pass out the nails when they
do. That's assuming your 'bad call' lets any of us get off this
chunk of gravel alive. Think about that for a while." She
stepped away from him, shaking with anger.

At least the aliens' motivations were comprehensible.

Burke straightened his back and his shirt, pity in his
voice. "You just can't see the big picture, can you? Your
worldview is restricted exclusively to the here and now. You've
no interest in what your life could be like tomorrow."

"Not if it includes you, I don't."

"I expected more of you, Ripley. I thought you would
be smarter than this. I thought I'd be able to count on you
when the time came to make the critical decisions."

"Another bad call on your part, Burke. Sorry to disap-
point you." She spun on her heel and abandoned the observation room, the door closing behind her. Burke followed her
with his eyes, his mind a whirl of options.

Breathing hard, she strode toward Operations as the alarm
began to sound. It helped to take her mind off the confrontation with Burke. She broke into a run.

XI

Hudson had the portable tactical console set up next to the colony's main computer terminal. Wires trailed from the console to the computer, a rat's nest of connections that enabled whoever sat behind the tactical board to interface with the colony's remaining functional instrumentation. Hicks looked up as Ripley entered Operations and slapped a switch to kill the alarm. Vasquez and Hudson joined her in clustering around the console.

"They're coming," he informed them quietly. "Just thought you'd like to know. They're in the tunnel already."

Ripley licked her lips as she stared at the console readouts. "Are we ready for them?"

The corporal shrugged, adjusted a gain control. "Ready as we can be. Assuming everything we've set up works. Manufacturers' warranties aren't going to be a lot of use to us if something shorts out when it's supposed to be firing, like those sentry guns. They're about all we've got."

"Don't worry, man, they'll work." Hudson looked better than at any time since the initial assault on the processing station's lower levels. "I've set up hundreds of those suckers. Once the ready lights come on, you can leave 'em and forget 'em. I just don't know if they'll be enough."

"No use worrying about it. We're throwing everything we've got left at them. Either the RSS guns'll stop them or they won't. Depends on how many of them there are." Hicks thumbed a couple of contact switches. Everything read out on-line and operational. He glanced at the readouts for the motion sensors mounted on A and B guns. They were blinking rapidly, the strobe speeding up until both lights shone steadily. At the same time a crash of heavy gunfire made the floor quiver slightly.

"Guns A and B. Tracking and firing on multiple targets." He looked up at Hudson. "You give good firepower."

The comtech ignored Hicks, watching the multiple readouts. "Another dozen guns," he muttered under his breath. "That's all it would take. If we had another dozen guns..."

A steady rumble echoed through the complex as the automatic weapons pounded away beneath them. Twin ammo counters on the console shrank inexorably toward single digits.

"Fifty rounds per gun. How are we going to stop them with only fifty rounds per gun?" Hicks murmured.

"They must all be wall-to-wall down there." Hudson gestured at the readouts. "Look at those ammo counters go. It's a shooting gallery down there."

"What about the acid?" Ripley wondered. "I know those guns are armored, but you've seen that stuff at work. It'll eat through anything."

"As long as the guns keep firing, they ought to be okay," Hicks told her. "Those RSS shells have a lot of impact. If it keeps blowing them backward, that'll keep the acid away. It'll spray all over the walls and floor, but the guns should stay clear."

That certainly seemed to be what was happening in the service tunnel because the robot sentries kept up their steady barrage. Two minutes went by; three. The counter on B gun reached zero, and the thunder below was reduced by half. Its motion sensor continued to flicker on the tactical readout as the empty weapon tracked targets it could no longer fire upon.

"B gun's dry. Twenty left on A." Hicks watched the counter, his throat dry. "Ten. Five. That's it."

A grim silence descended over Operations. It was shattered by a reverberating boom from below. It was repeated at regular intervals like the thunder of a massive gong. Each of them knew what the sound meant.

"They're at the fire door," Ripley muttered. The booming increased in strength and ferocity. Audible along with the deeper rumble was another new sound: the nerve-racking scrape of claws on steel.

"Think they can break through there?" Ripley thought Hicks looked remarkably calm. Assurance—or resignation?

"One of them ripped a hatch right off the APC when it tried to pull Gorman out, remember?" she reminded him.

Vasquez nodded toward the floor. "That ain't no hatch down there. It's a Class double-A fire door, three layers of steel alloy with carbon-fiber composite laid between. The door will hold. It's the welds I'm worried about. We didn't have much time. I'd feel better if I'd had a couple bars of chromite solder and a laser instead of a gas torch to work with."

"And another hour," Hudson added. "Why don't you wish for a couple of Katusha Six antipersonnel rockets while you're at it. One of those babies would clean out the whole tunnel."

The intercom buzzed for attention, startling them. Hicks clicked it on.

"Bishop here. I heard the guns. How are we doing?"

"As well as can be expected. A and B sentries are out of ammo, but they must've done some damage."

"That's good, because I'm afraid I have some bad news."

Hudson made a face and leaned back against a cabinet. "Well, now, that's a switch."

"What kind of bad news?" Hicks inquired.

"It will be easier to explain and show you at the same time. I'll be right over."

"We'll be here." Hicks flipped the intercom off. "Charming."

"Hey, no sweat," said the jaunty comtech. "We're already in the toilet, so why worry?"

The android arrived quickly and moved to the single high window that overlooked much of the colony complex. The wind had picked back up and blown off the clinging fog. Visibility was still far from perfect, but it was sufficient to permit them a glimpse of the distant atmosphere-processing station. As they stared, a column of flame unexpectedly jetted skyward from the base of the station. For an instant it was brighter than the steady glow that emanated from the top of the cone itself.

"What was that?" Hudson pressed his face closer to the glass.

"Emergency venting," Bishop informed him.

Ripley was standing close to the comtech. "Can the construction contain the overload?"

"Not a chance. Not if the figures I've been monitoring are half accurate, and I have no reason to suppose that they are anything other than completely accurate."

"What happened?" Hicks spoke as he walked back to the tactical console. "Did the aliens cause that, monkeying around inside?"

"There's no way to tell. Perhaps. More likely someone hit something vital with a smartgun shell or a blast from a pulse-rifle during the fight on C-level. Or the damage might have been done when the dropship smashed into the base of the complex. The cause is of no import. All that matters is the result, which is not good."

Ripley started to tap her fingers on the window, thought better of it, and brought her hand back to her side. There might be something out there listening. As she stared, another gush of superheated gas flared from the base of the processing station.

"How long before it blows?"

"There's no way to be sure. One can extrapolate from the available figures but without any degree of certainty. There are too many variables involved that can only be roughly compensated for, and the requisite calculations are complex."

"How long?" Hicks asked patiently.

The android turned to him. "Based on the information I've been able to gather, I'm projecting total systems failure in a little under four hours. The blast radius will be about thirty kilometers. It will be nice and clean. No fallout, of course. About ten megatons."

"That's very reassuring," said Hudson dryly.

Hicks sucked air. "We got problems."

The comtech unfolded his arms and turned away from his companions. "I don't believe this," he said disconsolately. "Do you believe this? The RSS guns blow a pack of them to bits, the fire door's still holding, and it's all a waste!"

"It's too late to shut the station down? Assuming the instrumentation necessary to do it is still operational?" Ripley stared at the android. "Not that I'm looking forward to jogging across the tarmac, but if that's the only chance we've got, I'll take a shot at it."

He smiled regretfully. "Save your legs. I'm afraid it's too late. The dropship impact, or the guns, or whatever, did too much damage. At this point overload is inevitable."

"Terrific. So what's the recommended procedure now?"

Vasquez grinned at her. "Bend over, put your head between your legs, and kiss your ass goodbye."

Hudson was pacing the floor like a caged cat. "Oh, man. And I was getting short too! Four more weeks and out. Three of that in hypersleep. Early retirement. Ten years in the Marines and you're out and sitting pretty, they said. Recruiters. Now I'm gonna buy it on this rock. It ain't fair, man!"

Vasquez looked bored. "Give us a break, Hudson."

He spun on her. "That's easy for you to say, Vasquez. You're a lifer. You love mucking around on these alien dirtballs so you can blow away anything that sticks up bug eyes.

Me, I joined for the pension. Ten years and out, take the credit, and buy into a little bar somewhere, hire somebody else to run the joint so I can kick back and jabchat with the customers while the money rolls in."

The smartgun operator looked back toward the window as another gas jet lit up the mist-shrouded landscape. Her expression was hard. "You're breaking my heart. Go cross a wire or something."

"It's simple." Ripley looked over at Hicks. "We can't stay here, so we've got to get away. There's only one way to do that: We need the other dropship. The one that's still on the *Sulaco*. Somehow we have to bring it down on remote. There's got to be a way to do that."

"There *was*. You think I haven't been thinking about that ever since Ferro rolled ours into the station?" Hudson stopped pacing. "You use a narrow-beam transmitter tuned just for the dropship's controls."

"I know," she said impatiently. "I thought about that, too, but we can't do it that way."

"Right. The transmitter was on the APC. It's wasted."

"There's got to be another way to bring that shuttle down. I don't care how. Think of a way. You're the comtech. Think of something."

"Think of what? We're dead."

"You can do better than that, Hudson. What about the colony's transmitter? That uplink tower down at the other end of the complex? We could program it to send that dropship a control frequency. Why can't we use that? It looked like it was intact."

"The thought had occurred to me earlier." All eyes turned toward Bishop. "I've already checked it out. The hardwiring between here and the tower was severed in the fighting between the colonists and the aliens—one more reason why they were unable to communicate with the relay satellite overhead, even if only to leave a warning for anyone who might come to check on them."

Ripley's mind was spinning like a dynamo, exploring options, considering and disregarding possible solutions until only one was left. "So what you're saying is that the transmitter itself is still functional but that it can't be utilized from here?"

The android looked thoughtful, finally nodded. "If it is receiving its share of emergency power, then yes, I don't see why it wouldn't be capable of sending the requisite signals. A lot of power would not be necessary, since all the other channels it would normally be broadcasting are dead."

"That's it, then." She scanned her companions' faces. "Somebody's just going to have to go out there. Take a portable terminal and go out there and plug in manually."

"Oh, right, right!" said Hudson with mock enthusiasm. "With those things running around. No way."

Bishop took a step forward. "I'll go." Quiet, matter of fact. As though there was no alternative.

Ripley gaped at him. "What?"

He smiled apologetically. "I'm really the only one present who is qualified to remote-pilot a dropship, anyway. And the outside weather won't bother me the way it would the rest of you. Nor will I be subject to quite the same degree of ... mental distractions. I'll be able to concentrate on the job."

"If you aren't accosted by any passing pedestrians," Ripley pointed out.

"Yes, I will be fine if I am not interrupted." His smile widened. "Believe me, I'd prefer not to have to attempt this. I may be synthetic, but I'm not stupid. As nuclear incineration is the sole alternative, however, I am willing to give it a try."

"All right. Let's get on it. What'll you need?"

"The portable transmitter, of course. And we'll need to check to make sure the antenna is still drawing power. Since we're making an extra-atmospheric broadcast on a narrow beam, the transmitter will have to be realigned as precisely as possible. I will also need some—"

Vasquez interrupted sharply. "Listen!"

"To what?" Hudson turned a slow circle. "I don't hear anything."

"Exactly. It's stopped."

The smartgun operator was right. The booming and scratching at the fire door had ceased. As they listened, the silence was broken by the high-pitched trill of a motion-sensor alarm. Hicks looked at the tactical console.

"They're into the complex."

It didn't take long to get together the equipment Bishop needed. Finding a safe way out for him was another matter entirely. They debated possible exit routes, mixing information from the colony computer with suggestions from the tactical console, and spicing the results with their own heated personal opinions. The result was a consensual route that was the best of an unpromising bunch.

It was presented to Bishop. Android or not, he had the final say. Along with a multitude of other human emotions the new synthetics were also fully programmed for self-preservation. Or as Bishop ventured when the discussion of possible escape paths grew too heated, on the whole he would rather have been in Philadelphia.

There was little to argue about. Everyone agreed that the route selected was the only one that offered half a chance for him to slip out of Operations without drawing unwelcome attention. An uncomfortable silence ensued once this course was agreed upon, until Bishop was ready to depart.

One of the acid holes that was part of the colonists' losing battle with the aliens had formed a sizable gap in the floor of the medical lab. The hole offered access to the maze of subfloor conduits and serviceways. Some of these had been added subsequent to the colony's original construction and tacked on as required by Hadley's industrious inhabitants. It was one of these additions that Bishop was preparing to enter.

The android lowered himself through the opening, sliding and twisting until he was lying on his back, looking up at the others.

"How is it?" Hicks asked him.

Bishop looked back between his feet, then arched his neck to stare straight ahead. The chosen path. "Dark. Empty. Tight, but I guess I can make it."

You'd better, Ripley mused silently. "Ready for the terminal?"

A pair of hands lifted, as if in supplication. "Pass it down." She handed him the heavy, compact device.

Turning with an effort, he shoved it into the constricted shaft ahead of him. Fortunately the instrument was sheathed in protective plastic. It would make some noise as it was pushed along the conduit but not as much as metal scraping on metal. He turned on his back and raised his hands a second time.

"Let's have the rest."

Ripley passed him a small satchel. It contained tools, patch cables and replacement circuit boards, energy bypasses, a service pistol, and a small cutting torch, together with fuel for same. More weight and bulk, but it couldn't be helped. Better to take a little more time reaching the uplink tower than to arrive short of some necessary item.

"You're sure about which way you're going?" Ripley asked him.

"If the updated colony schematic is correct, yes. This duct runs almost out to the uplink assembly. One hundred eighty meters. Say, forty minutes to crawl down there. It would be easier on treads or wheels, but my designers had to go and get sentimental. They gave me legs." No one laughed.

"After I get there, one hour to patch in and align the antenna. If I get an immediate response, thirty minutes to prep the ship, then about fifty minutes' flight time."

"Why so long?" Hicks asked him.

"With a pilot on board the dropship it would take half

that, but remote-piloting from a portable terminal's going to be damn tricky. The last thing I want to do is rush the descent and maybe lose contact or control. I need the extra time to bring her in slow. Otherwise she's liable to end up like her sister ship."

Ripley checked her chronometer. "It's going to be close. You'd better get going."

"Right. See you soon." His farewell was full of forced cheerfulness. Entirely for their benefit, Ripley knew. No reason to let it get to her. He was only a synthetic, a near-machine.

She turned away from the hole as Vasquez slid a metal plate over the opening and began spot-welding it in place. There wasn't any maybe about what Bishop had to do. If he failed, they wouldn't have to worry about holding off the aliens. The bonfire that was slowly being ignited inside the processing station would finish them all.

Bishop lay on his back, watching the glow from Vasquez's welder transcribe a circle over his head. It was pretty, and he was sophisticated enough to appreciate beauty, but he was wasting time enjoying it. He rolled onto his belly and began squirming forward, pushing the terminal and the sack of equipment ahead of him. Push, squirm, push, squirm: slow going. The conduit was barely wide enough for his shoulders. Fortunately he was not subject to claustrophobia, any more than he suffered from vertigo or any of the other mental ills mankind was heir to. There was much to be said for artificial intelligence.

In front of him the conduit dwindled toward infinity. This is how a bullet must feel, he mused, lodged in the barrel of a gun. Except that a bullet wasn't burdened with feelings and he was. But only because they'd been programmed into him.

The darkness and loneliness gave him plenty of time for thinking. Moving forward didn't require much mental effort, so he was able to spend the rest considering his condition.

Feelings and programming. Organic tantrums or byte snits? Was there in the last analysis that much difference between himself and Ripley or, for that matter, any of the other humans? Beyond the fact that he was a pacifist and most of them were warlike, of course. How did a human being acquire its feelings?

Slow programming. A human infant came into the world already preprogrammed by instinct but could be radically reprogrammed by environment, companions, education, and a host of other factors. Bishop knew that his own programming was not affected by environment. What had happened to his earlier relative, then, the one that had gone berserk and caused Ripley to hate him so? A breakdown in programming—or a deliberate bit of malicious reprogramming by some still unidentified human? Why would a human do such a thing?

No matter how sophisticated his own programming or how much he learned during his allotted term of existence, Bishop knew that the species that had created him would remain forever shrouded in mystery. To a synthetic mankind would always be an enigma, albeit an entertaining and resourceful one.

In contrast to his companions there was nothing mysterious about the aliens. No incomprehensible mysteries to ponder, no double meanings to unravel. You could readily predict how they would act in a given situation. Moreover, a dozen aliens would likely react in the same fashion, whereas a dozen humans might do a dozen completely different and unrelated things, at least half of them illogical. But then, humans were not members of a hive society. At least they chose not to think of themselves as such. Bishop still wasn't sure he agreed.

Not all that much difference between human alien, and android. All hive cultures. The difference was that the human hive was ruled by chaos brought about by this peculiar thing called individuality. They'd programmed him with it. As a result he was part human. An honorary organic. In some respects he was better than a human being, in others, less. He felt best of all when they acted as though he were one of them.

He checked his chronometer. He'd have to crawl faster or he'd never make it in time.

The robot guns guarding the entrance to Operations opened up, their metallic clatter ringing along the corridors. Ripley picked up her flamethrower and headed for computer central. Vasquez finished welding the floor plate that blocked Bishop's rabbit hole into place with a flourish, put the torch aside, and followed the other woman.

Hicks was staring at the tactical console, mesmerized by the images the video pickups atop the guns were displaying. He barely glanced up long enough to beckon to the two arrivals.

"Have a look at this," he said quietly.

Ripley forced herself to look. Somehow the fact that they were distant two-dimensional images instead of an immediate reality made it easier. Each time a gun fired, the brief flare from the weapon's muzzle whited out the video, but they could still see clearly enough and often enough to watch the alien horde as it pushed and stumbled up the corridor. Each time one was struck by an RSS shell, the chitinous body would explode, spraying acid blood in all directions. The gaping holes and gouges in the floor and walls stood out sharply. The only thing the acid didn't chew through was other aliens.

Tracer fire lit the swirling mist that poured into the corridor from jagged gashes in the walls as the automatic weapons continued to hammer away at the invaders.

"Twenty meters and closing." Hicks's attention was drawn to the numerical readouts. "Fifteen. C and D guns down about fifty percent." Ripley checked the safety on her flamethrower

to make sure it was off. Vasquez didn't need to check her
pulse-rifle. It was a part of her.

The readouts flickered steadily. Between the bursts of
fire a shrill, inhuman screeching was clearly audible.

"How many?" Ripley asked.

"Can't tell. Lots. Hard to tell how many of them are
alive and which are down. They lose arms and legs and keep
coming until the guns hit them square." Hudson's gaze flicked
to another readout. "D gun's down to twenty rounds. Ten."
He swallowed. "It's out."

Abruptly all firing ceased as the remaining gun ran out
of shells. Smoke and mist obscured the double pickup view
from below. Small fires burned where tracers had set flammable material ablaze in the corridor. The floor was littered
with twisted and blackened corpses, a biomechanical bone-
yard. As they stared at the monitors several bodies collapsed
and disappeared as the acid leaking from their limbs chewed
a monstrous hole in the floor.

Nothing lunged from the clinging pall of smoke to rip
the silent weapons from their mounts. The motion-sensor
alarm was silent.

"What's going on?" Hudson fiddled uncertainly with his
instruments. "What's going on, where are they?"

"I'll be..." Ripley exhaled sharply. "They gave up.
They retreated. The guns stopped them. That means they can
reason enough to connect cause and effect. They didn't just
keep coming mindlessly."

"Yeah, but check this out." Hicks tapped the plastic
between a pair of readouts. The counter that monitored D
gun rested on zero. C gun was down to ten—a few seconds
worth of firepower at the previous rate. "Next time they can
walk right up to the door and knock. If only the APC hadn't
blown."

"If the APC hadn't blown, we wouldn't be standing here
talking about it. We'd be driving somewhere talking with the
turret gun," Vasquez pointed out sharply.

Only Ripley wasn't discouraged. "But *they* don't know how far the guns are down. We hurt them. We actually hurt them. Right now they're probably off caucusing somewhere, or whatever it is they do to make group decisions. They'll start looking for another way to get in. That'll take them awhile, and when they decide on another approach, they'll be more cautious. They're going to start seeing those sentry guns everywhere."

"Maybe we got 'em demoralized." Hudson picked up on her confidence. He had some color back in his face. "You were right, Ripley. The ugly monsters aren't invulnerable."

Hicks looked up from the console and spoke to Vasquez and the comtech. "I want you two walking the perimeter. Operations to Medical. That's about all we can cover. I know we're all strung-out, but try to stay frosty and alert. If Ripley's right, they'll start testing the walls and conduits. We've got to stop any entries before they get out of hand. Pick them off one at a time as they try to get through."

The two troopers nodded. Hudson abandoned the console, picked up his rifle, and joined Vasquez in heading for the main corridor. Ripley located a half cup of coffee, picked it up, and drained the tepid contents in a single swallow. It tasted lousy but soothed her throat. The corporal watched her, waited until she'd finished.

"How long since you slept? Twenty-four hours?"

Ripley shrugged indifferently. She wasn't surprised by the question. The constant tension had drained her. If she looked half as tired as she felt, it was no wonder that Hicks had expressed concern. Exhaustion threatened to overwhelm her before the aliens did. When she replied, her voice was distant and detached.

"What difference does it make? We're just marking time."

"That's not what you've been saying."

She nodded toward the corridor that had swallowed Hudson and Vasquez. "That was for their benefit. Maybe a little for myself too. We can sleep but *they* won't. They won't slow down and they won't back off until they have what they want, and what they want is us. They'll get us too."

"Maybe. Maybe not." He smiled slightly.

She tried to smile back but wasn't sure if she accomplished it or not. Right then she'd have traded a year's flight salary for a hot cup of fresh coffee, but there was no one to trade with, and she was too tired to work on the dispenser. She slung the flamethrower over her shoulder.

"Hicks, I'm not going to wind up like those others. Like the colonists and Dietrich and Crowe. You'll take care of it, won't you, if it comes to that?"

"*If* it comes to that," he told her softly, "I'll do us both. Although if we're still here when the processing station blows, it won't be necessary. That'll take care of everything, us and them. Let's see that it doesn't."

This time she was sure she managed a grin. "I can't figure you, Hicks. Soldiers aren't supposed to be optimists."

"Yeah, I know. You're not the first to point it out. I'm a freakin' anomaly." Turning, he picked something up from behind the tactical console. "Here, I'd like to introduce you to a close personal friend of mine."

With the smoothness and ease of long practice he disengaged the pulse-rifle's magazine and set it aside. Then he handed her the weapon.

"M-41A 10-mm pulse-rifle, over and under with a 30-mm pump-action grenade launcher. A real cutie-pie. The Marine's best friend, spouses notwithstanding. Almost jam-proof, self-lubricating, works under water or in a vacuum and can blow a hole through steel plate. All she asks is that you keep her clean and don't slam her around too much and she'll keep you alive."

Ripley hefted the weapon. It was bulky and awkward, stuffed with recoil-absorbent fiber to counter the push from the high-powered shells it fired. It was much more impressive than her flamethrower. She raised the muzzle and pointed it experimentally at the far wall.

"What do you think?" Hicks asked her. "Can you handle one?"

She looked back at him, her voice level. "What do I do?"

He nodded approvingly and handed her the magazine.

No matter how quiet he tried to be, Bishop still made noise as the portable flight terminal and his sack of equipment scraped along the bottom of the conduit. No human being could have maintained the pace he'd kept up since leaving Operations, but that didn't mean he could keep going indefinitely. There were limits even to a synthetic's abilities.

Enhanced vision enabled him to perceive the walls of the pitch-dark tunnel as it continued receding ahead of him. A human would have been totally blinded in the cylindrical duct. At least he didn't have to worry about losing his way. The conduit provided almost a straight shot to the transmitter tower.

An irregular hole appeared in the right-hand wall, admitting a feeble shaft of light. Among the emotions that had been programmed into him was curiosity. He paused to peer through the acid-etched crack. It would be nice to be able to take a bearing in person instead of having to rely exclusively on the computer printout of the service-shaft plans.

Drooling jaws flashed toward his face to slam against the enclosing steel with a vicious scraping sound.

Bishop flattened himself against the far side of the conduit as the echo of the attack rang along the metal. The curve of the wall where the jaws had struck bent slightly inward. Hurriedly he resumed his forward crawl. To his considerable surprise the attack was not repeated, nor could he sense any apparent pursuit.

Maybe the creature had simply sensed motion and had struck blindly. When no reaction had been forthcoming from inside the duct, there was no reason for it to strike again. How did it detect potential hosts? Bishop went through the motions of breathing without actually performing respiration. Nor did he smell of warmth or blood. To a marauding alien an android might seem like just another piece of machinery. So long as one didn't attack or offer resistance, you might be able to walk freely among them. Not that such an excursion appealed to Bishop, since the reactions and motives of the aliens remained unpredictable, but it was a useful bit of information to have acquired. If the hypothesis could be verified, it might offer a means of studying the aliens.

Let someone else study the monsters, he thought. Let someone else seek verification. A bolder model than himself was required. He wanted off Acheron as much for his own sake as for that of the humans he was working with.

He glanced at his chronometer, faintly aglow in the darkness. Still behind schedule. Pale and strained, he tried to move faster.

Ripley had the stock of the big gun snugged up against her cheek. She was doing her best to keep pace with Hicks's instructions, knowing that they didn't have much time, knowing that if she had to use the weapon, she wouldn't be able to ask a second time how something worked. Hicks was as patient with her as possible, considering that he was trying to compress a complete weapons instruction course into a couple of minutes.

The corporal stood close behind her, positioning her arms as he explained how to use the built-in sight. It required a mutual effort to ignore the intimacy of their stance. There was little enough warmth in the devastated colony, little enough humanity to cling to, and this was the first physical, rather than verbal, contact between them.

"Just pull it in real tight," he was telling her. "Despite the built-in absorbers, it'll still kick some. That's the price you have to pay for using shells that'll penetrate just about anything." He indicated a readout built into the side of the stock. "When this counter reads zero, hit this." He ran a thumb over a button, and the magazine dropped out, clattering on the floor.

"Usually we're required to recover the used ones: they're expensive. I wouldn't worry about following regs just now."

"Don't worry," she told him.

"Just leave it where it falls. Get the other one in quick." He handed her another magazine, and she struggled to balance the heavy weapon with one hand while loading with the other. "Just slap it in hard, it likes abuse." She did so and was rewarded with a sharp click as the magazine snapped home. "Now charge it." She tapped another switch. A red telltale sprang to life on the side of the arming mechanism.

Hicks stepped back, eyed her firing stance approvingly. "That's all there is to it. You're ready for playtime again. Give it another run-through."

Ripley repeated the procedure: release magazine, check, reload, arm. The gun was awkward physically, comforting mentally. Her hands were trembling from supporting the weight. She lowered the barrel and indicated the metal tube that ran underneath.

"What's this for?"

"That's the grenade launcher. You probably don't want to mess with that. You've got enough to remember already. If you have to use the gun, you want to be able to do it without thinking."

She stared back at him. "Look, you started this. Now show me everything. I can handle myself."

"So I've noticed."

They ran through sighting procedures again, then grenade loading and firing, a complete course in fifteen minutes. Hicks showed her how to do everything short of breaking down and cleaning the weapon. Satisfied that she'd missed nothing, she left him to ponder the tactical console's readouts as she headed for Medical to check on Newt. Slung from its field straps, her newfound friend bounced comfortingly against her shoulder.

She slowed when she heard footsteps ahead, then relaxed. Despite its greater bulk, an alien would make a lot less noise than the lieutenant. Gorman emerged from the doorway, looking weak but sound. Burke was right behind him. He barely glanced at her. That was fine with Ripley. Every time the Company representative opened his mouth, she had an urge to strangle him, but they needed him. They needed every hand they could get, including those stained with blood. Burke was still one of them, a human being.

Though just barely, she thought.

"How do you feel?" she asked Gorman.

The lieutenant leaned against the wall for support and put one hand to his forehead. "All right, I guess. A little dizzy. One beauty of a hangover. Look, Ripley, I—"

"Forget it." No time to waste on useless apologies. Besides, what had happened wasn't entirely Gorman's fault. Blame for the fiasco beneath the atmosphere-proessing station needed to be apportioned among whoever had been foolish or incompetent enough to have put him in command of the relief team. Gorman's lack of experience aside, no amount of training could have prepared anyone for the actuality of the aliens. How do you organize combat along accepted lines of battle with an enemy that's as dangerous when it's bleeding to death as it is when it's alive? She pushed past him and into the Med lab.

Gorman followed her with his eyes, then turned to head up the corridor. As he did so he encountered Vasquez approaching from the other direction. She regarded him out of cold, slitted eyes. Sweat stained her colorful bandanna and plastered it to her dark hair and skin.

"You still want to kill me?" he said quietly.

Her reply mixed contempt with acceptance. "It won't be necessary." She continued past him, striding toward the next checkpoint.

With Gorman and Burke gone, Medical was deserted. She crossed through to the operating theater where she'd left

Newt. The light was dim, but not so weak that she couldn't make out the empty bed. Fear racing through her like a drug, she spun, her eyes frantically scanning the room, until a thought made her bend to look beneath the cot.

She relaxed, the tension draining back out of her. Sure enough, the girl was curled up against the wall, jammed as far back in as she could get. She was fast asleep, Casey clutched tightly in one small hand.

The angelic expression further reassured Ripley, innocent and undisturbed despite the demons that had plagued the child through waking as well as through sleeping hours. Bless the children, she thought, who can sleep anyplace through anything.

Carefully she laid the rifle on the cot. Getting down on hands and knees, she crawled beneath the springs. Without waking the girl she slipped both arms around her. Newt twitched in her sleep, instinctively snuggling her body closer to the adult's comforting warmth. A primal gesture. Ripley turned slightly on her side and sighed.

Newt's face contorted with the externalization of some private, tormented dreamscape. She cried out inarticulately, a vague dream-distorted plea. Ripley rocked her gently.

"There, there. Hush. It's all right. It's all right."

Several of the high-pressure cooling conduits that encircled the massive atmosphere-processing tower had begun to glow red with excess heat. High-voltage discharges arced around the conical crown and upper latticework, strobing the blighted landscape of Acheron and the silent structures of Hadley town with irregular, intense flashes of light. It would have been obvious to anyone that something was drastically wrong with the station. Damping units fought to contain a reaction that was already out of control. They continued, anyway. They were not programmed for futility.

Across from the landing platform a tall metal spire poked

toward the clouds. Several parabolic antennae clustered around the top, like birds flocking to a tree in wintertime.

At the base of the tower a solitary figure stood hunched over an open panel, his back facing into the wind.

Bishop had the test-bay cover locked in the open position and had managed to patch the portable terminal console into the tower's instrumentation. Thus far everything had gone as well as anyone dared hope. It hadn't started out that way. He'd arrived late at the tower, having underestimated the length of time it would take him to crawl through the conduit. As if by way of compensation, the preliminary checkout and testing had come off without a hitch, enabling him to make up some of that lost time. Whether he'd made up enough remained to be seen.

His jacket lay draped over the keyboard and monitor of the terminal to shield them from blowing sand and dust. The electronics were far more sensitive to the inclement weather than he was. The last several minutes had seen him typing frenetically, his fingers a blur on the input keys. He accomplished in a minute what would have taken a trained human ten.

Had he been human he might have uttered a small prayer. Perhaps he did anyway. Synthetics have their own secrets. He surveyed the keyboard a last time and muttered to himself.

"Now, if I did it right, and nothing's busted inside . . ." He punched a peripheral function key inscribed with the signal word ENABLE.

Far overhead, the *Sulaco* drifted patiently and silently in the emptiness of space. No busy figures moved through its empty corridors. No machines hummed efficiently as they worked the huge loading bay. Instruments winked on and off silently, maintaining the ship in its geo-stationary orbit above the colony.

A klaxon sounded, though there were none to hear it. Rotating warning lights came to life within the vast cargo hold, though there was no one to witness the interplay of red, blue, and green. Hydraulics whined. Immensely powerful lifters rumbled along their tracks as the second dropship was trundled out on its overhead rack. Wheels locked in place, and pulleys and levers took over. The shuttle was lowered into the gaping drop bay.

As soon as it was locked in drop position, service booms and automatic decouplers extended from walls and floor to plug into the waiting vessel. Predrop fueling and final check-out commenced. These were mundane, routine tasks for which human attention was unnecessary. Actually the ship could do the job better without any people around. They would only get in the way and slow down the operation.

Engines were brought on-line, shut down, and restarted. Locks were cycled open and sealed shut. Internal communications flared to life and exchanged numerical sequences with the *Sulaco*'s main computer. A recorded announcement boomed across the vast, open chamber. Procedure required it, even though there was no one present to listen.

"Attention. Attention. Final fueling operations have begun. Please extinguish all smoking materials."

Bishop witnessed none of the activity, saw no lights rotating rapidly, heard no warning. He was satisfied nonetheless. The tiny readouts that came alive on the portable guidance console were as eloquent as a Shakespearean sonnet. He knew that the dropship had been prepared and that fueling was taking place because the console told him so. He'd done more than make contact with the *Sulaco*: he was communicating. He didn't have to be there in person. The portable was his electronic surrogate. It told him everything he needed to know, and what it told him was good.

XII

She hadn't intended to go to sleep. All she'd wanted was to share a little space, some warmth, and a few moments of quiet with the girl. But her body knew what she needed better than she did. When she relinquished control and allowed it the chance to minister to its own requirements, it took over immediately.

Ripley awoke with a start and just missed banging her head against the underside of the cot. She was wide-awake instantly.

Dim light from the Med lab filtered into the operating room. Checking her watch, she was startled to see that more than an hour had passed. Death could have visited and departed in that much time, but nothing seemed to have changed. No one had come in to wake her, which wasn't surprising. Their minds were occupied with more important matters. The fact that she'd been left alone was in itself a good sign. If the final assault had begun, Hicks or someone else surely would have rousted her out of the warm corner beneath the bed by now.

Gently she disengaged herself from Newt, who slept on, oblivious to adult obsessions with time. Ripley made sure the small jacket was pulled up snugly around the girl's chin before turning to crawl out from beneath the cot. As she turned to roll, she caught another glimpse of the rest of the Med lab— and froze.

The row of stasis cylinders stood just inside the doorway that led toward the rest of Hadley central. Two of them were dark, their tops hinged open, the stasis fields quiescent. Both were empty.

Hardly daring to breathe, she tried to see into every dark corner, under every counter and piece of freestanding equipment. Unable to move, she frantically tried to assess the situation as she nudged the girl sleeping behind her with her left hand.

"Newt," she whispered. Could the things sense sound waves? They had no visible ears, no obvious organs of hearing, but who could tell how primitive alien senses interpreted their environment? "Newt, wake up."

"What?" The girl rolled over and rubbed sleepily at her eyes. "Ripley? Where are—"

"Shssh!" She put a finger to her lips. "Don't move. We're in trouble."

The girl's eyes widened. She responded with a single nod, now as wide-awake and alert as her adult protector. Ripley didn't have to tell her a second time to be quiet. During her solitary nightmare sojourn deep within the conduits and service ducts that honeycombed the colony, the first thing Newt had learned was the survival value of silence. Ripley pointed to the sprung stasis tubes. Newt saw and nodded again. She didn't so much as whimper.

They lay close to each other and listened in the darkness. Listened for sounds of movement, watching for lethal low-slung shapes skittering across the polished floor. The compact space heater hummed efficiently nearby.

Ripley took a deep breath, swallowed, and started to move. Reaching up, she grabbed the springs that lined the underside of the cot and began trying to push it away from the wall. The squeal of metal as the legs scraped across the floor was jarringly loud in the stillness.

When the gap between bed rail and wall was wide enough, she cautiously slid herself up, keeping her back pressed against the wall. With her right hand she reached across the mattress for the pulse-rifle. Her fingers groped among the sheets and blanket.

The pulse-rifle was gone.

Her eyes cleared the rim of the bed. Surely she'd left it lying there in the middle of the mattress! A faint hint of movement caught her attention, and her head snapped around to the left. As it did so, something that was all legs and vileness jumped at her from its perch on the foot of the bed. She uttered a startled, mewling cry of pure terror and ducked back down. Horny talons clutched at her hair as the loathsome shape struck the wall where her head had been a moment earlier. It slid, fighting for a grip while simultaneously searching for the vulnerable face that had shown itself a second ago.

Rolling like mad and digging her bare fingers into the springs, Ripley slammed the cot backward, pinning the teratoid against the wall only centimeters above her face. Its legs twitched and writhed with maniacal ferocity while the muscular tail banged against springs and wall like a demented python. It emitted a shrill, piercing noise, a cross between a squeal and a hiss.

Ripley heaved Newt across the floor and, in a frenzied scramble, rolled out after her. Once clear, she put both hands against the side of the cot and shoved harder against the imprisoned facehugger. Timing her move carefully, she flipped the cot and managed to trap it underneath one of the metal rails.

Clutching Newt close to her, she backed away from the overturned bed. Her eyes were in constant motion, darting from shadow to cupboard, searching out every corner. The whole lab area was fraught with fatal promise. As they retreated, the facehugger, displaying terrifying strength for something so small, shoved the bulk of the bed off its body and scuttled away beneath a bank of cabinets. Its multiple legs were a blur of motion.

Trying to keep to the center of the room as much as possible, Ripley continued backing toward the doorway. As soon as her back struck the door, she reached up to run a hand over the wall switch. The barrier at her back should have rolled aside. It didn't move. She hit the switch again then started pounding on it, regardless of the noise she was making. Nothing. Deactivated, broken, it didn't matter. She tried the light switch. Same thing. They were trapped in the darkness.

Trying to keep her eyes on the floor in front of them, she used one fist to pound on the door. Dull thunks resounded from the acoustically dampened material. Naturally the entrance to the operating theater would be soundproofed. Wouldn't want unexpected screams to unsettle a queasy colonist who happened to be walking past.

Keeping Newt with her, she edged away from the door and around the wall until they were standing behind the big observation window that fronted on the main corridor. Hardly daring to spare a glance away from the threatening floor, she turned and shouted.

"Hey—hey!"

She hammered desperately on the window. No one appeared on the other side of the triple-glazed transparency. A scrabbling noise from the floor made her whirl. Now Newt began to whimper, feeding off the adult's fear. Desperately Ripley stepped out in line with the wall-mounted video surveillance pickup and began waving her arms.

"Hicks! Hicks!"

There was no response, not from the pickup, nor from the empty room on the other side of the glass. The camera didn't pan to focus on her and no curious voice came from its speaker. In frustration Ripley picked up a steel chair and slammed it against the observation window. It bounced off without even scarring the tough material. She kept trying.

Wasting her strength. The window wasn't going to break, and there was no one in the outer lab to witness her frantic efforts. She put the chair aside and struggled to control her breathing as she surveyed the room.

A nearby counter yielded a small, high-beam examination light. Switching it on, she played the narrow beam over the walls. The circle of light whipped over the stasis tubes, past tall assemblies of surgical and anaesthesiological equipment, over flush-mounted storage bins and cabinets and research instrumentation. She could feel Newt shaking next to her as she clung to the tall woman's leg.

"Mommy—Mommmmyyyy . . ."

Perversely it helped to steady Ripley. The child was completely dependent on her, and her own obvious fear was only making the girl panic. She swept the beam across the ceiling, brought it back to something. An idea took hold.

Removing her lighter from a jacket pocket, she hastily crumpled together a handful of paper gleaned from the same cabinet that had provided the beam. Moving as slowly as she dared, she boosted Newt up onto the surgical table that occupied the center of the room, then clambered up after her.

"Mommy—I mean, Ripley—I'm scared."

"I know, honey," she replied absently. "Me too."

Twisting the paper tightly, she touched the lighter's flame to the top of her improvised torch. It caught instantly, blazing toward the ceiling. She raised her hand and held the fire toward the temperature sensor at the bottom of one of the Med lab's fire-control sprinkler heads. Like much of the self-contained safety equipment that was standard issue for frontier worlds, the sprinkler had its own battery-powered backup power supply. It wasn't affected by whatever had killed the door and the lights.

The flames rapidly consumed her handful of paper, threatening to burn her ungloved skin. She gritted her teeth and held tight to the torch as it illuminated the room, bouncing off the mirror-bright surface of the globular surgical instrument cluster that hung suspended above the operating table.

"Come on, come _on_," she muttered tightly.

A red light winked to life on the side of the sprinkler head as the flames from her makeshift torch finally got hot enough to trigger internal sensors. As it was activated, the sensor automatically relayed its information to the other sprinklers set into the ceiling. Water gushed from several dozen outlets, flooding cabinets and floor with an artificial downpour. Simultaneously the Operations complex fire alarm came to life like a waking giant.

In Operations central, Hicks jumped at the sound of the alarm. His gaze darted from the tactical console to the main computer screen. One small section of the floor plan was flashing brightly. He rose and bolted for the exit, shouting into his headset pickup as he ran.

"Vasquez, Hudson, meet me in Medical! We got a fire!" Both troopers abandoned their guard positions and moved to rendezvous with the corporal.

Ripley's clothes clung to her as the sprinklers continued to drench the room and everything in it. The siren continued to hoot wildly. Between its steady howl and the splatter of water on metal and floor, it was impossible to hear anything else.

She tried to see through the heavy spray, wiping water and hair away from her eyes. One elbow banged against the surgical multiglobe and its assortment of cables, high-intensity lights, and tools, setting it swaying. She glanced at it and turned away to resume her inspection of the room. Something made her look a second time.

The something leapt at her face.

Falling water and the shrieking siren drowned out the sound of her scream as she stumbled backward, falling off the table and splashing to the floor, arms flailing, legs kicking wildly. Newt screamed and scrambled clear as Ripley hurled the chittering facehugger away. It slammed into a wall, clung there like an obscene parody of a climbing tarantula, then leapt back at her as though propelled by a steel spring.

Ripley scrambled desperately, pulling equipment down

on herself, trying to put something solid between her and the
abomination as she retreated. It went over, under, or around
everything she heaved in its path, its multijointed legs a frenzy
of relentless motion. Claws caught at her boots and it scuttled
up her body. She pushed at it again, the feel of the slick,
leathery hide making her nauseous. The one thing she dared
not do was throw up.

It was unbelievably strong. When it had jumped at her
from atop the multiglobe, she'd managed to fling it away
before it could get a good grip. This time it refused to be
dislodged, hung on tight as it ascended her torso. She tried
to rip at it, to pull it away, but it avoided her hands as it
climbed toward her head with single-minded purpose. Newt
screamed abjectly, backing away until she was pressed up
against a desk in one corner.

With a last, desperate gesture Ripley slid both hands up
her chest until they blocked her face, just as the facehugger
arrived. She pushed with all her remaining strength, trying
to force it away from her. As she fought, she stumbled blindly,
knocking over equipment, sending instruments flying. On the
wet floor her feet threatened to slip out from under her. Water
continued to pour from the ceiling, flooding the room and
blinding her. It also hindered the facehugger's movements
somewhat, but it made it impossible for her to get a strong
grip on its body or legs.

Newt continued to scream and stare. In consequence she
failed to see the crablike legs that appeared above the rim of
the desk she was leaning against. But her ability to sense
motion had become almost as acute as that of the sentry-gun
sensors. Whirling, she jammed the desk against the wall, fear
lending strength to her small form. Pinned against the wall,
the creature writhed wildly, fighting to free itself with its legs
and tail as she leaned against the desk and wailed.

"Ripleyyy!"

The desk bounced and shuddered with the teratoid's

struggles. It slipped one leg free, then another. A third, as it began to squeeze itself out of the trap.

"*Ripleeyyy!*"

The facehugger's legs clawed at Ripley's head, trying to reach behind it to interlock even as she whipped her face from side to side. As it fought for an unbreakable grip it extruded the ovipositorlike tubule from its ventral opening. The organ pushed wetly at Ripley's arms, trying to force its way between.

A shape appeared outside the observation window, dim behind mist-shrouded glass. A hand wiped a clear place. Hicks's face pressed against the glass. His eyes grew wide as he saw that was happening inside. There was no thought of trying to repair the inoperative door mechanism. He stepped back and raised the muzzle of his pulse-rifle.

The heavy shells shattered the triple-paned barrier in several places. The corporal then dove at the resulting spiderweb patterns and exploded into the room in a shower of glittering fragments, a human comet with a glass tail. He hit the floor rolling, his armor grinding through the shards and protecting him from their sharp edges, sliding across to where the facehugger finally got its powerful tail secured around Ripley's throat. It began to choke her and pull itself closer to her face.

Hicks slipped his fingers around the thrashing arachnoidal limbs and pulled with superhuman force. Between the two of them they forced the monstrosity away from her face.

Hudson followed Hicks into the room, stared a moment at Ripley and the corporal as they struggled with the facehugger. Then he spotted Newt leaning against the desk. He shoved her aside, sending her spinning across the damp floor, and, in the same motion, raised his rifle to blast the second parasite to bits before it could crawl free of the desk's imprisoning bulk. Acid splattered, chewing into desk, wall, and floor as the crablike body was blown apart.

Gorman leaned close to Ripley and got both hands around

the end of the facehugger's tail. Like a herpetologist removing a boa constrictor from its favorite branch, he unwound it from her throat. She gasped, swallowing air and water and choking spasmodically. But she kept her grip on it as the three of them held it between them.

Hicks blinked against the spray, nodded to his right. "The corner! Together. Don't let it keep a grip on you." He glanced over his shoulder toward the watching Hudson. "Ready?"

"Do it!" The comtech raised his weapon.

The three of them threw the thing into the empty corner. It scrabbled upright in an instant and jumped back at them with demented energy. Hudson's shot caught it in midair, blowing it apart. The heavy downpour from the sprinklers helped to localize the resultant gush of acid. Smoke began to mix with water vapor as the yellow liquid ate into the floor.

Gagging, Ripley fell to her knees. Red streaks like rope burns scarred her throat. As she knelt next to Hicks and Hudson the sprinklers finally shut down. Water dripped from cabinets and equipment, racing away through the holes the acid had eaten in the floor. The fire siren died.

Hicks was staring at the stasis cylinders. "How did they get out of there? You can't break a stasis field from the inside." His gaze rose to the security pickup mounted on the far wall. "I was watching the monitors. Why didn't I see what was going on here?"

"Burke." It came out as a long wheeze. "It was Burke."

It was very quiet in Operations. Everyone's thoughts were racing at breakneck speed, but no one spoke. None of the thoughts were pleasant. Finally Hudson gestured at the subject of all this solemn contemplation and spoke with his usual eloquence.

"I say we grease him right now."

Burke tried hard not to stare at the menacing muzzle of the comtech's pulse-rifle. One twitch of Hudson's finger and the Company rep knew his head would explode like an overripe melon. He managed to maintain an icy calm betrayed only by the isolated beads of sweat that dotted his forehead. The last five minutes had seen him compose and discard half a dozen speeches as he decided it was best to say nothing. Hicks might listen to his arguments, but the wrong word, even the wrong movement, could set any of the others off. In this he was quite correct.

The corporal was pacing back and forth in front of the Company rep's chair. Occasionally he would look down at him and shake his head in disbelief.

"I don't get it. It doesn't make any sense."

Ripley crossed her arms as she regarded the man-shape in the chair. In her eyes it had ceased to be human. "It makes plenty of sense. He wanted an alien, only he couldn't figure out a way to sneak it back through Gateway quarantine. I guaranteed him I'd inform the appropriate authorities if he tried it. That was *my* mistake."

"Why would he want to try something like that?" Hicks bemusement was plain on his face.

"For weapons research. Bioweapons. People—and I use the word advisedly—like him do things like that. If it's new and unique, they see a profit in it to the exclusion of every-thing else." She shrugged. "At first I thought he might be different. When I figured otherwise, I made the mistake of not thinking far enough ahead. I'm probably being too hard on myself. I couldn't think beyond what a sane human being might do."

"I don't get it," said Vasquez. "Where's his angle if those things killed you? What's that get him?"

"He had no intention of letting them kill us—right away. Not until we got his toys back to Earth for him. He had it timed just right. Bishop'll have the dropship down pretty soon. By then the facehuggers would've done their job, and Newt and I would be flat-out with nobody knowing the cause. The rest of you would have hauled us unconscious onto the dropship. See, if we were impregnated, parasitized, whatever you want to call it, and then frozen in hypersleep before we woke up, the effects of hypersleep would slow down the embryonic alien's growth just like it does ours. It wouldn't mature during the flight home. Nobody would know what we were carrying, and as long as our vital signs stayed stable, no one would think anything was radically wrong. We'd unload at Gateway, and the first thing the authorities would do is ship us Earthside to a hospital.

"That's where Burke and his Company cronies would step in. They'd claim responsibility, or bribe somebody, and check us into one of their own facilities where they could study us in private. Me and Newt."

She looked over at the frail figure of the girl sitting nearby. Newt hugged her knees to her chest and watched the proceedings with somber eyes. She was all but lost in the adult jacket someone had scrounged for her, scrunched down inside the copious padding and high collar. Her still-damp hair was plastered to her forehead and cheeks.

Hicks stopped pacing to stare at Ripley. "Wait a minute. *We*'d know about it. Maybe we wouldn't be sure, but we'd sure have it checked out the instant we arrived at the Station. No way would we let anybody ship you Earthside without a complete medical scan."

Ripley considered this, then nodded. "The only way it would work is if he sabotaged the sleep capsules for the trip back. With Dietrich gone, each of us would have to put ourselves into hypersleep. He could set his timer to wake him a few days down the road, climb out of his capsule, shut down everybody else's bio-support systems, and jettison the bodies. Then he could make up any story he liked. With most of your squad already killed by the aliens, and the details of the fight over on C-level recorded by your suit scanners and stored in the *Sulaco*'s records, it would be an easy matter to attribute your deaths to the aliens as well."

"He's *dead*." Hudson switched his attention from Ripley

back to the Company rep. "You hear that? You're dog meat, pal."

"This is a totally paranoid delusion." Burke saw no harm in finally speaking out, convinced that he couldn't hurt himself any more than he already had. "You saw how strong those things are. I had nothing to do with their escaping."

"Bullcrap. Nothing's strong enough to force its way out of a stasis tube," Hicks said evenly.

"I suppose after they climbed out they locked the operating room from the outside, shut down the emergency power to the overhead lights, hid my rifle, and killed the videoscan too." Ripley looked tired. "You know, Burke, I don't know which species is worse. You don't see *them* killing each other for a percentage."

"Let's waste him." Hicks's expression was unreadable as he gazed down at the Company rep. "No offense."

Ripley shook her head. Inside, the initial rage was giving way to a sickened emptiness. "Just find someplace to lock him up until it's time to leave."

"Why?" Hudson was shaking with suppressed anger, his finger taut on the trigger of his rifle.

Ripley glanced at the comtech. "Because I'd like to take him back. I want people to know what he's done. They need to know what happened to the colony here, and why. I want—"

The lights went out. Hicks turned immediately to the tactical console. The screen still glowed on battery power, but no images flashed across it because the power to the colony's computer had been cut. A quick check of Operations revealed that everything was out: power doors, videoscreens, sensor cameras, the works.

"They cut the power." Ripley stood motionless in the near blackness.

"What do you mean, *they* cut the power?" Hudson turned a slow circle and started backing toward a wall. "How could they cut the power, man? They're dumb animals."

"Who knows what they really are? We don't know enough about them to say that for sure yet." She picked up the pulse-rifle that Burke had taken and thumbed off the safety. "Maybe they act like that individually, but they could also have some kind of collective intelligence. Like ants or termites. Bishop talked about that, before he left. Termites build mounds three meters high. Leaf-cutter ants have agriculture. Is that just instinct? What is intelligence, anyway?" She glanced left.

"Stay close, Newt. The rest of you, let's get some trackers going. Come on, get moving. Gorman, keep an eye on Burke."

Hudson and Vasquez switched on their scanners. The glow of the motion-tracker sensors was comforting in the darkness. Modern technology hadn't failed them completely yet. With the two troopers leading the way, they headed for the corridor. With all power out to Operations, Vasquez had to slide the barrier aside manually.

Ripley's voice sounded behind the smartgun operator. "Anything?"

"Nothing here." Vasquez was a shadow against one wall.

She didn't have to put the same question to Hudson because everyone heard the comtech's tracker beep loudly. All eyes turned in his direction.

"There's something. I've got something." He panned the tracker around. It beeped again, louder this time. "It's moving. It's *inside* the complex."

"I don't see anything." Vasquez's tracker remained silent. "You're just reading me."

Hudson's voice cracked slightly. "No. No! It ain't you. They're inside. Inside the perimeter. They're in *here*."

"Stay cool, Hudson." Ripley tried to see to the far end of the corridor. "Vasquez, you ought to be able to confirm."

The smartgun operator swung her tracker and her rifle in a wide arc. The last place she pointed both of them was directly behind her. The portable sensor let out a sharp beep.

"Hudson may be right."

Ripley and Hicks exchanged a glance. At least they wouldn't have to stand around anymore waiting for something to happen.

"It's game time," the corporal said tightly.

Ripley called to the pair of troopers. "Get back here, both of you. Fall back to Operations."

Hudson and Vasquez started to backtrack. The comtech's eyes nervously watched the dark tunnel they were abandoning. The tracker said one thing, his eyes another. Something was wrong.

"This signal's weird. Must be some interference or something. Maybe power arcing unevenly somewhere. There's movement all over the place, but I don't see a thing."

"Just get back here!" Ripley felt the sweat starting on her forehead, under her arms. Cold, like the pit of her stomach. Hudson turned and broke into a run, reaching the door a moment before Vasquez. Together they pulled it closed and locked the seal-tight.

Once inside, they began sharing out the remnants of their pitifully small armory. Flamethrowers, grenades, and lastly, a fair distribution of the loaded pulse-rifle magazines. Hudson's tracker continued to beep regularly, rising in a gradual crescendo.

"Movement!" He looked around wildly, saw only the silhouettes of his companions in the shadowed room. "Signal's clean. Can't be an error." Picking up the scanner, he panned the business end around the room. "I've got full range of movement at twenty meters."

Ripley whispered to Vasquez. "Seal the door."

"If I seal the door, how do we get to the dropship?"

"Same way Bishop did. Unless you want to try to walk out."

"Seventeen meters," Hudson muttered. Vasquez picked up her handwelder and moved to the door.

Hicks handed one of the flamethrowers to Ripley and began priming the other for himself. "Let's get these things

lit.". A moment later his sprang to life, a small, steady blue
flame hissing from the weapon's muzzle like an oversize
lighter. Ripley's flared brilliantly as she nudged the button
marked IGNITE, which was set in the side of the handgrip.

Sparks showered around Vasquez as she began welding
the door to the floor, ceiling, and walls. Hudson's tracker
was going like mad now, though still not as fast as Ripley's
heart.

"They learned," she said, unable to stand silence. "Call
it instinct or intelligence or group analysis, but they learned.
They cut the power and they've avoided the guns. They must
have found another way into the complex, something we
missed."

"We didn't miss anything," Hicks growled.

"Fifteen meters." Hudson took a step away from the
door.

"I don't know how they did it. An acid hole in a duct.
Something under the floors that was supposed to be sealed
but wasn't. Something the colonists added or modified and
didn't bother to insert into the official schematics. We don't
know how up-to-date those plans are or when they were last
revised to include all structural additions. I don't know, but
there has to be something!" She picked up Vasquez's tracker
and aimed it in the same direction as Hudson's.

"Twelve meters," the comtech informed them. "Man,
this is one big signal. Ten meters."

"They're right on us." Ripley stared at the door. "Vasquez, how you coming?"

The smartgun operator didn't reply. Molten droplets
singed her skin and landed, smoking, on her suit. She gritted
her teeth and tried to hurry the welder along with some choice
imprecations.

"Nine meters. Eight." Hudson announced the last number on a rising inflection and looked around wildly.

"Can't be." Ripley was insistent, despite the fact that

the tracker she was holding offered the same impossible readout. "That's inside the room."

"It's right, it's right." He turned his instrument sideways
so she could see the tiny screen and its accompanying telltales.
"Look!"

Ripley fiddled with her own tracker, rolling the fine-
tuning controls as Hicks crossed to Hudson's position in a
single stride.

"Well, you're not reading it right."

"I'm not!" The comtech's voice bordered on hysteria.
"I know these little babies, and they don't lie, man. They're
too simple to screw up." He was staring bug-eyed at the
flickering readouts. "Six meters. Five. What the fu—?"

His eyes met Ripley's, and the same realization hit them
simultaneously. Both bent their heads back, and they angled
the trackers in the same direction. The beeping from both
instruments became a numbing buzz.

Hicks climbed onto a file cabinet. Slinging his rifle over
his shoulder and clutching the flamethrower tightly, he raised
one of the acoustical ceiling panels and shined his flashlight
inside.

It illuminated a vision Dante could not have imagined
in his wildest nightmares, nor Poe in the grasp of an uncon-
trollable delirium.

XIII

The serviceway between the suspended acoustical ceiling and the metal roof was full of aliens. More aliens than he could quickly count. They clung upside down to pipes and beams, crawling like bats toward his light, glistening metallically. They covered the serviceway as far back as his light could shine.

He didn't need a motion tracker to sense movement behind him. As he snapped light and body around, the beam picked out an alien less than a meter away. It lunged at his face. Ducking wildly, the corporal felt claws capable of rending metal rake across the back of his armor.

As he tumbled back into Operations the army of infiltrating creatures detached en masse from their grips and claw holds. The flimsy suspended ceiling exploded, raining debris and nightmare shapes into the room below. Newt screamed, Hudson opened fire, and Vasquez gave Hicks a hand up as she let go with her flamethrower. Ripley scooped up Newt and stumbled backward. Gorman was at her side in an instant, pumping away with his own rifle. No one had time to notice Burke as the Company rep bolted for the only unblocked corridor, the one that connected Operations to Medical.

Flamethrowers brightened the chaos as they incinerated one attacker after another. Sometimes the burning aliens would stumble into one another, screeching insanely and adding to the confusion and conflagaration. They sounded much more

209

like screams of anger than of pain. Acid poured from seared bodies, chewing gaping holes in the floor and adding to the danger.

"Medical!" Ripley was backing up slowly, keeping Newt close to her. "Get to Medical!" She turned and dashed for the connecting corridor.

The walls blurred around her, but at least the ceiling overhead stayed intact. She was able to concentrate on the corridor ahead. She caught a glimpse of Burke just as the Company rep cleared the heavy door into the lab area and slid it shut behind him. Ripley slammed into it and wrenched at the outside latch, just as it clicked home on the other side.

"Burke! Open the door! Burke, open the door!"

Newt tugged on Ripley's pants as she slipped behind her, pointing down the corridor. "Look!"

An alien was striding up the passageway toward them. A *big* alien. A shaking Ripley raised her rifle, trying to recall in an instant everything Hicks had taught her about the powerful weapon. She aimed the barrel straight at the middle of the glistening, skeletal chest and squeezed the trigger.

Nothing happened.

A hiss came from the advancing abomination. The outer jaws parted, slime splattering on the floor. Calm, calm, don't lose it, Ripley told herself. She checked the safety. It was off. A glance revealed a full magazine. Newt clung desperately to her leg and began to wail. Ripley's hands were trembling so violently, she nearly dropped the gun.

It was almost on top of them when she remembered that the first high-powered round had to be injected into the breech manually. She did so, jerked convulsively on the trigger. The rifle went off in the thing's face, hurling it backward. She turned away and covered her face as best she could in what had by now become an instinctive defensive gesture. But the energy of the shell impacting on the alien's body at point-blank range had thrown it back with such force that the spraying acid missed them completely.

The dampened recoil was still strong enough to send her off-balance body stumbling into the locked door. Her sight had been temporarily wiped by the nearness of the explosion, and she blinked furiously, trying to bring her eyes back into focus. Her ears rang with the concussion.

In Operations, Hicks looked up just in time to fire at a leaping outline, the force of the pulse shell hurling his assailant backward into a blazing cabinet. By this time the combined efforts of the flamethrowers had activated the fire-control system, and the overhead spinkler jets deluged the room. Water cascaded around the corporal, drenched the other soldiers. Some of it penetrated the central colony computer, ruining it for future use. But at least it didn't pool up around their legs. By now there were enough acid holes to drain it off. The fire siren wailed mindlessly, making it difficult for the combatants to hear each other and rendering any thought of unifed tactics impossible.

Hudson was screaming at the top of his lungs, his shrill tone audible over the siren's moan. "Let's go, let's go!"

"Medical!" Hicks yelled to him. He gestured frantically as he retreated toward the corridor. "Come on!"

As the comtech turned toward him the floor panels erupted under his feet. Clawed arms seized him, powerful triple fingers locking around his ankles and dragging him down. Another towering shape fell on him from behind, and he was gone in seconds, swallowed by the subfloor crawlway. Hicks let loose a rapid-fire burst in the direction of the cavity, hoping he got the comtech as well as his abductors, then turned and ran. Vasquez and Gorman were right behind him, the smart-gun operator laying down a murderous arc of fire as she covered their retreat.

Ripley was fumbling with the door handle when Newt pulled on her arm to attract her attention. The girl pointed silently to where the bleeding, half-blown-away alien was trying to rise to advance on them again. Flinching away from the blast and glare, Ripley drilled it a second time. The pulse-

ALAN DEAN FOSTER

rifle's muzzle jerked ceilingward, and Newt covered her ears against the roar. This time the nightmare stayed down.

A voice sounded behind them. "Hold your fire!" Hicks and the others materialized out of the smoke and dust. They were grime-streaked and soaking wet. She stepped aside, gestured at the door.

"Locked." It wasn't necessary to explain how. Hicks just nodded.

"Stand clear." From his belt he removed a cutting torch that was a miniature of the one Vasquez had used earlier to seal first the fire-tunnel door and then the one leading into Operations. It made short work of the lock.

Inhuman shapes appeared at the far end of the corridor. Ripley wondered how they could track their prey so efficiently. They had no visible eyes or ears, no nostrils. Some unknown, special, alien sensing organ? Someday maybe some scientist would dissect one of the monstrosities and produce an answer. Someday after she was long dead, because she had no intention of being around when it was attempted.

Vasquez passed her flamethrower to Gorman and unslung her rifle. From a pouch she extracted several small egg-shaped objects and dumped them into the underslung barrel of the M-41A.

Gorman's eyes widened as he watched her load the grenades. "Hey, you can't use those in here!" He backed away from her.

"Right. I'm in violation of close-quarter combat regulations ninety-five through ninety-eight. Put me on report." She aimed the muzzle of the gun at the oncoming horde. *"Fire in the hole!"* She pumped up a round and let fly, turning her head slightly as she did so.

The blast from the grenade staggered Ripley and almost knocked Vasquez off her feet. Ripley was sure that she could see the smartgun operator smiling as the light from the explosion illuminated her battle-streaked face. Hicks wavered, the blue-hot flame of his torch shooting wildly upward for a moment. Then he straightened and resumed cutting.

The lock fell away from the door a moment later, clattering inside Medical. He reholstered the torch, stood up, and kicked the door open. Molten droplets went flying. Hicks and his companions ignored them. They were used to dodging spraying acid.

He turned just long enough to shout back at Vasquez. "Thanks a lot! Now I can't hear at all!"

She affected a look of bewilderment that was as genuine and heartfelt as her gentle nature, cupping a hand to one ear. "Say what?"

They stumbled into the ruined Med lab. Vasquez was the last one through. She turned, slid the heavy door halfway closed behind her, and in rapid succession fired three grenades through the resultant gap. An instant before they went off, she shut the door the rest of the way and ran. The triple boom sounded like a giant gong going off. The heavy metal security door was bent inward off its track.

Ripley had already crossed to the far side of the annex to try the door. This time she wasn't surprised to find it locked. She worked on it as Hicks used his torch to seal the bent door they'd just come through.

In the main lab Burke found himself backing across the dark floor. This time there would be no discussion of hypothetical iniquities, no polite give-and-take. He would be shot on sight. Maybe Hicks would hold off, and Gorman, but they would be unable to restrain Hudson or that crazy Vasquez woman.

Gasping, he crossed to the door that led out into the main complex. If the aliens were wholly preoccupied with his former colleagues, he might have a chance, might pull it off in spite of everything that had gone so dreadfully wrong. He could slip back into the colony proper, away from the fight, and make a roundabout run for the landing field. Bishop was amenable to argument and reason, as any good synthetic ought to be. Maybe he could convince him that everyone else was dead. If he could manage that small semantic feat and disable the android's communicator so that the others couldn't contact him to dispute the assertion, they'd have no choice but to take off immediately. If the directive was delivered with enough force and with no one to counter it, Bishop should comply.

His fingers reached for the door latch, froze without touching the metal. The latch was already turning, seemingly by itself. Almost paralyzed with fear, he staggered backward as the door was slowly opened from the *other* side.

The loud crack of a descending stinger was not heard by those in the annex.

Vasquez's grenade party had cleared the corridor long enough for Hicks to get the door sealed. It assured them of a few secure minutes, a holding gesture and no more. Now the corporal backed away from the doorway and readied his rifle for the final confrontation as something whammed against the barrier from outside, dimpling it in the middle. A second crash made metal squeal as the door began to separate from its frame.

Newt tugged insistently at Ripley's hand. Finally the adult took notice, forcing her attention away from the failing door.

"Come on! This way!" Newt was pulling Ripley toward the far wall.

"It won't work, Newt. I could barely fit in your hide-away. The others have armor on, and some of them are bigger. They won't be able to fit in there at all."

"Not *that* way," the girl said impatiently. "There's another."

Behind a desk an air vent was a dark rectangle against the wall. Newt expertly unlatched the protective grille and swung it open. She bent to duck inside, but Ripley pulled her back.

She glanced petulantly up at the adult. "I know where I'm going."

"I don't doubt that for a minute, Newt. You're just not going first, that's all."

"I've always gone first before."

"I wasn't here before, and you didn't have every alien on Acheron chasing you before." She walked over to Gorman and swapped her rifle for his flamethrower before he could think to protest. Pausing just long enough to tousle Newt's hair affectionately, she dropped to her knees and pushed into the shaft. Darkness unknown confronted her. At the moment it felt like a comforting old friend.

She looked back past her shoulder. "Get the others. You stay behind me."

Newt nodded vigorously and disappeared. She was back in seconds, diving into the duct to crowd close to Ripley as the older woman started forward. The girl was followed by Hicks, Gorman, and Vasquez. Between their armor and the big pulse-rifles they were hauling, it was a tight squeeze for the soldiers, but everyone cleared the opening. Vasquez paused long enough to pull the grille shut behind them.

If the tunnel narrowed down ahead or split off into smaller subducts, they'd be trapped, but Ripley wasn't worried. She had a great deal of confidence in Newt. At worst they'd have time to exchange polite farewells before drawing straws, or something similar, to decide who got to deliver the final coup de grace. A glance showed that the girl was right behind her.

Closer than that. Used to moving through the labyrinth of ducts at a much faster pace, Newt was all but crawling up Ripley's legs.

"Come on," the girl urged her repeatedly, "crawl faster."

"I'm doing the best I can. I'm not built for this, Newt. None of us are, and we don't have your experience. You're sure you know where we are?"

"Of course." The girl's voice was tinged with gentle

contempt, as though Ripley had just stated the most obvious thing in the world.

"And you know how to get to the landing field from here?"

"Sure. Keep going. A little farther on and this turns into a bigger tunnel. Then we go left."

"A bigger duct?" Hicks's voice reverberated from the metal walls as he spoke to Newt. "Girl, when we get home, I'm going to buy you the biggest doll you ever saw. Or whatever you want."

"Just a bed will be fine, Mr. Hicks."

Sure enough, another several minutes of rapid crawling brought them into the colony's main ventilation duct, right where Newt said it would be. It was spacious enough to allow them to rise from a crawl to a low crouch. Ripley's hands and knees screamed in relief, and their pace increased markedly. She kept banging her head on the low ceiling, but it was such a relief to be off all fours that she hardly noticed the occasional contact.

Despite their increased speed, Newt kept up easily. Where the adults had to bend to clear the top of the duct, she was able to stand and run. Armor clattered and banged in the confined tunnel, but at this point it was agreed that speed was more important than silence. For all they knew, the aliens had poor hearing and located them by smell.

They were coming up on an intersection where two main ducts crossed. Ripley slowed to fire a preventative blast from the flamethrower, methodically searing both passageways.

"Which direction?"

Newt didn't have to think. "Go right here." Ripley turned and started up the right-hand tunnel. The new duct was somewhat smaller than the colony main but still larger than the one they'd used to flee Medical.

Behind her and Newt, Hicks was addressing his headset pickup as they scuttled along. "Bishop, this is Hicks, do you read? Do you read, Bishop? Over." Silence greeted his initial query, but eventually his persistence was rewarded by a static-distorted but still recognizable voice.

"Yes, I read you. Not very well."

"Well enough," Hicks told him. "It'll get better the closer we come. We're on our way. Taking a route through the colony ductwork. That's why the bad connection. How are things at your end?"

"Good and bad," the synthetic replied. "Wind's picked up a lot. But the dropship's on its way. Just reconfirmed drop and release with the *Sulaco*. Estimated time of arrival: sixteen minutes plus. I've got my hands full trying to remote-fly in this wind." An electronic roar distorted the end of his sentence.

"What was that?" Hicks fiddled with his headset controls. "Say again, Bishop. Wind?"

"No. The atmosphere-processing station. Emergency venting system is approaching overload. It'll be close, Corporal Hicks. Don't stop for lunch."

In the darkness the soldier grinned. Not all synthetics were programmed for a sense of humor, and not all those that were knew how to make use of it. Bishop was something else.

"Don't worry. None of us are real hungry right now. We'll make it in time. Stand by out there. Over."

Preoccupied with his communication, he almost ran over Newt. The girl had halted in the duct. Looking beyond the girl, he saw that Ripley had stopped in front of her.

"What is it, what's wrong?"

"I'm not sure." Ripley's voice was ghostly in the darkness. "I could swear I saw—there!"

At the extreme limit of her flashlight Hicks made out a moving, obscene shape. Like a ferret, the alien had somehow managed to flatten its body just enough for it to fit inside the duct. There was additional movement visible beyond the intruder.

"Back, go back!" Ripley yelled.

Everyone tried to comply, jamming into each other in the confined tunnel. Behind them the sound of a grating being torn apart echoed through the duct. The grating collapsed with a sharp *spanggg*, and a deadly silhouette flowed through the resultant opening. Vasquez unlimbered her flamethrower and bathed the tunnel behind them in fire. Everyone knew it was a temporary victory. They were trapped.

Vasquez leaned to one side and stared upward. "Vertical shaft right here. Slick, no handholds." Her tone was clipped, matter-of-fact. "Too smooth to try a chimney ascent."

Hicks broke out his cutting torch, snapped it alight, and began slicing through the wall of the duct. Molten metal spattered his armor as sparks filled the confined tunnel with lurid light. Vasquez's flamethrower roared again, then sputtered out.

"Losing fuel." From the other direction the column of aliens continued to close on them, their advance slowed by their need to squeeze through the narrow walls.

Hicks had three-quarters of an exit cut in the side of the tunnel when the portable torch flickered and went out. Cursing, he braced his back against the opposite wall of the duct and kicked hard. The metal bent. He kicked again and it gave way. Without pausing to see what lay on the other side, he grabbed his rifle and dove through the opening . . .

. . . to emerge into a narrow serviceway thick with pipes and exposed conduits. Ignoring the still-hot edges of the cavity, he reached back inside to pull Newt to safety. Ripley followed, turned to aid Gorman. He hesitated at the opening long enough to see Vasquez's flamethrower run dry. The smartgun operator dumped it aside and drew her service revolver.

There was movement above her as a grotesque shape dropped down the vertical overhead duct. As the alien landed in the tunnel she rolled clear and let fly with the automatic pistol. The alien tumbled toward her as the small projectiles ripped into its skeletal body. Vasquez snapped her head to one side just in time to avoid the stinger. It buried itself into the metal wall next to her cheek. She kept firing, emptying the pistol into the thrashing form as she kicked at the powerful legs and quivering tail.

A gush of acid finally cut through her armor to sear her thigh. She let out a soft moan of pain.

Gorman froze in the tunnel. He glanced at Ripley. "They're right behind me. Get going." Their eyes met for as long as either of them dared spare. Then she turned and raced up the serviceway with Newt in tow. Hicks followed reluctantly, staring back at the opening he'd cut in the ventilation duct. Hoping. Knowing better.

Gorman crawled toward the immobilized smartgun operator. When he reached her, he saw the smoke pouring from the hole in her armor, shut out the gruesome smell of scarred flesh. His fingers locked around her battle harness, and he started dragging her toward the opening.

Too late. The first alien coming from the other direction had already reached and passed the hole Hicks had made. Gorman stopped pulling, leaned forward to look at Vasquez's leg. Where armor, harness, and flesh had been eaten away by the acid, bone gleamed whitely.

Her eyes were glazed when she looked up at him. Her voice was a harsh whisper. "You always were stupid, Gorman."

Her fingers seized his in a death grip. A special grip shared by a select few. Gorman returned it as best he was able. Then he handed her a pair of grenades and armed another couple for himself as the aliens closed in on them from both ends of the tunnel. He grinned and raised one of the humming explosives. She barely had enough strength to mimic the gesture.

"Cheers," he whispered. He couldn't tell if she was grinning back at him because he had closed his eyes, but he had a feeling she was. Something sharp and unyielding stroked his back. He didn't turn to see what it was.

"Cheers," he whispered feebly. He clicked one of his grenades against one of Vasquez's in the final toast.

Behind them, the serviceway lit up like the sun as Ripley, Newt, and Hicks pounded along full tilt. They were a long way from the opening the corporal had cut in the wall of the duct, but the shock wave from the quadruple explosion was still powerful enough to rock the whole level. Newt kept her balance best and broke out in front of the two adults. It was all Ripley and Hicks could do to keep up with her.

"This way, this way!" she was shouting excitedly. "Come on, we're almost there!"

"Newt, wait!" Ripley tried to lengthen her stride to catch up to the girl. The sound of her heart was loud in her ears, and her lungs screamed in protest with every step she took. The walls blurred around her. She was dimly aware of Hicks pounding along like a steam engine just behind her. Despite his armor, he probably could have outdistanced her, but he didn't try. Instead he laid back so he could protect against an attack from behind.

Ahead the corridor forked. At the end of the left-hand fork a narrow, angled ventilation chute led upward at a steep forty-five degrees. Newt was standing at its base, gesturing frantically.

"Here! This is where we go up."

Her body grateful for a respite no matter how temporary, Ripley slowed to a halt as she examined the shaft. It was a steep climb but not a long one. Dim light marked the end of the ascent. From above she could hear the wind booming like air blowing across the lip of a bottle. Narrow climbing ribs dimpled the smooth sides of the shaft.

She looked down to where the chute punched a hole in the floor and disappeared into unknown depths lost in darkness. Nothing stirred down there. Nothing came climbing toward them. They were going to make it.

She put her foot onto the first climbing rib and started

up. Newt followed as Hicks emerged from the main corridor behind them.

The girl turned to wave. "Just up here, Mr. Hicks. It's not as far as it looks. I've done it lots of tim—"

Rusted out by seeping water, worn through by the corrosive elements contained in Acheron's undomesticated atmosphere, the rib collapsed beneath her feet. She slipped, managed to catch another rib with one hand. Ripley braced herself against the dangerously slick surface of the chute, turned, and reached back for her. As she did so, she dropped her flashlight, watched it go skittering and bumping down the opening until its comforting glow faded from sight.

She strained until she was sure her arm was separating from her shoulder, her fingers groping for Newt's. No matter how far over she bent, they remained centimeters apart.

"Riiipplleeee . . ."

Newt's grip broke. As she went sliding down the chute Hicks made a dive for her, laying himself out, flat and indifferent to the coming impact. He slammed into the floor next to the chute, and his fingers dug into the collar of the girl's oversize jacket, holding the material in a death grip.

She slipped out of it.

Her scream reverberated up the chute as she vanished, plummeting down into darkness.

Hicks threw the empty jacket aside and stared at Ripley. Their eyes met for just a second before she released her own grasp and went sliding down the chute after Newt. As she slid, she pushed out with her feet, braking her otherwise uncontrolled descent.

Like the corridor above, the chute forked where it intersected the lower level. Her flashlight gleamed off on her right, and she shifted her weight so she would slide in that direction.

"Newt. Newt!"

A distant wail, plaintive and distorted by distance and intervening metal, floated back to her.

"Mommy—where are you?" Newt was barely audible. Had she taken the other chute?

The shaft bottomed out in a horizontal service tunnel. Her undamaged flashlight lay on the floor, but there was no sign of the girl. As Ripley bent to recover the light the cry reached her again, bouncing off the narrow walls.

"Moommmeee!"

Ripley started down the tunnel in what she hoped was the right direction. The wild slide down the chute had completely disoriented her. Newt's call came again. Fainter? Ripley couldn't tell. She turned a circle, panic growing inside her, her light illuminating only grime and dampness. Every projection contained grinning, slime-lubricated jaws, every hollow was a gaping alien mouth. Then she remembered that she was still wearing her headset. And she remembered something else. Something the corporal had given her that she'd given away in turn.

"Hicks, get down here. I need the locator for that bracelet you gave me." She cupped her hands to her mouth and shouted down the serviceway. "Newt! Stay wherever you are. We're coming!"

The girl was in a low, grottolike chamber where the other branch of the chute had dumped her. It was crisscrossed with pipes and plastic conduits and was flooded up to her waist. The only light came from above, through a heavy grating. Maybe Ripley's voice had also, she thought. Using the network of pipes, she started to climb.

A large, bulky object came sliding down the chute. Hicks wouldn't have found the description flattering, but Ripley was immensely relieved to see him no matter how rumpled he looked. The mere presence of another human being in that stygian, haunted tunnel was enough to push back the fear a little way.

He landed on his feet, clutching his rifle in one hand, and unsnapped the emergency location unit from his battle harness. "I gave *you* that bracelet," he said accusingly, even as he was switching the tracker on.

"And I gave it to Newt. I figured she'd need it more than I would, and I was right. It's a good thing I did it or we'd never find her in this. You can bawl me out later. Which way?"

He checked the tracker's readout, turned, and started off down the tunnel. It led them into a section of serviceway where the power hadn't been cut. Emergency lights still brightened ceiling and walls. They switched off their lights. Water dripped somewhere nearby. The corporal's gaze rarely strayed from the tracker's screen. He turned left.

"This way. We're getting close."

The locator led them to a large grate set in the floor— and a voice from below.

"Ripley?"

"It's us, Newt."

"Here! I'm here, I'm down here."

Ripley knelt at the edge of the grating, then wrapped her fingers around the center bar and pulled. It didn't budge. A quick inspection revealed that it was welded into the floor instead of being latched for easy removal. Peering down, she could just make out Newt's tear-streaked face. The girl reached upward. Her small fingers wriggled between the closely set bars. Ripley gave them a reassuring squeeze.

"Climb down off that pipe, honey. We're going to have to cut through this grate. We'll have you out of there in a minute."

The girl obediently backed clear, shinnying down the pipe she'd ascended as Hicks fired up his hand torch. Ripley glanced significantly in its direction, then met his eyes as she lowered her voice.

"How much fuel?" She was remembering how Vasquez's flamethrower had run out at a critical moment.

He looked away. "Enough." Bending, he began cutting through the first of the bars.

From below Newt could watch sparks shower blindingly as Hicks sliced through the hardened alloy. It was cold in the tunnel, and she was standing in the water again. She bit her lip and fought back tears.

She did not see the glistening apparition rising silently from the water behind her. It would not have mattered if she had. There was nowhere to run to, no safe air duct to duck into. For a moment the alien hovered over her, motionless, dwarfing her tiny form. Only when it moved again did she sense its presence and whirl. She barely had enough time to scream as the shadow engulfed her.

Ripley heard the scream and the brief splashing below and went completely berserk. The grating had been half cut away. She and Hicks wrenched and kicked at it until a portion bent downward. Another kick sent the chunk of crumpled metal tumbling into the water. Heedless of the red-hot edges, Ripley lunged through the opening, her light clutched in one hand, its beam slashing over pipes and conduits.

"Newt! Newt!"

The surface of the dark water reflected the light back up at her. It was placid and still after having swallowed the section of grille. Of the girl there was no sign. All that remained to show that she'd ever been there was Casey. As Ripley looked on helplessly, the doll head sank beneath the oily blackness.

Hicks had to drag her bodily out of the opening. She struggled blindly, trying to rip free of his embrace.

"No, noooo!"

It took all his strength and greater mass to wrestle her away from the opening. "She's *gone*," he said intensely. "There's nothing you or I or anybody else can do now. Let's go!" A glance showed something moving at the far end of the corridor that had led them to the grating. It might be nothing more than his eyes playing tricks on him. Eye tricks on Acheron could prove fatal.

Ripley was sliding rapidly into hysteria, screaming and

crying and flailing her arms and legs. He had to lift her clear
of the floor to keep her from diving through the gap. A wild
plunge into the water-filled darkness below was a short course
to suicide.

"No! No! She's still alive! We have to—"

"All right!" Hicks roared. "She's alive. I believe it. But
we gotta get moving. Now! You're not going to be able to
catch her that way." He nodded at the hole in the floor. "She
won't be waiting for you down there, but they will. Look."
He pointed, and she stopped struggling. There was an elevator
at the far end of the tunnel.

"If there's emergency power to the lights in this section,
then maybe that's functioning too. Let's get out of here. Once
we're up top, we can try to think this through where they
can't sneak up on us."

He still had to half drag her to the elevator and push her
inside.

The movement he'd detected at the far end of the tunnel
coalesced into the advancing outline of an alien. Hicks practically broke the plastic as he jammed a thumb on the "up"
button. The elevator's double doors began to close—not quite
fast enough. The creature slammed one huge arm between
them. As both humans looked on in horror, the automatic
safety built into the elevator doors buzzed and began to part.
The machine could not discriminate between human and alien.

The drooling abomination lunged toward them, and Hicks
blew it away, firing his pulse-rifle at point-blank range. Too
close. Acid sluiced between the closing doors to splash across
his chest as he shielded Ripley with his armor. Fortunately
none of the acid struck the elevator cables. The elevator began
to ascend, clawing its way toward the surface on lingering
emergency power.

Hicks tore at the quick-release catches on the harness as
the powerful liquid ate through the composite-fiber armor.
His plight was enough to galvanize Ripley out of her panic.
She clawed at his straps, trying to help as much as she could.

Acid reached his chest and arm, and he yelled, shucking out of the combat armor like an insect shedding its old skin. The smoking plates fell to the floor, and the relentless acid began to eat through the metal underfoot. Acrid fumes filled the air inside the elevator, searing eyes and lungs.

After what seemed like a thousand years, the elevator ground to a halt. Acid ate through the floor and began to drip onto the cables and support wheels.

The doors parted and they stumbled out. This time it was Ripley who had to support Hicks. Smoke continued to rise from his chest, and he was doubled over in agony.

"Come on, you can make it. I thought you were a tough guy." She inhaled deeply, coughed, and inhaled again. Hicks choked, gritted his teeth, and tried to grin. After the foulness of the tunnels and ductways the less-than-idyllic air of Acheron smelled like perfume. "Almost there."

Not far ahead of them the sleek, streamlined shape of Dropship Two was descending erratically toward the landing grid like a dark angel, side-slipping as it fought its way through the powerful wind gusts just above the surface. They could see Bishop, his back to them, standing in the lee of the transmitter tower as he struggled with the portable guidance terminal to bring the dropship in. It sat down hard and slid sideways, coming to a halt near the middle of the landing pad. Except for a bent landing strut, the inelegant touchdown appeared to have left it undamaged.

She yelled. The synthetic turned to see the two of them stumbling out of a doorway in the colony building behind him. Putting the terminal down carefully, he ran to help, getting one powerful arm under Hicks and helping him toward the ship. As they ran, Ripley shouted to the android, her words barely audible over the gale.

"How much time?"

"Plenty!" Bishop looked pleased. He had reason to be. "Twenty-six minutes."

"We're not leaving!" She said this as they were staggering up the loading ramp into the warmth and safety of the ship.

Bishop gaped at her. "What? Why not?"

She studied him carefully, searching for the slightest suggestion of deception in his face and finding none. His question was perfectly understandable under the circumstances. She relaxed a little.

"Tell you in a minute. Let's get Hicks some medical and close this sucker up, and then I'll explain."

Lightning crackled around the upper rim of the failing atmosphere-processing station. Steam blasted from emergency vents. Columns of incandescent gas shot hundreds of meters into the sky as internal compensators struggled futilely to adjust temperature and pressure overloads that were already beyond correction.

Bishop was careful not to drift too close to the station as he guided the dropship toward the upper-level landing platform. As they approached, they passed over the ruined armored personnel carrier. A shattered, motionless hulk outside the station entryway, the APC had finally stopped smoking. Ripley stared as it slipped past beneath him, a monument to overconfidence and a misplaced faith in the ability of modern technology to conquer any obstacle. Soon it would evaporate along with the station and the rest of Hadley colony.

About a third of the way up the side of the enormous

cone that formed the processing station, a narrow landing platform jutted out into the wind. It was designed to accommodate loading skimmers and small atmospheric craft, not something the size of a dropship. Somehow Bishop managed to maneuver them in close. The platform groaned under the shuttle's weight. A supporting beam bent dangerously but held.

Ripley finished winding metal tape around the bulky project that had occupied her hands and mind for the past several minutes. She tossed the half-empty tape roll aside and inspected her handiwork. It wasn't a neat job, and it probably violated twenty separate military safety regulations, but she didn't give a damn. She wasn't going on parade, and there was no one around to tell her it was dangerous and impossible.

What she'd done while Bishop was bringing them in close to the station was to secure Hicks's pulse-rifle to the side of a flamethrower. The result was a massive, clumsy siamese weapons package with tremendous and varied firepower. It might even be enough to get her back to the ship alive—if she could carry it.

She turned back to the dropship's armory and began loading a satchel and her pockets with anything that might kill aliens: grenades; fully charged pulse-rifle magazines; shrapnel clips; and more.

Having programmed the dropship for automatic lift-off should the landing platform show signs of giving way, Bishop made his way aft from the pilot's compartment to help Hicks treat his injuries. The corporal lay sprawled across several flight seats, the contents of a field medical kit strewn around him. Working together, he and Ripley had managed to stanch the bleeding. With the aid of medication his body would heal. The dissolved flesh was already beginning to repair itself. But in order to reduce the pain to a tolerable level, he'd been forced to take several injections. The medication kept him halfway comfortable but blurred his vision and slowed his reactions. The only support he could give to Ripley's mad plan was moral.

Bishop tried to remonstrate. "Ripley, this isn't a very efficacious idea. I understand how you feel—"

"Do you?" she snapped at him without looking up.

"As a matter of fact, I do. It's part of my programming. It's not sensible to throw one life after another."

"She's *alive*." Ripley found an empty pocket and filled it with grenades. "They brought her here just like they brought all the others, and you know it."

"It seems the logical thing for them to do, yes. I admit there is no obvious reason for them to deviate from the pattern they have demonstrated thus far. That is not the point. The point is that even if she is here, it is unlikely that you can find her, rescue her, and fight your way back out in time. In seventeen minutes this place will be a cloud of vapor the size of Nebraska."

She ignored him, her fingers flying as she sealed the overstuffed satchel. "Hicks, don't let him leave."

He blinked weakly at her, his face taut with pain. The medication was making his eyes water. "We ain't going anywhere." He nodded toward her feet. "Can you carry that?"

She hefted her hybrid weapon. "For as long as I have to." Picking up the satchel, she slung it over one shoulder, then turned and strode to the crew door. She thumbed it open, waiting impatiently for it to cycle. Wind and the roar from the failing atmosphere processor rushed the gap. She stepped to the top of the loading ramp and paused for a last look back.

"See you, Hicks."

He tried to sit up, failed, and settled for rolling onto his side. One hand held a wad of medicinal gauze tight against his face. "Dwayne. It's Dwayne."

She walked back over to grab his hand. "Ellen."

That was enough. Hicks nodded, leaned back, and looked

satisfied. His voice was a pale shadow of the one she'd come to be familiar with. "Don't be long, Ellen."

She swallowed, then turned and exited, not looking back as the hatch closed behind her.

The wind might have blown her off the platform had she not been so heavily equipped. Set in the station wall opposite the dropship were the doors of a large freight elevator. The controls responded instantly to her touch. Plenty of power here. Too much power.

The elevator was empty. She entered and touched the contact switch opposite C-level. The bottom. The seventh level, she thought as the elevator began to descend.

It was slow going. The elevator had been designed to carry massive, sensitive loads, and it would take its time. She stood with her back pressed against the rear wall, watching bars of light descend. As the elevator descended into the bowels of the station the heat grew intense. Steam roared everywhere. She had difficulty breathing.

The slow pace of the descent allowed her time to remove her jacket and slip the battle harness she'd appropriated from the dropship's stores on directly over her undershirt. Sweat plastered her hair to her neck and forehead as she made a last check of the weaponry she'd brought with her. A bandolier of grenades fit neatly across the front of the harness. She primed the flamethrower, made sure it was full. Same for the magazine locked into the underside of the rifle. This time she remembered to chamber the initial round to activate the load.

Fingers nervously traced the place where marking flares bulged the thigh pockets of her jumpsuit pants. She fumbled with an unprimed grenade. It slipped between her fingers and fell to the floor, bouncing harmlessly. Trembling, she recovered it and slid it back into a pocket. Despite all of Hicks's detailed instructions, she was acutely aware that she didn't know anything about grenades and flares and such.

Worst of all was the fact that for the first time since

they'd landed on Acheron she was alone. Completely and utterly alone. She didn't have much time to think about it because the elevator motors were slowing.

The elevator hit bottom with a gentle bump. The safety cage enclosing the lift retracted. She raised the awkward double muzzle of rifle and flamethrower as the doors parted.

An empty corridor lay before her. In addition to the illumination provided by the emergency lighting, faint reddish glows came from behind thick metal bulges. Steam hissed from broken pipes. Sparks flared from overloaded, damaged circuits. Couplings groaned while stressed machinery throbbed and whined. Somewhere in the distance a massive mechanical arm or piston was going *ka-rank*, *ka-rank*.

Her gaze darted left, then right. Her knuckles were white above the dual weapon she carried. She had no flexible battle visor to help her, though in the presence of so much excess heat its infrared-imaging sensors wouldn't have been of much use, anyway. She stepped out into the corridor, into a scene designed by Piranesi, decorated by Dante.

She was struck by the aliens' presence as soon as she turned the first bend in the walkway. Epoxy-like material covered conduits and pipes, flowing smoothly up into the overhead walkways to blend machinery and resin together, creating a single chamber. She had Hicks's locator taped to the top of the flamethrower, and she looked at it as often as she dared. It was still functioning, still homing in on its single target.

A voice echoed along the corridor, startling her. It was calm and efficient and artificial.

"Attention. Emergency. All personnel must evacuate immediately. You now have fourteen minutes to reach minimum safe distance."

The locator continued to track; range and direction spelled out lucidly by its LED display.

As she advanced, she blinked sweat out of her eyes. Steam swirled around her, making it difficult to see more than a short distance in any direction. Flashing emergency lights lit an intersecting passageway just ahead.

Movement. She whirled, and the flamethrower belched napalm, incinerating an imaginary demon. Nothing there. Would the blast of heat from her weapon be noticed? No time to worry about maybes now. She resumed her march, trying not to shake as she concentrated on the locator's readouts.

She entered the lower level.

In the inner chambers now. The walls around her subsumed skeletal shapes, the bodies of the unfortunate colonists who had been brought here to serve as helpless hosts for embryonic aliens. Their resin-encrusted figures gleamed like insects frozen in amber. The locator's signal strengthened, leading her off to the left. She had to bend to clear a low overhang.

At each turning point or intersection she was careful to ignite a timed flare and place it on the floor behind her. It would be easy to get lost in the maze without the markers to help her find her way back. One passageway was so narrow, she had to turn sideways to slip through it. Her eyes touched upon one tormented face after another, each entombed colonist caught in a rictus of agony.

Something grabbed her. Her knees sagged, and the breath went out of her before she could even scream. But the hand was human. It was attached to an imprisoned body, surmounted by a face. A familiar face. Carter Burke.

"Ripley." The moan was barely human. "Help me. I can feel it inside. It's moving..."

She stared at him, beyond horror now. No one deserved this.

"Here." His fingers clutched convulsively around the grenade she handed him. She primed it and hurried on. The voice of the station boomed around her. There was a rising note of mechanical urgency in its tone.

"You now have eleven minutes to reach minimum safe distance."

According to the locator, she was all but on top of the target. Behind her the grenade went off, the concussion nearly knocking her off her feet. It was answered by a second, more forceful, eruption from deep within the station itself. A siren began to wail, and the whole installation shuddered. The locator led her around a corner. She tensed in anticipation. The locator's range finder read out zero.

Newt's tracer bracelet lay on the tunnel floor, the metal fabric shredded. The glow from its sender module was a bright, cheerless green. Ripley sagged against a wall.

It was over. All over.

Newt's eyes fluttered open, and she became aware of her surroundings. She had been cocooned in a pillarlike structure at the edge of a cluster of ovoid shapes: alien eggs. She recognized them right away. Before they'd been carried off or killed, the last desperate adult colonists had managed to acquire a few for study.

But those had all been empty, open at the tops. These were sealed.

Somehow the egg nearest her prison became aware of her stirrings. It quivered and then began to open, an obscene flower. Something damp and leathery stirred within. Transfixed by terror, Newt stared as jointed, arachnoid legs appeared over the lip of the ovoid. They emerged one at a time. She knew what was going to happen next, and she reacted the only way she could, the only way she knew how—she screamed.

Ripley heard, turned toward the sound, and broke into a run.

With horrible fascination Newt watched as the facehugger climbed out of the egg. It paused for a moment on the rim, gathering its strength and taking its bearings. Then it turned toward her. Ripley came pounding into the chamber as it poised to leap. Her finger tensed on the pulse-rifle's trigger. The single shell tore the crouching creature apart.

The flash from the muzzle illuminated the figure of a mature alien standing nearby. It spun and charged the intruder just in time for twin bursts from the rifle to catapult it backward. Ripley advanced on the corpse, firing again and again, a murderous expression on her face. The alien jerked onto its back, and she finished it with the flamethrower.

While it burned, she ran to Newt. The resinous material of the girl's cocoon hadn't hardened completely yet, and Ripley was able to loosen it enough for Newt to crawl free.

"Here." Ripley turned her back to the girl and bent her knees. "Climb aboard." Newt clambered up onto the adult's hips and locked her hands around Ripley's neck. Her voice was weak.

"I knew you'd come."

"So long as I could still breathe. Okay, we're getting out of here. I want you to hang on, Newt. Hang on real tight. I'm not going to be able to hold you, because I've got to be able to use the guns."

She didn't see the nod, but she felt it against her back. "I understand. Don't worry. I won't let go."

Ripley sensed movement off to their right. She ignored it as she blasted the eggs with the flamethrower. Only then did she turn it on the advancing aliens. One almost reached her, a living fireball, and she blew it apart with two bursts from the rifle. Ducking beneath a glistening cylindrical mass, she retreated. A piercing shriek filled the air, rising above the pounding of failing machinery, the wail of the emergency siren and the screech of attacking aliens.

She'd have seen it earlier if she'd looked up instead of straight ahead when she'd entered the egg chamber. It was just as well that she hadn't because, despite her determination, she might have faltered. A gigantic silhouette in the ruddy mist, the alien queen glowered above her egg cache like a great, gleaming insectoid Buddha. The fanged skull was horror incarnate. Six limbs, two legs and four taloned arms, were folded grotesquely over a distended abdomen. Swollen with eggs, it comprised a vast, tubular sac that was suspended from the latticework of pipes and conduits by a weblike membrane, as though an endless coil of intestine had been draped along the supporting machinery.

Ripley realized she'd passed right beneath part of the sac a moment earlier.

Inside the abdominal container countless eggs churned toward a pulsating ovipositor in a vile, organic assembly line. There they emerged, glistening and wet, to be picked up by tiny drones. These miniature versions of the alien warriors scuttled back and forth as they attended to the needs of both eggs and queen. They ignored the staring human in their midst as they concentrated with single-minded intensity on the task of transferring newly deposited eggs to a place of safety.

Ripley remembered how Vasquez had done it as she pumped the slide on the grenade launcher: pumped and fired four times. The grenades punched deep into the flimsy egg sac and exploded, blowing it to shreds. Eggs and tons of noisome, gelatinous material spilled over the floor of the chamber. The queen went berserk, screeching like a psychotic locomotive. Ripley laid about with the flamethrower, methodically igniting everything in sight as she retreated. Eggs shriveled in the inferno, and the figures of warriors and drones vanished amid frenzied thrashing.

The queen towered above the carnage, struggling in the flames. Two warriors closed in on Ripley. The pulse-rifle clicked empty. Smoothly she ejected the magazine, slammed another one home, and held the trigger down. Her attackers vanished in the homicidal hail of fire.

It didn't matter if it moved or not. She blasted everything that didn't look wholly mechanical as she ran for the elevator, setting fire to equipment and destroying controls and instrumentation together with attacking aliens. Sweat and steam half blinded her, but the flares she'd dropped to mark her path shone brightly, jewels set among the devastation. Sirens howled around her, and the station rocked with internal convulsions.

She almost ran past one flare, skidded to a halt, and turned toward it. She staggered on as if in a dream, her lungs straining no longer. Her body was so pumped up, she felt as though she were flying across the metal floor.

Behind her, the queen detached from the ruined egg sac, ripping it away from her abdomen. Rising on legs the size of temple pillars, she lumbered forward, crushing machinery, cocoons, drones, and anything else in her path.

Ripley used the flamethrower to sterilize the corridor ahead, letting loose incinerating blasts at regular intervals, firing down side corridors before she crossed them to keep from being surprised. By the time she and Newt reached the freight elevator, the weapon's tank was empty.

The elevator she'd used for the descent had been demolished by falling debris. She hit the call button on its companion and was rewarded by the whine of a healthy motor as the second metal cage commenced its slow fall from the upper levels. An enraged shriek made her turn. A distant, glistening shape like a runaway crane was trying to batter its way through intervening pipes and conduits to reach them. The queen's skull scraped the ceiling.

She checked the pulse-rifle. The magazine was empty, and she was out of refills, having spent shells profligately while rescuing Newt. No more grenades, either. She tossed the useless dual weapon aside, glad to be rid of the weight.

The cage's descent was too slow. There was a service ladder set inside the wall next to the twin elevator shafts, and she scrambled up the first rungs. Newt was as light as a feather on her back.

As she dove into the stairwell a powerful black arm shot through the doorway like a piston. Razor-sharp talons slammed into the floor centimeters from her legs, digging into the metal.

Which way now? She was no longer fearful, had no time

to panic. Too many other things to concentrate on. She was too busy to be terrified.

There: an open stairwell leading to the station's upper levels. It rocked and shuddered as the huge installation began tearing itself to bits beneath her. Behind her, the floor buckled as something incredibly powerful threw itself insanely against the metal wall. Talons and jaws pierced the thick alloy plates.

"You now have two minutes to reach minimum safety distance," the sad voice of the station informed any who might be listening.

Ripley fell, banging one knee against the metal stairs. Pain forced her to pause. As she caught her breath the sound of the elevator motors starting up made her look back down through the open latticework of the building. The elevator cage had begun to ascend. She could hear the overloaded cables groaning in the open shaft.

She resumed her heavenward flight, the stairwell becoming a mad blur around her. There was only one reason why the elevator would resume its ascent.

At last they reached the doorway that led out onto the upper-level landing platform. With Newt still somehow clinging to her, Ripley slammed the door open and stumbled out into the wind and smoke.

The dropship was gone.

"*Bishop*!" The wind carried her scream away as she scanned the sky. "Bishop!" Newt sobbed against her back.

A whine made her turn as the straining elevator slowly rose into view. She backed away from the door until she was leaning against the narrow railing that encircled the landing platform. It was ten levels to the hard ground below. The skin of the heaving processing station was as smooth as glass. They couldn't go up and they couldn't go down. They couldn't even dive into an air duct.

The platform shook as an explosion ripped through the bowels of the station. Metal beams buckled, nearly throwing her off her feet. With a shriek of rending steel a nearby cooling tower collapsed, keeling over like a slain sequoia. The explosions didn't stop after the first one this time. They began to sequence as backup safety systems failed to contain the expanding reaction. On the other side of the doorway the elevator ground to a halt. The safety cage enclosing the cargo bay began to part.

She whispered to Newt. "Close your eyes, baby." The girl nodded solemnly, knowing what Ripley intended as she put one leg over the railing. They would hit the ground together, quick and clean.

She was just about to step off into open air when the dropship rose into view almost beneath them, its hovering thrusters roaring. She hadn't heard it approach because of the howling wind. The ship's loading boom was extended, a single, long metal strut reaching toward them like the finger of God. How Bishop held the vessel steady in the rippling gale Ripley didn't know—and didn't care. Behind her, she could just hear the voice of the station. It, like the installation it served, had almost run out of time.

"You now have thirty seconds to reach..."

She jumped onto the loading boom and hung on as it retracted into the dropship's cargo bay. An instant later a tremendous explosion tore through the station. The resultant wind shear slammed the hovering craft sideways. Extended landing legs ripped into a complex of platform, wall, and conduit. Metal squealed against metal, the entanglement threatening to drag the ship downward.

Inside the hold Ripley threw herself into a flight seat, cradling Newt against her as she strapped both of them in. Glancing up the aisle, she could just see into the cockpit where Bishop was fighting the controls. As they retracted, the sound of the landing legs pulling free echoed through the little vessel. She slammed home the latches on her seat harness, wrapped both arms tightly around Newt.

"Punch it, Bishop!"

The entire lower level of the station vanished in an ex-

panding fireball. The ground heaved, earth and metal va-
porizing as the dropship erupted skyward. Its engines fired
hard, and the resultant gees slammed Ripley and Newt back
in their seat. No comfortable, gradual climb to orbit this time.
Bishop had the engines open full throttle as the dropship
clawed its way through the blighted atmosphere. Ripley's
back protested even as she mentally urged Bishop to increase
the velocity.

As they left blue for black, the clouds lit up from beneath. A bubble of white-hot gas burst through the tropo-
sphere. The shock wave from the thermonuclear explosion
rattled the ship but didn't damage it, and they continued to
climb toward high orbit.

Within the metal bottle Ripley and Newt stared out a
viewport, watching as the blinding flare dissipated behind
them. Then Newt slumped against Ripley's shoulder and began to cry quietly. Ripley rocked her and stroked her hair.

"It's okay, baby. We made it. It's over."

Ahead of them the great, ungainly bulk of the *Sulaco*
hung in geo-synchronous orbit, awaiting the arrival of its
smaller offspring. On Bishop's command the dropship rose
until docking grapples snapped home, lifting them into the
cargo bay. The outer lock doors cycled shut. Automatic warning lights swept the dark, deserted chamber, and a warning
horn ceased hooting. Excess engine heat was vented as the
cavernous hold filled with air.

Within the ship Bishop stood behind Ripley while she
knelt beside the comatose Hicks. She glanced questioningly
at the android.

"I gave him another shot for the pain. He kept insisting
that he didn't need it, but he didn't fight the injection. Strange
thing, pain. Stranger to me still, this peculiar inner need of
certain types of humans to pretend that it doesn't exist. Many
are the times I'm glad I'm synthetic."

"We need to get him to the *Sulaco*'s medical ward," she
replied, rising. "If you can get his arms, I'll take his feet."

Bishop smiled. "He is resting comfortably now. It will be better for him if we jostle him as little as possible. And you are tired. For that matter, *I'm* tired. It'll be easier if we get a stretcher."

Ripley hesitated, looking down at Hicks, then nodded. "You're right, of course."

Picking up Newt, she preceded the android down the aisle leading to the extended loading ramp. They could have a self-propelling stretcher back for Hicks in a few minutes. Bishop continued to talk.

"I'm sorry if I gave you a scare when you emerged onto the landing platform and saw the ship missing, but the site had simply become too unstable. I was afraid I'd lose the ship if I remained docked. It was simpler and safer to hover a short distance away. Close to the ground, the wind is not as strong. I had a monitor on the exit all the time so that I'd know when you arrived."

"Wish I'd known that at the time."

"I know. I had to circle and hope that things didn't get too rough to take you off. In the absence of human direction I had to use my own judgment, according to my programming. I'm sorry if I didn't handle it the best way."

They were halfway down the loading ramp. She paused and put a hand on his shoulder, stared evenly into artificial eyes.

"You did okay, Bishop."

"Well, thanks, I—" He stopped in mid-sentence, his attention focused on something glimpsed out of the corner of one eye. Nothing, really. An innocuous drop of liquid had splashed onto the ramp next to his shoe. Condensate from the skin of the dropship.

The droplet began to hiss as it started to eat into the metal ramp. Acid.

Something sharp and glistening burst from the center of his chest, spraying Ripley with milky android internal fluid. An alien stinger, queen-size, driving straight through him from behind. Bishop thrashed, uttering meaningless machine noises and clutching the protruding point of the spear as it slowly lifted him off the landing ramp.

The queen had concealed herself among the landing mechanism inside one strut bay. The atmospheric plates that normally sealed the bay flush with the rest of the dropship's skin had been bent aside or ripped away. She'd blended in perfectly with the rest of the heavy machinery until she began to emerge.

Seizing Bishop in two huge hands, she ripped him apart and flung the two halves aside. Rotating warning lights flashed on her shining dark limbs as she slowly descended to the deck, still smoking where Ripley had half fried her. Acid dripped from minor wounds that were healing rapidly. Sextuple limbs unfolded in unhuman geometries.

Breaking out of her paralysis, Ripley lowered Newt to the deck without taking her eyes off the descending nightmare.

"Go!"

Newt bolted for the nearest cluster of packing crates and equipment. The alien dropped to the deck and pivoted in the direction of the movement. Ripley backed clear, waving her arms and shouting, making faces, jumping up and down— doing anything and everything she could think of to draw the monster's attention away from the fleeing child.

Her decoying action was successful. The giant whirled, moving much too quickly for anything so huge, and sprang as Ripley sprinted for the oversize internal storage door that dominated the far end of the cargo hold. Massive feet boomed on the deck behind her.

She cleared the door and flailed at the "close" switch. The barrier whirred as it complied with the command, moving much faster than the doors of the now vanished station. An echoing *whang* reverberated through the storage room as the alien struck the solid wall an instant too late.

Ripley didn't have time to stand around to see if the

door would hold. She moved rapidly among bulky, dark shapes, searching for a particular one.

Outside, the queen's attention was drawn from the stubborn barrier to visible movement. A network of trenchlike service channels protected by heavy metal grillwork underlaid the cargo bay deck like the tributaries of a river system. The channels were just deep enough for Newt to enter. She'd dropped through one service opening and had begun crawling, scurrying toward the other end of the cargo bay like a burrowing rabbit.

The alien tracked the movement. Talons swooped, ripped up a section of grillwork just behind the frantic child. Newt tried to move faster, scrambling desperately as another piece of grille disappeared right at her heels. The next to go would be directly above her.

The alien paused in mid-reach at the sound of the heavy storage room door grinding open behind her. In the opening stood a massive, articulated silhouette.

Riding two tons of hardened steel, Ripley strode out in the powerloader. Her hands were inside waldo gloves while her feet rested in similar receptacles attached to the floor controls of the safety cab. Wearing the loader like high-tech armor, she advanced on the watching queen. The loader's ponderous feet boomed against the deck plates. Ripley's face was a mask of maternal fury devoid of fear.

"Get away from her, *you*!"

The queen emitted an inhuman screech and leapt at the oncoming machine.

Ripley threw her arm in a movement not normally associated with the activities of powerloaders or similar devices, but the elegant machine reacted perfectly. One massive hydraulic arm slammed into the alien's skull and threw it back against the wall. The queen reacted instantly and charged again, only to crash into a backhand that literally landed like a ton. She fell backward into a pile of heavy loading equipment.

"Come on!" Ripley wore a frenzied, distorted smile. "Come on!"

Tail lashing with rage, the queen charged the loader a third time. Four biomechanical arms swung at the loader's two. The great stinger stabbed at the flanks and underside of the loader, glancing harmlessly off solid metal. Ripley parried and struck with sweeping blows of the steel tines, backing up the loader, then advancing, pivoting to keep the machine's arms between her and the queen. The battle moved across the deck, demolishing packing crates, portable instrumentation, small machinery, everything in the path of the fight. The cargo bay echoed with the nightmarish sounds of two dragons battling to the death.

Getting the two powerful mechanical hands around a pair of alien arms, Ripley clenched her own fingers tight inside the waldoes, crushing both biomechanical limbs. The queen writhed with outrage, the talons of her other hands coming within inches of penetrating the safety cage to tear the tiny human apart. Ripley raised her arms, lifting the queen off the deck. The loader's engine groaned as it protested against the excessive weight. Hind legs ripped at the machine, denting the safety cage protecting its operator. The alien skull inclined toward her, and the outer jaws began to part. Ripley clung grimly to her controls.

The inner striking teeth exploded toward her. She ducked, and they slammed into the seat cushion behind her in an explosion of gelatinous drool. Yellow acid foamed over the hydraulic arms, crawling toward the safety cage. The queen tore at high-pressure hoses. Purple fluid sprayed in all directions, machine blood mixing with alien blood.

As it lost hydraulic pressure on one side the loader crumpled and fell over. The queen immediately rolled to get on top of it, avoiding the crushing metal arms, trying to find a way to penetrate the safety cage. Ripley hit a switch on the loader's console, and its cutting torch came to life, the intense blue flame firing straight into the alien's face. It screamed and drew back, dragging the loader with it. As she fell and the world was turned upside down around her, Ripley's safety harness kept her secured to the driver's seat.

Together machine, biomechanoid, and human rolled into the rectangular pit of the loading dock. The loader landed on top of the alien, crushing part of its torso and pinning it beneath its great weight. Acid began to seep in a steady flow from the badly damaged body.

Ripley's eyes widened as she fought with the loader's controls. The dripping acid spread out over the airlock doors and began to smoke as it started eating its way through the superstrong alloy. Beyond the outer lock lay void.

As the first tiny holes appeared, she struggled to unstrap herself from the driver's seat. Air began to leave the *Sulaco* as the insatiable emptiness of space sucked at the ship. A rising wind tore at Ripley as she stumbled clear of the loader. Jumping a puddle of smoking acid, she grabbed at the bottom rungs of the ladder that was built into the wall of the airlock. One hand slapped the inner door's emergency override. Above, the heavy inner airlock doors began rumbling toward each other like steel jaws. She climbed wildly.

Beneath her, the first holes widened, were joined by others as the acid did its work. The flow of escaping air around her increased in volume, slowing her ascent.

Newt had emerged from the network of subfloor channels to hide among a forest of gas cylinders. When the powerloader, Ripley, and the alien had tumbled into the airlock, she'd slipped out for a better look.

Now the suction from below pulled her legs out from under her and dragged her, kicking and screaming, across the smooth deck. Bishop, or rather his upper half, saw her coming. He grabbed a support stanchion with one hand. With the other he reached out, and thanks to perfect synthetic timing, just managed to get his fingers entwined in the girl's belt as she slid by. She hung there in his grasp, floating in the intensifying gale like a Newt-flag as the wind sucked at her.

Ripley's head emerged above deck level. As she tried to kick up and out with her right leg, something caressed her left ankle and latched hold. An experimental tug almost tore Ripley's arms from their sockets. Desperately she threw both arms around the ladder's upper rung, which was mounted a foot away on the deck. The inner airlock doors continued rumbling toward one another. If she didn't pull herself clear or drop back down within a couple of seconds, she'd end up looking just like Bishop.

Below, the acid-weakened outer lock doors groaned. A portion of the inner reinforcing collapsed. The interlocked powerloader and alien queen settled a few centimeters. Ripley felt her arms giving way as she was dragged down, but it was her shoe that came away first. Her leg was free.

Summoning strength from unknown depths, she dragged herself onto the deck just as the inner airlock doors slammed shut. Beneath her, the alien queen uttered another scream of rage and exerted all her incomprehensible strength. The heavy loader squealed as she began to push it aside.

It was half off when the outer doors, honeycombed by acid, fell apart, sending chunks of metal, bubbles of acid, the queen, and the powerloader spilling out into space. Ripley rose and stumbled to the nearest viewport. The queen's efforts were enough to propel her clear of the *Sulaco*'s artificial gravity field. Still screaming and tearing at the powerloader, the queen tumbled slowly back toward the inhospitable world she'd recently fled.

Ripley stared as her nemesis faded to a dot, then a dim point, and was at last swallowed by the rolling clouds. Within the cargo bay turbulent air eddied and settled as the *Sulaco*'s cyclers worked to replenish the atmosphere that had been lost.

Bishop was still holding Newt with one hand. His bisected torso trailed artificial inner organs and sparking conduits. His eyelids fluttered, and his head sometimes jerked unpredictably, bumping against the deck. His internal regulators had managed to shut off the flow of android blood, fighting a holding action against the massive injury. White encrustation sparkled along the edge of the tear.

He managed a small, grim smile as he eyed the approaching Ripley. "Not bad for a human." He regained control of his eyelids long enough to give her an unmistakable wink.

Ripley stumbled over to Newt. The girl looked dazed. "Mommy—mommy?"

"Right here, baby. I'm right here." Sweeping the girl up in her arms, she hugged her as hard as she could. Then she headed toward the *Sulaco*'s crew quarters.

Around them, the big ship's systems hummed reassuringly. She found her way up to Medical and returned to the cargo hold with a stretcher in tow. Bishop assured her that he could wait. With the stretcher's aid she gently loaded the sleeping Hicks and trundled him back to the hospital ward. His expression was peaceful, content. He'd missed the whole thing, luxuriating in the effects of the injection Bishop had given him.

As for the android, he lay on the deck, his hands crossed over his chest and his eyes closed. She couldn't tell if he was dead or sleeping. Better minds than hers would determine that once they got back to Earth.

In sleep Hicks's face lost much of its macho Marine toughness. He looked much like any other man. Handsomer though, and certainly more tired. Except that he wasn't like any other man. If it hadn't been for him, she'd be dead, Newt would be dead, all dead. Only the *Sulaco* would have lived on, an empty receptacle awaiting the return of humans who would never come.

She thought of waking him, decided against it. In a little while, when she was sure that his vital signs were stabilized and the repairs to his acid-scarred flesh well under way, she'd place him in one of the empty, waiting hypersleep capsules.

She turned to inspect the sleeping chamber. Three capsules to prep. If he still lived, Bishop wouldn't need one.

The synthetic would probably have found hypersleep confining.

Newt looked up at her. She held two of Ripley's fingers as they strode together up the corridor.

"Are we going to sleep now?"

"That's right, Newt."

"Can we dream?"

Ripley gazed down at the bright, upturned face and smiled. "Yes, honey. I think we both can."

ALIEN³

novelization by Alan Dean Foster

based on a screenplay by
David Giler and Walter Hill and Larry Ferguson

story by Vincent Ward

Here, even the wind screams. Abandoned hulks of
machinery rust in the colourless landscape. Dark, oily seas
beat against a jagged black shore. And the remnants of a
reentry space vehicle crash into the rough waves.

In it sleeps Ripley, a woman who has battled the Enemy
twice. It killed her whole crew the first time. The second
time, it slaughtered a spaceload of death-dealing Marines.
No on this prison planet that houses only a horde of
defiant, captive men, she will have to fight the ultimate
alien horror one more time.

Before it rips apart a whole world ...

FICTION

Warner now offers an exciting range of quality titles by both established and new authors. All of the books in this series are available from:
Little, Brown and Company (UK) Limited,
Cash Sales Department,
P.O. Box 11,
Falmouth,
Cornwall TR10 9EN.

Alternatively you may fax your order to the above address. Fax No. 0326 376423.

Payments can be made as follows: Cheque, postal order (payable to Little, Brown and Company) or by credit cards, Visa/Access. Do not send cash or currency. UK customers: and B.F.P.O.: please send a cheque or postal order (no currency) and allow £1.00 for postage and packing for the first book, plus 50p for the second book, plus 30p for each additional book up to a maximum charge of £3.00 (7 books plus).

Overseas customers including Ireland, please allow £2.00 for postage and packing for the first book, plus £1.00 for the second book, plus 50p for each additional book.

NAME (Block Letters) ....

ADDRESS...

....

☐ I enclose my remittance for _____

☐ I wish to pay by Access/Visa Card

Number [ ][ ][ ][ ][ ][ ][ ][ ][ ][ ][ ][ ][ ][ ][ ][ ][ ][ ][ ]

Card Expiry Date [ ][ ][ ][ ]